ACCLAIM FOR THE SEAL ISLAND...

"Fresh, vibrant writing and a delightful, heart-felt story that only feeds the craving to visit Ireland!"
(Review for "The Selkie Spell")
~ *Bella Street, Author of "Kiss Me, I'm Irish"* ~

"With her excellent pacing, gorgeous descriptive prose, and wonderfully fleshed out characters, Sophie Moss' writing style reminds me of Nora Roberts'."
(Review for "The Selkie Spell")
~ *Tracie Banister, Author of "In Need of Therapy"* ~

"Sophie does an amazing job of creating a highly developed plot in which you're taken into this magical world, but it feels real."
(Review for "The Selkie Enchantress")
~ *Rachel Kall, Author of "Legally Undercover"* ~

"I could almost smell the scent of roses and taste the salt in the air while reading, and I felt like I was transported to a windswept Irish island."
(Review for "The Selkie Enchantress")
~ *Kristy Atkinson, Reader* ~

"I was totally swept off my feet by this book...I loved the way reality and magic were beautifully interwoven..."
(Review for "The Selkie Enchantress")
~ *Roberta Capizzi, Author of "The Melody In Our Hearts"* ~

"The setting and images are just as lush and magical as in the first book, and the emotions of the characters are rendered poignantly."
(Review for "The Selkie Enchantress")
~ *Lori Fitzgerald, Reader* ~

Also by Sophie Moss

The Selkie Spell
Book one of The Seal Island Trilogy

The Selkie Enchantress
Book two of The Seal Island Trilogy

THE
SELKIE
SORCERESS

BOOK THREE OF THE SEAL ISLAND TRILOGY

SOPHIE MOSS

Sea Rose
Publishing

Cover design, interior book design and eBook design
by Blue Harvest Creative
www.blueharvestcreative.com

THE SELKIE SORCERESS

Published by
Sea Rose Publishing

ISBN-13: 978-0615801056
ISBN-10: 0615801056

Visit the author at:
www.sophiemosswrites.com
www.facebook.com/SophieMossAuthor
www.twitter.com @SMossWrites

Contact the author at:
sophiemosswrites@gmail.com

FOR MY MOM

THE
SELKIE
SORCERESS

CHAPTER 1

S am Holt stripped off his jacket and laid it over the railing of the ferry. He stood at the helm, watching the rocky cliffs of Seal Island come into view. A beat-up pair of aviator glasses shaded his eyes from the reflection of the midmorning sun. He hadn't expected to be gone this long.

Or to return with so little.

The ancient motor hummed, cutting a slow path over the surface of the ocean. Inside the leather satchel at his feet was the only clue he'd found so far in his search for Dominic and Liam O'Sullivan's mother, a woman who'd left them over twenty years ago.

Brigid O'Sullivan had done a damn good job of covering her tracks.

Not that that had ever stopped him before. But there was something about this case that nagged at him, that reminded him too much of *Tara* O'Sullivan. It was Tara's case that had first led him to this island. He'd come in search of a runaway wife, only to find an innocent woman seeking shelter from her deranged husband. He'd realized too late that his client—her husband—had no desire to reunite with Tara; he had wanted to kill her.

Tara had managed to defeat her husband, and Sam had switched sides at the last minute to help her, but he'd come far too close to getting her killed. Sam rolled his neck, working out the kinks. He'd fallen asleep at his desk the night before, as he did most nights now. He glanced at the captain, eyeing the sheen of sweat on the elderly man's forehead. "It's rather warm for January."

"Aye." Finn spoke out of one side of his mouth, a pipe dangling from his cracked lips. "But it's been good for the cleanup." He rested his leathery hand on the wheel. "The village is almost back to the way it was before the storm."

Sam nodded. When he'd left the island in November, it had been to the sound of hammers patching broken shutters and splintered fences, the bark of sheepdogs herding animals from flooded pastures to the highest fields.

Now, he took in the cluster of white-washed cottages dotting the sunlit hillside. Stone walls crisscrossed the blankets of moss leading up to the soaring limestone cliffs. The deep blue waters around the island were calm and surprisingly deserted.

"It's a nice enough day for fishing," Sam remarked. "How come we're the only boat out on the water?"

Finn puffed on his wooden pipe, and the sweet scent of tobacco floated into the salty air. "Haven't seen a fish in these waters for weeks."

"Weeks?" Sam picked up the paper cup he'd set down when he'd taken off his jacket, eyeing the instant coffee grounds lying on the bottom. He was starting to get used to the coffee in Ireland. It was the only thing keeping him awake at this point. "I thought the waters around these islands were some of the best fishing on the west coast?"

"They are." Finn steered them toward the quiet harbor, where the crumbling ruins of an ancient stronghold dipped into the sea. "At least, they used to be."

Sam knocked back the rest of the coffee. "Until what?"

Finn sent him a sideways glance. "You don't know?"

Sam shook his head slowly.

Seagulls alighted from a thin sliver of white beach, their cries echoing over the water. Finn glanced up, following the path of the birds. "It's fallout from the white selkie curse."

Sam lowered the cup. Last fall, when Liam had uncovered an ancient Irish fairy tale, it had trapped him in a dangerous enchantment. The white selkie, who was every bit as real as the pages in that tale, had chosen Liam as her mate. She had come on land for three days to tempt him into following her back into the sea. It had been a very close call, but in the end they *had* managed to save him. "I thought we broke that curse?"

"We thought so, too," Finn admitted. "Turns out, it's not that simple." The motor propelled them through the water, the wake fanning out behind them the only ripple in the glassy surface. "When Nuala failed to bring a suitable land-man into the sea, the selkies lost their ruler."

"What about Liam's grandmother?" Sam turned to face Finn. "I thought she held the throne until the next white selkie came?"

"She passed."

"When?"

"About six weeks ago." Finn shifted gears, slowing the ferry. The ocean churned beneath them. "The white selkie and her land-man have kept the peace between these islands and the sea for thousands of years. Without them, everything falls out of balance."

"What about the king?"

Finn shook his head. "The selkies need a queen."

Sam's gaze shifted back to the island. Long strands of kelp curled on the sand, cooking in the sun. The stench of dried seaweed floated over the sea and he noticed for the first time how low the tide was.

A lone seal bobbed in the water at the edge of the shallow harbor. She dove, disappearing from sight, but when she resurfaced several meters behind the boat, she bobbed in the water until their eyes met.

Sam took a step back. He would recognize those pale eyes anywhere. But what the hell was Nuala doing here, so close to the island?

The sound of laughter drifted down from the village and Nuala slid underwater, her sleek black shadow darting away toward the deeper waters.

Sam turned to see if Finn had seen her, but the captain's filmy eyes were gazing up at the village, at the woman walking out of *O'Sullivan's* pub.

"Glenna's doing well," Finn said over the hum of the motor. "Almost fully recovered."

Glenna. The coffee grounds in Sam's throat turned to dust. The mere mention of that woman's name could spark every nerve-ending inside him until all he could hear was the pop and sizzle of his own flesh burning with need.

"I thought she might have mentioned something to you," Finn said, glancing back at Sam, "about the curse."

Sam pushed back from the railing, crumpling the paper cup in his hand. "I haven't spoken with Glenna since I left."

GLENNA MCCLURE STOOD outside *O'Sullivan's* pub in the village, watching the ferry motor up to the pier. She knew Sam would be on it. She'd prepared herself for this moment. But she hadn't expected the wave of emotions that would sweep through her at the first sight of him in two months—like a thousand moonflowers unfurling at dusk.

Her fingers closed around the fire agate pendant hanging from a long silver chain around her neck. She breathed in the calming energy of the stone and let its protective powers ground her. The last thing she needed right now was a distraction. She couldn't afford to lose focus.

Behind her, the door to the pub was propped open. Dominic was writing up the day's specials on a chalkboard. A handful of children chased a soccer ball through the streets, their cheerful shouts echoing over the water.

From the outside eye, it would appear things had gone back to normal on Seal Island. The villagers had spent weeks cleaning up the island and riding out the aftershocks of the storm in November. But that storm was only the beginning of what the people on this island were going to have to face.

Glenna watched Sam step off the ferry, his long purposeful strides carrying him toward the one road leading up to the village. She heard Kelsey O'Sullivan's excited squeal when she spotted him and Sam's deep gravelly laugh as the children ran down to meet him.

She gripped the pendant tighter, her knuckles turning white around the fiery red stone. The man was trouble. He'd brought nothing but trouble since the moment he'd set foot on this island last summer. The sooner he left, the better it would be for all of them.

The children's chatter grew louder as they climbed the hill, surrounding Sam. And then there he was, not twenty feet away from her, batting the ball back and forth with the kids, without a care in the world.

Ronan O'Shea let out a triumphant cheer as he knocked the ball free from under Sam's foot. It rolled down the rutted street toward Glenna. She released the stone, lowering her hand to her side and lifting the toe of her heeled boot to stop the ball.

Sam's eyes followed the path of the ball, then cruised up the front of her, wandering up every inch of her body. He lowered his glasses from his face and those tawny eyes—the same eyes that had haunted her dreams for weeks now—met hers. She felt a punch of heat swim all the way through her. "Sam."

"Glenna." She expected him to say something witty, something clever to break the ice. But she saw only raw concern and something else—something she couldn't place—in his eyes. "You look well."

Glenna nodded. She hadn't forgotten how he'd stayed with her every night until she recovered, how he hadn't left her side until she was strong enough to walk back and forth to the pub on her own.

Sam kept his eyes on hers as he walked slowly toward her, easing the ball free. With a twitch of his boot, it sailed lightly up into the air and he caught it, tucking it under his arm.

Glenna lifted a brow. "I didn't know you could play football."

Sam leaned in so she could catch his scent—earthy with a touch of wood smoke. "I bet there are a lot of things you don't know about me."

Desire pooled inside her, but she could see the fatigue in his eyes now that he was so close. He hadn't shaved in days and his thick blond hair, tousled from the ferry ride, had grown even longer.

The case was wearing at him. She could sense the tension in his muscles, the frustration building inside him. Good. She wanted him tense. Frustrated. On edge.

He was more likely to make mistakes that way.

They both glanced up as Dominic O'Sullivan walked out of the pub. He slipped his hands in the pockets of his worn jeans, leaning against the doorway. He didn't offer Sam even a hint of a smile. "We thought we'd hear from you. A call. Something."

Sam hooked his sunglasses in the neck of his shirt. "That's not the way I work."

No, Glenna thought. It wasn't. Sam didn't waste time with phone calls to update his clients when he could be working. He wouldn't stop until he got his answers, until he found out the truth. She knew how hard he'd been working.

Because she'd been working just as hard to stop him.

"Do you have any news?" Dominic asked.

Sam nodded, peeling back the flap of his tattered satchel. He walked over to Dominic, pulling out a bulky object. "I thought you should have this."

Dominic breathed out a curse when Sam unfolded the battered seal-skin.

THEY WAITED UNTIL everyone was gathered at the pub. Sam helped Dominic and Glenna pull up enough seats for Tara O'Sullivan, Dominic's wife; Liam O'Sullivan, Dominic's younger brother; and Caitlin Conner, Liam's fiancée. Fiona O'Sullivan, Dominic and Liam's grandmother, coaxed the children back out into the street to play. As soon as Fiona closed the door behind them, Sam laid the pelt on the table.

Tara gasped at the burn marks singed into the leather. There were cracks along the creases where it had been folded for so long, and teeth marks where rats had nibbled at the edges.

"Where did you find it?" Dominic asked.

"Inside your old house," Sam replied. "The one where you grew up."

"Was anyone living there?"

Sam shook his head. "The neighbors said a building down the block caught fire several years ago and it spread to the rest of the houses. Yours was right on the edge of the worst of the damage, but the city condemned them all. They haven't gotten around to rebuilding."

"I'm not surprised," Dominic murmured. "It wasn't the best section of town."

No, Sam thought. It wasn't. It was about as bad as it gets.

Tara reached out, brushing the tips of her fingers over the pelt. It crackled when she touched it. She jerked her hand back as a moldy dust puffed up from the table.

Caitlin looked at Sam. "If it was boarded up, how did you get in?"

Dominic pushed away from the table and walked to the open window. "I'm sure Sam has his ways."

A balmy breeze blew into the room, ruffling a stack of cocktail napkins on the bar. A few fluttered to the floor. No one bothered to pick them up.

Liam pulled out the chair beside Caitlin. He reached for her hand, lacing their fingers together. "What else did you find?"

"Not much," Sam admitted. "I searched the place twice, but something kept nagging at me to go back. I found a tear in the ceiling of one of the bedrooms last night. I thought it was water damage, but when I touched it, it fell away. The pelt was hidden inside, behind about three layers of insulation."

Dominic gazed out at the fields. "If our mother never went back for her pelt, that means she's still on land."

"But why wouldn't she go back for her pelt?" Liam asked. "Doesn't every selkie need to return to the sea?" His gaze met Tara's across the table. "Isn't that what they are desperate for?"

"Unless she couldn't go back for it," Tara said slowly, "because she was in some kind of trouble."

Sam looked at Glenna. She'd been uncharacteristically quiet, her gaze never leaving the pelt. Her hands were clasped calmly in her lap, but Sam could tell something was wrong. "Glenna, what do you think?"

"I think," she said, lifting her amber eyes to his, "that you have a knack for finding people who don't want to be found."

CHAPTER 2

Dominic watched Glenna rise, excusing herself. Their eyes met across the room. They were both thinking the same thing...*Tara.* Sam had led Tara's psychotic ex-husband to this island. Sam had almost gotten Tara killed.

When Dominic voiced his concerns at the beginning of this investigation, Glenna was the only one who'd sided with him. She was the only one who'd understood that if Brigid *wanted* to be found, she'd have tracked *them* down.

But that was before he'd seen the pelt.

Dominic's gaze shifted to the battered seal-skin. It was easier to blame someone for abandoning you as a child when you couldn't picture her anymore, when you didn't know anything about her.

He'd had his doubts—even after everything that happened in November—that his mother was really a selkie. That somehow she'd been forced onto land by his father and trapped against her will.

But the moment Sam pulled that pelt from the satchel, she became real. She became one of them. It didn't change the fact that she'd left them. But it did make him *feel* something toward her for the first time. And he didn't know what to do about that.

The heavy cobalt blue door clicked shut behind Glenna, and Dominic dipped his hands in his pockets, strolling back to join the others.

"Last fall," Liam said, breaking the silence, "when I asked the librarians at the Trinity College Library to research the white selkie legend, it took them weeks to track down the only story they had in their database. When they finally found it, it was shelved in an odd section, far away from the selkie legends."

"And your mother was listed as the last person to sign for it," Caitlin added. "That was the first thing that made you wonder if she could be involved."

"I've been to the library," Sam said. "But none of the staff remembers your mother. I have the name of a retired librarian who managed the place in the eighties, but she's been out of the country traveling for weeks."

Liam drummed his fingers over the table. "If we can find out why her name was connected to that book, I'm sure we'll know something."

"Do you still think she might have moved it on purpose?" Sam asked.

"I don't know," Liam admitted. "I've been thinking about this a lot. If she was hiding it so I wouldn't find it, why hide it somewhere in the library? Why not destroy it? Why leave it in a place where it could be found at all?"

"Maybe she moved the book to leave you a clue so you would look for her," Tara suggested as Dominic settled into the chair beside her. "Maybe she wanted you to find the story, but in a strange way that would raise your suspicions."

Caitlin frowned. "That's pretty far-fetched."

Liam nodded. "I agree with Cait. How could she have known I'd be a professor, that my line of work would take me on a path of uncovering ancient fairy tales?"

"She couldn't," Sam said. "And we won't know anything until that librarian gets back." He stood, rubbing a hand over his eyes. He needed a shower, and about thirty-six hours of sleep. "If you think of anything else, tell me tonight. I'm heading back to Dublin first thing in the morning."

TARA SQUEEZED DOMINIC'S hand and rose, following Sam outside. The sun sparkled over the ocean and the ebbing tide lapped at the shoreline, but it was strange not to see the waves breaking against the cliffs and the seagulls diving in and out of the jagged crevasses. And it was even stranger not to be wearing a sweater in January.

"Sam, wait," she called after him as he strode across the road, shouldering his satchel. "Don't you want to stay for lunch? You can't possibly have anything in your fridge at home."

"I'll pick up something at the market." He nodded to Sarah Dooley's shop on the other side of the street.

Tara trailed after him. "I'm worried about you," she said, when he stopped and turned to face her. She took in the thin lines at the corners of his mouth, the puffy rims around his eyes and the stress marks etched between them. "I don't like how this case is affecting your health."

"I'm fine, Tara."

"You said you were done," she said gently. "That you didn't want to do anymore investigations. It was wrong of me to ask you to do this." She shielded her eyes from the sun as she looked up at him. "We can hire someone else—"

"No." He cut her off, more sharply than he intended. Dragging a hand through his hair, he gazed out at the ocean. "Things aren't clicking like they used to, Tara. I'm not finding the clues I need to get the job done. It's harder this time, like something's stopping me from what I need to do."

Tara frowned when Sam continued to scan the horizon, almost like he was looking for an answer in the sea.

"I'll find her," he said. "Besides, it's the least I can do."

"Sam—"

"No. I mean it, Tara." He looked back down at her. "I owe you, and I won't let you down."

"We've forgotten it." Tara waved him off. "It's over."

"Has Dominic forgotten it?"

"He will," Tara said stubbornly. But she stole a glance back at the pub and sighed. "This investigation is hard on him. He's still not completely sold on the idea."

"How could he be?" Sam rolled his shoulders, relieving some of the tension. "Brigid left him with a father who beat him for years until he and Liam escaped. I wouldn't have warm feelings toward the woman either."

Snatches of Dominic and Liam's conversation drifted into the street. Sam lowered his voice. "You know when you came to me in November, after Nuala and Owen arrived? You said you didn't know what was going on, but you felt something was off?"

Tara nodded.

"I've got that feeling now."

"So do I."

An alley cat tiptoed across the street, winding itself around Sam's ankle. Tara pulled something out of her pocket and held it out to him.

Sam took the small glass vial wrapped in blue and silver ribbon. "What's this?"

"I've been working with herbs lately," Tara explained. "Trying different combinations to see what works and what doesn't work. This one has sage, bergamot, rose petals, and oil. It's supposed to have protective powers in it."

Sam tested the weight of the tiny vial in his hand. "Do you think I need protecting?"

"I don't know. Those are the herbs that worked their way into your tincture. I follow their lead and research the combinations later to see what they mean." Tara eyed the small tincture dwarfed in Sam's broad palm. "I know it seems silly. How could something so small protect anyone? But I'd feel better if you kept it on you."

"I don't think it's silly." Sam tucked it in his shirt pocket. "But I might take the ribbon off later." His lips twitched. "It could hurt my reputation."

Tara rolled her eyes. At least he still had his sense of humor. "You can take the bow off. It was only on there because it was supposed to be a Christmas present."

Sam lowered his hand to his side, his expression suddenly guarded. "You made me a Christmas present?"

Tara nodded. "I thought you'd come back for Christmas."

"Why?"

Tara held his gaze. "I figured we were your closest friends, your family." When Sam looked away, Tara angled her head. "Who did you spend Christmas with, Sam?"

Sam lifted a shoulder. "It's just another day of the year."

It was as she'd suspected; he'd spent Christmas alone. He'd probably spent a lot of Christmases alone. She knew what it was like to be alone, to not have anyone. "You could have come back, Sam. You could have spent the holidays with us."

Sam slipped his sunglasses back on. "Thank you for the present, Tara." He tipped his head at her. "I'll be on my way."

GLENNA STOOD AT her window, scanning the fields leading back to the village to see if she'd been followed, but there were only a few blonde cows grazing in the sunlight. Yanking her scarlet curtains closed, she strode to the hearth. She didn't have time for matches and sod.

She threw out her arms. Sparks hissed from her fingertips. Flames sizzled and crackled to life. They rose, licking at the paint around the hearth, stretching up to the mantle where a dozen black candles were lit. Heat filled the cottage, and fingers of smoke curled into the room.

The flames shifted, grabbing at the air with greedy hands. The black candles flickered erratically. The red curtains flapped, reaching toward her mother as she stepped out of the flames. Moira's green-gold eyes met Glenna's. "Hello, darling."

"Mother," Glenna said, taking in the waves of gold silk that formed to her mother's lush figure. Blond waves tumbled to Moira's waist, where her dress gathered before pooling down from a glittering topaz clasp.

Her mother's hair had lightened over the years, as her magic grew. But when Moira had stolen Nuala's powers in November, her hair had warmed to the color of pale corn silk. It didn't help that Moira had also obtained Nuala's incomparable beauty. Her skin was smooth, her lips full, her eyes wide and luminous.

She looked almost the same age as Glenna now.

Teacups quivered, clattering in the cupboard as Moira sashayed into the room. She lifted one of Glenna's orange pillar candles, tipping it and letting the hot wax drip onto the bronze plate. "What have they found so far?"

"They found Brigid's pelt."

"Did they?" Moira didn't even bother to look up. "How nice."

"It wasn't in very good shape."

"What a pity." Moira set the candle down and wandered over to the window facing the sea. Beneath the sill, Glenna's altar was covered in herbs, satchels, stones and spells. "You've been working hard, my dear."

"I have."

Moira glanced up. "Sam is very good at what he does, isn't he?"

"He is. But her pelt is the only clue he's found so far."

Glenna tensed when Moira picked up her athame—a ceremonial dagger used only for spells. Moira tested the sharpness of the blade against her crimson fingernail and set it back down. Glenna let out a breath when she walked away from it. "He still has no idea where she is?"

"None."

"Good." Moira's lips curved as she walked to Glenna and brushed a long brown lock back over her daughter's shoulder. To anyone else the gesture might have seemed mothering. But it made Glenna sick.

"Don't worry, darling. He'll tire after a while." Moira took one last look around the cottage and nodded, satisfied. "I'm happy to see you're holding up your end of the bargain. I was worried at first that your feelings for him would interfere with your ability to stop him."

Glenna went very still. "I don't have feelings for Sam."

Moira smiled. "Don't you?"

CHAPTER 3

The flames died and Moira vanished in the black smoke. Glenna hurried into her bedroom, sliding a Moleskine sketchbook from the shelf behind her bed. It looked like the other sketchbooks beside it, but the blank pages fluttered when she opened it. A warm light spread from her fingertips and the book grew heavier, changing shape in her hands. The leather binding creaked, the pages crinkling and yellowing with age as she sank to the bed.

Ancient words, scrawled in Gaelic, leaked onto the parchment. She traced a black and white sketch of a leafy bush at the top of the page marked by a red ribbon. In three days the blackthorn would bloom—the first sign of spring in Ireland. Pagans called it Imbolc. Christians celebrated it as St. Brigid's Day. Both would light fires all over the countryside and give thanks for renewed warmth and fertility.

But Moira was planning a different celebration—a celebration that would change the fate of all their lives forever.

Glenna slid the faded map of Connemara from the back of the book, unfolding it and spreading it out on the mattress. She'd been searching the mountains for years—quietly, carefully, so as not to draw any attention to herself. Large red circles marked the spots where blackthorn grew. She crossed out another one, scanning the few that were left. If she could find the spot—the one spot where everything had started—she might have a chance of saving them.

She set the map down when she heard the knock on her front door. She knew Sam would come. Once he'd found his first clue, more would follow. That was how it worked with Sam. She'd used all her powers the last two months to keep those clues out of his reach. But he was breaking through. Every step closer put him, and all of them, in more danger.

She rose, folding the map and sliding the book back onto the shelf. She stalked to the door and opened it, taking in the tall, broad-shouldered man on the other side. He'd changed into clean clothes—a faded blue T-shirt and jeans. His sun-streaked hair was still wet from the shower and he'd shaved, revealing the jagged scar that etched through his strong jaw.

His perceptive eyes swept past her, assessing the cottage. "Do I smell smoke?"

"It's the candles."

He took in the ashes scattered in front of the hearth, the fresh streaks of soot climbing up the paint. "It doesn't smell like candle smoke."

Glenna kept her hand lightly on the doorknob, standing between him and the cottage. "What are you doing here, Sam?"

Sam pulled his gaze from the charred underside of the mantle, fishing a small glass vial out of his pocket. "Tara thinks I need protection."

Glenna recognized the vial—one of Tara's tinctures. Good, she thought. She didn't want to hurt Sam. She just wanted him off this case. She was glad Tara was protecting him.

He held it out to her. "I want you to keep it."

Glenna's gaze flickered up to his. "Tara already gave me one."

"For protection?"

Glenna looked back down at the tincture. "Not exactly."

"What is yours for?"

"I'd rather not say," Glenna admitted. Hers had been to attract love into her life. She had hurled it over the edge of the cliff on her way home Christmas night.

Sam hooked a finger in her belt loop and tugged her toward him. He held her surprised gaze, slipping the tincture into her pocket. "Somehow I don't think Tara's magic measures up to yours."

The air between them shimmered with heat. Glenna fought the urge to push up onto her toes and press her lips to that firm, perfectly-shaped mouth. "Tara's a healer. Her magic is just as powerful as mine, but in a different way."

He kept her close, inches away from him. It was hard to breathe, to think straight when he was this close, when she could see the little flecks of gold in his eyes. "Why do you think Tara thinks I need protection?"

"I imagine it's a precaution."

"Because of the fallout from the white selkie curse?"

Glenna stepped back, breaking the contact. As soon as he had her off-balance, he brushed past her, striding into her cottage.

Every candle was lit and the flames cast eerie shadows over the creamy yellow walls. The room was dark; the curtains drawn. The hiss of melted wax dripping to the plates had him pausing, gazing around at her things. "What's going on, Glenna? I thought we beat this thing."

She closed the door and turned to face him. After all the time he'd spent here last fall, he probably knew his way around her cottage as well as she did. And yet, he stood awkwardly, like he wasn't sure if he was welcome.

"Does life ever go back to normal here?" Sam asked.

It wouldn't, Glenna thought. Not if Moira won this battle. None of their lives would ever go back to normal. She crossed the room to the kitchen. She needed something to do with her hands. She pulled out two tumblers and a bottle of Jameson's.

"How long has Nuala been hanging around the island?"

Glenna fumbled the bottle, catching it before it fell. "What?"

Sam eyed her steadily from across the room. "Nuala," he repeated. "I saw her today on the ferry ride in. Her pelt is black now instead of white, but her eyes are the same color. It was definitely Nuala."

Glenna set the glasses down on the counter. "Where was she?"

"In the harbor." He walked over to the fireplace, gazing down at the pile of pale ash. "I didn't expect to see her so close to the island after everything that happened." He knelt, touching the cement hearth. It was still hot to the touch. "Do you think Liam and Caitlin know she's still hanging around?"

"No." Glenna shook her head. "Caitlin would have said something to me."

Sam drew his index finger through the soot mark on the wall. "Do you think Nuala still has contact with Owen?"

Owen. Glenna felt a wave of panic. The last thing she wanted was for Owen to get caught in the middle of this. But Nuala couldn't possibly want to rekindle a relationship with the child she stole from Caitlin and Liam so many years ago.

Nuala might have raised Owen for the first ten years of his life, but she hadn't shown the slightest bit of warmth toward him when they were both on the island last fall. She could only want one thing—revenge on Moira.

"Speaking of mothers..." Sam held up his black fingertips. "When was the last time you saw yours?"

"It's been a while," Glenna lied, pouring them each a glass of whiskey and handing him one.

Sam rose, taking it. "I imagine she's not very happy with how things turned out."

"No." Glenna gazed down at the warm brown liquid. "I imagine she's not."

"But she did get Nuala's powers," Sam said, watching her closely. "What is she planning to do with them?"

"My mother has only ever wanted one thing, Sam." Glenna lifted her gaze to his. "To rule the seas."

"The selkies don't have a ruler," Sam murmured.

"I know," Glenna said quietly.

Sam set down the glass. "I don't like that she's still out there. I don't like the thought of you living here alone when I know what she's capable of."

Glenna sipped the whiskey, the liquor warming her throat, soothing her nerves. "I can take care of myself, Sam."

"Can you?" Sam lifted a brow. "I seem to remember a different story."

"I'm fine now," Glenna said, setting her glass down sharply. She wanted him gone. "You can see that."

"Glenna," Sam cut in, frustrated. "You almost *died* the last time you stood up to her. I don't know what your mother wants with you. But I have a feeling she's not done trying to manipulate you and ruin all of our lives."

Glenna brushed past him, grinding her heel into the rug to scrub away any leftover remnants of ash. "How about you focus on finding Brigid, and I'll focus on dealing with my mother?" When she turned and saw a shadow cross his face, she angled her head. "Oh, right. You're not having much luck with that, are you?"

Sam narrowed his eyes. "Why do I get the feeling that makes you happy?"

"I'm on Dominic's side. I'm still not convinced Brigid should be found." She went to the table and started tidying up her stack of magazines. "It's been twenty years since she left them. She could have looked them up. It's not like they're hard to find. Liam is a well-known professor at the University of Ireland. Dominic hasn't left this island since he and Liam escaped here when they were boys. He owns a pub called, *O'Sullivan's*—the same last name as the man she ran from. It wouldn't take a genius to track them down."

"You don't think it's odd that Liam found her name connected to a legend he was researching?"

"I think Liam's reading too much into it, and he should spend more time worrying about how his new son is adjusting to life on land than tracking down a mother who left him twenty years ago with a father who beat him."

"What if it was you?"

"Excuse me?"

"Put yourself in Brigid's shoes. What if you were the one who was trapped in an abusive marriage? What if you found a way out, to save yourself, but you couldn't take the kids with you? Would you have the courage to reach out years later, to contact them after what you did? After the horrors you put them through?"

"I would never—"

"That's not the point. The point is that you *wouldn't* have the courage to reach out. You would think your children still blamed you for what you did. You would expect Dominic's reaction, which is sensible. But Dominic is only *one* of Brigid's sons. Liam *wants* to find her. Liam is ready to forgive her. To find out the truth."

"Liam is still hung up on that damn legend." Glenna threw the magazines back onto the table and turned to face him. "You told me the first day you came to this island, when you were looking for Tara, that you always find people who don't want to be found. Why do you think this case is going to be different?"

"This *is* different," Sam said tightly. "It's personal."

"Because you still feel guilty for tracking Tara here? For almost getting her killed?"

Sam picked up his drink, downing it in one sip. "Tara *asked* me to do this. This case isn't about money. It's about helping out a friend. I'm not going to screw it up."

"In my experience, friendship isn't usually based on one person's guilt to make up for something one has done to the other." Glenna saw the flash of anger that passed over Sam's eyes. She'd hit a nerve. Because that was exactly what Sam was doing. For all the kindness Tara had shown him, Sam wanted more than anything to absolve the guilt he still felt about leading her deranged husband to this island. "Have you ever considered that it might be easier to start over in a different place, Sam? One where you didn't have to prove yourself to everybody?"

"I never said I was starting over," Sam snapped. "I don't think in terms of putting down roots."

Glenna arched a brow, surprised. "If you're not planning to stay, then why are you still here? Is it really all because of Tara...?" She trailed off when she saw the shift in his eyes, when she saw the heat swim into them.

It wasn't Tara. It was her. *She* was the reason he was staying on the island. Glenna leveled her gaze at him. "You're wasting your time, Sam. I've made that clear."

Sam crossed the room to her. "I don't believe that."

"Sam—"

"No," he said sharply, cutting her off. "We had something before I left. You can't deny it."

She shook her head. "I was delirious with fever. I didn't know what I was thinking."

He took a step closer, and she retreated. The backs of her legs met the sofa behind her, and his strong hands landed on her hips. She could feel the heat, the intensity of his gaze only inches away. And then his mouth was on hers.

Sam. The man she had been avoiding for months. The one man who could unravel every one of her plans, who could break through all of her defenses. Who, if she gave him half a chance, could destroy them all.

She pressed her palms to his hard chest, intending to push him away. But his lips moved warm and insistent, and felt so damn good, against hers. He tasted of black coffee and sugar and...*Sam.*

He yanked her against him, locking them in place. And every bone in her body turned to molten lava. Her fingers twisted into his shirt, her nails digging into those hard muscles. Her lips parted under his, desperate for more than a taste.

She gasped, staggering back when he stepped away suddenly. The air between them turned cold. She reached for the arm of the sofa, steadying herself as Sam turned on his heel, stalking to the door.

He looked over his shoulder, his eyes on fire as he wrenched it open. "Think about *that*, Glenna."

A YELLOW FOG rolled over the rocks. The waves lapped at the shoreline. Moira gazed into a small driftwood fire, watching a vision of her daughter and Sam kissing. Glenna could pretend as much as she wanted, but she had feelings—*deep* feelings—for this man.

Sam Holt would be her daughter's undoing.

And Moira's ticket to the throne.

She laughed, low and wicked. Sam wouldn't let her down. He would lead her to Brigid without even knowing it. Her daughter would never be able to keep up this ploy to stop him, not when she fell for him.

It was already happening.

She smiled. Brigid would be found by Imbolc, before the fires burned.

And as soon as she got rid of Brigid, she would be the only one left to reclaim the throne. The only *rightful* queen.

Smoke twirled into the sky, taking on the shape of a rose. Flames brushed the flower, coloring the petals a blazing sunset orange. She let it hover, and gazed into the fiery petals.

She had assumed when she'd stolen Nuala's powers that she would be unstoppable. But Caitlin and Liam had proved her wrong. There was still one magic more powerful than hers—the magic of true love.

Good thing she knew where to find it.

Her lips curved as she watched the image of Sam stalk out of her daughter's cottage, slamming the door. She lifted her hand, blowing the wisp of rose-shaped smoke toward Glenna's cottage.

Sweet dreams, darling.

CHAPTER 4

L iam." Caitlin rubbed her eyes, walking out into the hallway. "It's after midnight."

Liam glanced up from the couch, where he was bent over his laptop, a single lamp burning beside him. "Is it that late?"

She nodded, peeking into the bedroom across the hall at Owen. Their son was tucked under a navy blue quilt, his face buried in his pillow. They'd decorated the room in an ocean theme, at Owen's request, with sea-green walls and paintings of starfish and dolphins. His collection of seashells twinkled in the moonlight bathing the windowsill.

She shut the door quietly, walking into the sitting room. "Why don't you come to bed?"

Liam pushed the computer off his lap, leaning back and pressing the heels of his hands to his eyes. "I need to figure out how it all connects."

"I know," Caitlin sighed, picking up the unfinished bottle of Harp on the table. The windows were open, the warm air teasing the curtains into the room. Goosebumps rose up on her bare arms despite the heat.

"She's out there somewhere," Liam said quietly. "He found her pelt, Cait. It's real now."

Caitlin set the bottle in the sink and sank to the couch beside him. "I know."

Liam's eyes were bloodshot from staring at the screen. "I've been researching the legends of these islands for years, but I'm only beginning to understand how closely linked they all are. And how fragile they are—both the islands and the selkies."

Caitlin took Liam's hand in hers. "Maybe you should give it a rest for a couple days. You've been working like this non-stop for weeks."

"I can't find what I'm looking for." Liam's gaze fell back to his computer. "I'm certain that my mother is the missing link in the puzzle. And as soon as we find her, we'll know how it all connects."

"Sam *will* find her." Caitlin closed the laptop and stood. "Come on," she said, tugging him gently up to his feet. "Let's get some sleep."

TARA LAY AWAKE, listening to the murmur of waves splashing against the cliffs far below. She welcomed the rhythm, as it usually lulled her to sleep. But tonight it felt off—more like a whisper than a song.

"Mum?"

Tara lifted her head off her pillow and peered through the crack in the door. Kelsey was standing in the hallway, the hem of her pink nightgown dragging on the floor. Tara put a finger to her lips, gesturing to Dominic who had fallen asleep only moments ago.

Kelsey backed into the hallway as Tara slipped out of bed and tiptoed out the door.

"You can't sleep?" Tara whispered.

Kelsey shook her head.

"Me neither." Tara guided Kelsey into the living room and switched on a light. "Hot chocolate?"

Kelsey nodded, climbing up onto the sofa. Tara warmed two mugs of milk and crushed mint leaves into the cocoa powder. She carried them over to the sofa and set them on the table, eyeing the book clutched in her daughter's arms. "Do you want me to read you a story?"

Kelsey nodded.

Tara lifted the collection of fairy tales into her lap, flipping through the pages. "How about something different...*The Twelve Dancing Princesses*?"

Kelsey shook her head. "I want to read *The Little Mermaid*."

Tara looked up. "I thought we'd moved past that story?"

Kelsey tugged on the crocheted blanket draped over the back of the sofa. "It's the only story with a sea witch in it."

Tara watched her daughter closely. "Why do you want to read about a sea witch?"

"Because Moira's a sea witch."

A prickle of uneasiness danced up Tara's spine. She knew Moira had unfinished business with Glenna—maybe with all of them—but she didn't want Kelsey getting involved. And it wouldn't be the first time her daughter had followed clues in a fairy tale that led her to danger. "If you have questions about Moira, I want you to ask me or your father."

Kelsey dug deeper under the covers, her fingers playing over the little bits of pale green yarn that stuck out of the corners of the blanket. "Don't you think it's strange that the sea witch in that story is a mermaid, when we know she's a selkie?"

"This story was written a long time ago."

"Do you think Moira is related to this sea witch?"

"I don't know. I'm not sure how that would be possible since one's a selkie and one's a mermaid."

Kelsey reached for her mug, cupping both of her small hands around the blue pottery. "How does somebody become a sea witch?"

"I don't know."

"No one wants to be a sea witch, do they?"

Tara breathed in the calming fragrance of mint and chocolate. "I imagine not."

Kelsey picked at a chip in the mug. "I wonder who Moira was before. If she wasn't born a sea witch, then she must have been a regular selkie once." She bit her lip. "There has to be some good in her, if she's Glenna's mum."

Tara thought of her ex-husband, the man who abused her for years before she got the courage to escape. "I think," she said slowly, "there are some people who don't have any good in them at all."

"We didn't think Nuala had any good in her," Kelsey said. "And we were wrong."

"That's different."

"Is it?" Kelsey asked, her eyes falling back to the book. "I think if we could figure out who Moira was before she was a sea witch, and what she wants, it might help us find my grandmother."

Tara closed the book. "I want you to leave this investigation to Sam."

"But—"

"No," Tara cut her off. "I don't want you getting involved in this. Besides, we don't even know if Moira's behind your grandmother's disappearance."

"There has to be a reason why she stole Nuala's powers," Kelsey protested. "Moira wants something." She reached for the book and Tara let it go reluctantly. "We need to figure out what it is."

Tara swallowed a lump in her throat. "What have you figured out so far?"

"Not much," Kelsey admitted, turning to an illustration of a mermaid in a dark cave hovering over a bubbling cauldron. "But I think parts of this story are wrong." She traced a finger over the words on the page. "It says that no plants or flowers could grow in the sea witch's lair. But whenever I read this part, I smell roses."

A BLACK ROOT pushed through the dusty soil. The earth cracked, crumbling as it grew. Tight orange buds stretched toward the moon, and sharp thorns latched onto the white walls of the cottage. They climbed up to the windowsill, scratching at the glass, ravenous.

Glenna heard the scraping, the thorns cutting grooves into the glass. She stirred as the pane shattered under the pressure, pieces of glass falling into the bedroom. The vines snaked into the dark room, coiling around her wrists.

She inhaled smoke, choking, struggling against the binds. But the vines trapped her, holding her down. The curtains burst into flames. Smoke poured in from under her closet door. Every candle in the room sparked aflame, melting to bubbling pools of hot wax.

She cried out as the heat from the flames scorched her bare skin. The thorns bit into her wrists and the smoke burned her eyes, blurring her vision. A hot wind blew in from the ocean, teasing the flames higher and slowly, one by one, the petals unfurled.

Brilliant coral roses blazed like beacons through the smoke. She kicked at her knotted sheets as the vines fell away from her wrists. The roses shrank back, retreating through the crack in the glass. She grabbed for the vine, clinging to it with both hands.

But when her fingers met the velvety petals, they turned black under her touch. They crinkled, fading to ash. She sank to the floor as the flames died and the smoke evaporated—her pounding heart the only sound over the whisper of black petals falling around her.

GLENNA WOKE, GASPING for air. She fumbled for her bedside lamp, almost knocking it over as she switched it on. Light flooded her bedroom and she searched the room frantically for signs of a fire. But there were no burn marks on her furniture. Her candles held their original shape. And her curtains were still intact. Her gaze fell to the windowpane. The glass wasn't broken.

Everything looked the same as when she'd turned out the light and gone to sleep.

But the roses. She threw off the covers and swung her feet to the floor. They were here.

She wrenched open the window and leaned out into the night, breathing in the familiar odor of salt and sea. She scanned the dark soil beneath her window. There were no black roots or curved thorns clinging to the whitewash.

She pushed back from the window, grabbing her robe. They had to be here somewhere. She stumbled through the darkness, feeling her way through the living room to the door and slipping out into the night.

Moss crackled under her bare feet as she circled the cottage. A hardy edging of rosemary skirted the foundation. Crocuses— confused by the unseasonably warm weather—were sprouting in a few of the beds. But there was no sign of the roses.

Which could only mean... Glenna's blood went cold. *Sam.*

That dream only ever meant one thing—her lover was in danger. But Sam wasn't her lover. It was all a mistake!

She ran back into the cottage, grabbing her boline—a ritual knife used for harvesting herbs—from the drawer beneath her altar. Moonlight glinted off the curved blade and she stood, stuffing her feet into the first pair of shoes she could find.

She'd been so careful to keep Sam at arm's length. Because every time a man fell for her, the same thing happened. She raced into the night, her heeled boots carrying her over the fields as the laces streamed out behind her.

The dream had found her here after all this time. She thought she had finally escaped it. She thought she was safe here.

She had been until Sam arrived.

She searched the village as she ran. Her gaze combed every cottage for a sign of them, for that tell-tale glow. But she knew deep down where they would be—growing outside the caretaker's cottage on Brennan Lockley's farm.

She crossed the island to the sloping hills of Brennan's land, passing sheep fields and horse pastures. Jagged stone walls lined the footpaths and dark shadows streaked over the moss. She spotted Sam's cottage and her hands gripped the white handle of her boline when she saw the coral flowers blooming against the whitewash.

SAM WOKE TO the scent of roses. He heard a faint scraping and rustling outside his window, and he sat up, dragging a shirt over his head. Snagging a pair of jeans off the floor, he stepped into them and crept through the house, slipping silently into the night, ready to confront whoever—or *whatever*—was out there.

Barefoot, he rounded the front of the cottage and blinked. Glenna knelt in front of a knotted vine, hacking at the dark roots with a sharp, hook-shaped blade. A sheen of sweat clung to her forehead and her long brown hair curled riotously around her shoulders. Her thin satin robe had slipped off one shoulder, revealing only a sheer cream slip underneath. Her legs were bare save the ankle high russet boots and long laces she hadn't bothered to tie.

"Glenna?"

She wouldn't look at him. Her heavy hair fell into her eyes and she kept stabbing at the base of the roots. Sam felt a cold knot form in his stomach when he noticed the magnificent blooms unfurling along the thorny vine—roses the color of an autumn sky on fire.

"Glenna," he said again, walking toward her. "Glenna, look at me."

She jammed the knife into the roots and Sam leaned down, putting his hand on her elbow. She jerked back and he cursed, sidestepping and narrowly missing the swing of the blade. He saw that her hands were bleeding and grabbed her by the shoulders, hauling her to her feet.

"Let go of me!" Glenna shouted, lurching out of his grip and reaching for her knife.

But his arms came around her and he held her tightly against him until she stopped struggling. "I need," she said, breathless, still staring at the flowers, "those roses."

He twisted her around to face him, keeping his grip firm on her upper arms. "What are you going to do with them?"

"Destroy them."

A chill crept down Sam's spine. He knew how dangerous it was when roses grew out of season on this island. "Why?"

She lifted her haunted eyes to his. "You need to leave the island, Sam. You're not safe here."

Sam shook his head. "You can't get rid of me that easily. Come on." He steered her toward the front of the house. She tried to twist out of his grasp, but he guided her through the door and into the small kitchen.

She flinched when he turned on the faucet and directed her hands under the spray. He washed her wounds with soap and she bit her lip to keep from whimpering. He knew it stung. He saw the scrapes as the blood washed down the sink, the long abrasions where the thorns had cut her.

He gave Glenna a clean towel to dry her hands and reached under the sink for a First Aid kit, unwinding a wad of gauze. "Are you going to tell me what this is about?"

"We were fine before you came here, Sam. You brought trouble to this island."

Sam shook his head. "That's not good enough." He took her hand and wrapped the gauze gently around it. "Besides, Liam *asked* to find his mother. Brennan *asked* me to help out on the farm." He lifted her hand to his mouth and cut the strip of gauze with his teeth. "You need me, even though you won't admit it yet."

Glenna stepped back, out of his reach. "No one needs you, Sam."

Sam set the gauze down. She might as well have jabbed the blade into his gut. Because the truth was, no one had *ever* needed Sam. He had only ever succeeded in bringing pain and heartache to everyone he loved by digging up awful truths and finding things that were better left buried.

But where he might have accepted that as truth before, he didn't anymore. Not after the friendships he'd made on this island. Not after everything that had happened since he'd arrived. He was finally starting to have faith again, to believe he could have a different life.

Part of the reason he'd agreed to take on this last case was to prove to everyone, especially Glenna, that he'd changed. "I'm not leaving, Glenna. I'm going to find Dominic and Liam's mother. And then I'm going to come back and help Brennan with the farm. Whether you like it or not, as long as we're both living on this island, I'm a part of your life."

Glenna looked down at her wrapped hand. "You need to stop this investigation. You need to stop it now."

"I can't." Sam said. "I won't. Not unless you tell me that this case is somehow putting *you* in danger."

Glenna's gaze shifted back to the window, where a ghostly glow illuminated those midnight-blooming roses. "I'm not the one you should be worried about."

CHAPTER 5

The bell on the door of the market jingled as Caitlin stepped into the street. The morning sun hung like a tarnished bronze ball in the hazy sky, and the warm winds blowing through the village smelled of sea salt and roasting ham. She headed for the pub, pausing when she spotted Glenna round the corner.

"Where are you going in such a hurry?" Caitlin asked.

Glenna glanced up, hesitating for only a second. "The ferry." She dug in her purse, her silver bracelets jangling as she pulled out her watch. "I'm headed to Galway to do some shopping."

"The ferry's gone," Caitlin said. "Finn and Sam left about a half hour ago."

Glenna stopped short. "What?"

Caitlin shifted the paper bag she was carrying to her other arm. "Sam finally got through to a librarian he's been trying to reach—the one who knew Brigid. She arrived home late last night from holiday and called him to set up a time to talk. He wanted to leave early so he could make it to Dublin on time."

Glenna looked out at the water, fear swimming into her eyes as she spotted the ferry, barely a dot in the distance.

Caitlin frowned. "I'm sure Finn would have waited if he'd known you wanted a ride."

Glenna pushed at her heavy hair. "Since when does Finn leave early for anyone? He always leaves at ten. *Exactly* at ten."

You might still be able to catch a ride with Donal." Caitlin glanced over her shoulder at the harbor to see if the fisherman's boat was still there. "I'm not sure if he's left yet."

"He's gone," Glenna murmured, her gaze already locked on the empty boat slip.

A gull cawed, circling the harbor. Caitlin watched it land on a piling, noticing how low the water mark was on the wood. A wave of uneasiness washed through her when she looked back at Glenna, noting the dark circles under her friend's eyes. Her thick brown waves were knotted around her silver necklace and a single garnet teardrop dangled from her left ear. She'd forgotten to put in her other earring.

"Is everything alright?"

Glenna slid her purse back onto her shoulder, looking back to the ferry. "I really needed to get to Galway today."

"Well," Caitlin said slowly. "You *could* help me shop instead."

"For what?"

Caitlin held open the bag so Glenna could see inside. "Sarah special ordered them for me. I know it seems silly—it's not like I'm planning some big fancy event—but I wanted to get some ideas."

Glenna pulled out one of the glossy bridal magazines. She looked at it for a long time with an unreadable expression on her face before lifting her eyes to Caitlin's. "I should have been the one to give you these."

Caitlin shrugged, tucking the bag back under her arm. "You've been busy."

"I have," Glenna admitted. "But not too busy to help my best friend shop for her wedding dress." She draped her arm around Caitlin's shoulders. With one last look at the retreating ferry, she steered her toward the pub.

GLENNA SETTLED ONTO one of the swivel stools at the bar as Caitlin went into the kitchen to ask Fiona to fix them a plate of scones. The last thing she wanted to do right now was look through bridal magazines, but her friend deserved this. She deserved to be happy, especially after the pain and heartache Moira—her *own* mother—had put Caitlin through.

She took a deep breath, running a hand through her hair. Maybe Sam would be okay on his own. Maybe it was proximity to *her* that caused the most danger. Maybe it would be best for all of them if she tried to act normal. She glanced up when Caitlin walked back out.

"Dominic's trying to fix the broken refrigerator," Caitlin explained as he started banging around in the back. "It blew a fuse this morning, probably because of this bizarre heat wave."

Glenna nodded, looking away. The heat would only get worse as the days passed. She spotted Owen and Brennan in the corner. They were sitting in the two arm chairs by the window, the elderly man puffing on a wooden pipe while Owen read aloud. "Shouldn't Owen be in school?"

Caitlin snagged two mugs from the rack above the bar, setting them on the counter. "Mary thinks we should wait until he's a bit farther along to introduce him into the classroom. I work with him in the morning and Liam at night, but Brennan's been chipping in a couple hours each day. He's been a big help."

Glenna took the magazines out of the bag, spreading them out on the counter. "Wouldn't he learn faster if he was exposed to other students, even if they aren't his age?"

"Yes." Caitlin dropped a bag of Earl Gray tea into each cup, her expression clouding. "But some of the kids have been giving him a hard time."

"Who?"

Caitlin poured hot water over the tea bags. "Well...Ronan, mostly."

"Ronan's always giving someone a hard time."

"Yes, but lately he has his sights set on Owen." Caitlin set the kettle down. Across the room Owen stumbled over a word as he read aloud. "Because he's...different."

Glenna's heart went out to him. Owen was learning to read for the first time because he'd spent the first ten years of his life underwater.

She had a pretty good understanding of what he was going through.

Caitlin pushed one of the cups toward her and Glenna took it, blowing on the steam rising out of the water. "But he's adjusting, right?"

"He is." Caitlin walked around the bar and settled onto the stool beside Glenna. "It'll take time. I have to keep reminding myself of that." Poking at the magazines, she sighed. "I have to admit, it feels strange to plan a wedding after all this time. Liam and I have such a history together. It's not like we met a couple years ago and this celebration is marking the start of our lives together. I gave birth to his son ten years ago."

"A son who you just got back," Glenna reminded her. "And who you're both just getting to know." She put her hand on Caitlin's. "You deserve this."

Caitlin's eyes widened when she looked down at their joined hands. "What happened to you?"

Glenna pulled her hand back quickly. She'd ditched the gauze from last night, using one of Tara's balms to seal the wounds. But she'd forgotten the red scratch marks on her skin. "I was digging in the garden yesterday. I had a bit of a misunderstanding with the rosemary."

"Since when does rosemary have claws?"

"I'm fine. The marks will be gone by tomorrow. I got carried away with the weather being so warm."

Caitlin pulled her gaze from Glenna's hand. "I know you like to garden, but take it easy, okay?"

"I will." Glenna smiled, opening one of the magazines and turning the picture to face Caitlin. "What about something like this?"

"You're kidding, right?"

"What?" Glenna asked. "It's pretty."

Caitlin made a face. "It's strapless. I have enough to worry about without my dress falling down." She picked up a magazine and flipped through it, frowning. She tossed it down and reached for the next one. "Who wears these dresses, anyway?"

Glenna stifled a laugh. "Lots of brides think these dresses are beautiful." She held up another picture of a model wearing a full-skirted gown with a heart-shaped neckline. "Like something out of a fairy tale."

"Right," Caitlin said sarcastically. "Come on, Glenna." She pointed to a picture of a woman wearing a veil that resembled a puffed-up cotton ball. "Would you wear any of these dresses to your wedding?"

Glenna looked down, brushing a hand over the magazine.

"Oh." Caitlin straightened. "Sorry. Sometimes I forget you were married before." She set the magazine down and glanced back up at her friend. "If you don't mind my asking, what *was* your wedding like?"

"I'd rather not..."

"Come on," Caitlin urged. "You can at least tell me about the dress."

Glenna's gaze shifted to the open door. A gull glided over the village, riding the salty breezes. "It was white silk. Armani."

Caitlin let out a low whistle. "Fancy."

"Yes." Glenna pulled her gaze back to the magazine, turning to the next page. "It was very fancy."

"I know it wasn't a friendly divorce, but do you ever hear from him? I mean, you guys *were* married."

"No."

"Do you ever wonder about him?" Caitlin pressed. "What he's up to?"

"No." Glenna paused in the middle of turning a page when she heard Owen reading a new story aloud. She swiveled in her chair. "What's Owen reading?"

"I'm not sure." Caitlin shrugged, eyeing Glenna strangely. "One of Brennan's books, maybe?"

OWEN SET THE book down in his lap. "Brennan, how come I never saw a mermaid when I was living underwater?"

Brennan puffed on a pipe. Smoke drifted out the open window. "I imagine Nuala was careful to keep you well hidden when there were mermaids nearby."

"Why? Don't mermaids and selkies get along?"

"Not exactly." Brennan leaned back in the chair, the leather creaking under his weight. "The mermaids are the protectors of the sea. The selkies are the connection between the sea folk and the land folk. They are supposed to maintain the peace between the two."

"Isn't that a good thing?"

"Aye." Brennan's lips closed over the pipe. "As long as the selkies hold up their end of the bargain."

"Why wouldn't they?" Owen tucked his legs under him, shifting to face Brennan. "Don't the selkies want peace?"

"Most of them, yes. But every now and then a selkie is born who has a different agenda."

Owen glanced across the room at Glenna. When he saw that she was watching him, he looked away quickly.

"Like Moira?" Owen asked, lowering his voice.

"Aye," Brennan said.

"Are there others?" Owen whispered. "Like Moira?"

"No. But there have been." Brennan glanced up as Fiona walked out of the bar, setting a plate of scones in front of Caitlin and Glenna. "In the past."

The two women turned around to chat with Fiona. Owen scooted closer to Brennan. "What happened?"

Brennan stretched out his legs, his knees cracking as his muddy work boots scuffed over the floorboards. "A long, long time ago, a selkie princess fell in love with a merman." Brennan dug in his pocket for his pipe tobacco. "Now, this was something that almost never happened," he added, packing a fresh pinch of sweet-smelling tobacco into his pipe. "It wasn't forbidden, but it wasn't encouraged either."

"Why? Because selkies are only supposed to fall in love with their own kind?"

"No." Brennan shook his head. "Because of how powerful their child would be."

Owen watched Brennan fumbling with his pack of matches. He took them from the elderly man's stiff fingers and lit a match for him, holding it over his pipe.

Brennan puffed on the pipe until the tobacco caught fire, then settled back into the chair. "Selkies and mermaids are powerful enough on their own. But a child of a union of these two creatures has unimaginable powers." He let the pipe dangle from the corner of his bearded mouth. "It's all about balance, you see. When any one person or creature gets too much power, everything shifts out of balance."

"Did they have a child?"

Brennan nodded. "They did. A daughter. And she grew up to be the most beautiful siren anyone had ever seen. Both families showered her with love and affection and the most precious jewels in all the sea. But after a while, she became greedy and spoiled. She wanted more than what her parents could give her, and she started to spend long hours on the surface by the busy sea ports, where the trading ships came and went.

"She began to abuse her powers, luring helpless men into the sea. She would sing to them from the rocks until they followed her into the waves and drowned. She got great pleasure from exploiting her power over men. She disrupted entire armies preparing a ship

for battle or sailing out of port. When she lured one of the great-
est warriors mankind has ever known into the sea, the men became
enraged and fought back."

"Did they catch her?" Owen asked.

Brennan shook his head. "They could never get close enough to
catch her, but they rounded up dozens of innocent seals and slaughtered them instead. They captured entire families of mermaids in
massive trolling nets and murdered them."

Owen shuddered, wrapping his arms around his stomach.

"You see," Brennan continued, "back then, mermaids and selkies
were more common in the shallow waters and men knew who and
what they were. They were not the creatures of legends and myths as
they are now. But men viewed selkies and mermaids as one and the
same—terrors to mankind, creatures to be feared."

"But it was only the one siren," Owen protested.

"It was," Brennan agreed. "But when the mermaids got word of
what was happening, they demanded the siren be handed over to
them. The selkies refused, and almost started a war between the two
species. As punishment, the mermaids corralled the selkies into the
waters around these islands and set up boundaries. They took away
their freedom to roam the seas and declared that if a child was ever
born of a selkie/merman union again, they would destroy it."

Owen's eyes went wide. "The selkies aren't allowed to leave the
waters around these islands?"

Brennan shook his head. "These waters are a sanctuary. They are
protected space for the selkies. As long as they stay inside the boundaries, they're safe."

"What happens if they try to leave?"

"The mermaids will kill any selkie who tries to leave the boundaries. It's the only way they can ensure that they maintain control,
and that everything stays balanced."

Owen's gaze fell to the book. He thought back to the years he'd
spent underwater with Nuala. He remembered how they'd lived in
that empty white palace, surrounded by tall locked gates. He remem-

bered how sometimes they would hide for days in one room, and she wouldn't let him come out. "It was really dangerous for Nuala and me to be banished from the safe haven, wasn't it?"

"Aye." Brennan said quietly. "I'm amazed you survived as long as you did."

"**HEY,**" **CAITLIN WHISPERED** as soon as the kitchen door swung shut behind Fiona. "What's going on with you? You hardly said two words the whole time she was out here."

"It's nothing." Glenna picked up a napkin, wiping at a nonexistent spot on the bar. "I guess I'm curious...why isn't Owen reading selkie stories? The legends of our islands, our culture? He should be reading those, not mermaid stories."

"Is that all?" Caitlin said, gathering up her magazines. "I don't care what story he reads as long as he's reading."

Glenna turned, catching a glimpse of Owen out of the corner of her eye. Caitlin's hands stilled on the magazines when she saw the look on her friend's face. "Glenna," Caitlin said quietly. "Is there some reason he shouldn't be reading that book?"

"Of course, not." Glenna lifted a shoulder lightly. "Owen should read whatever book he wants."

CHAPTER 6

The working class neighborhoods on the outskirts of Dublin were a jumble of gray stone buildings and winding streets. Remnants of Christmas still clung to some of the homes; tattered garlands drooped from metal railings and dried-out trees lay across the gritty sidewalk, waiting for the weekly trash pickup.

Sam pulled onto a narrow street and parked, cutting the engine. He took in the squat row house at the end of the block. Green shoots sprouted out of the tidy beds flanking a brick stoop and a stack of colorful pots leaned against a bag of soil.

Someone was hoping to get a jump start on spring.

Unfolding himself from the car, Sam ignored the dog barking at him from behind a barred window of one of the neighboring houses. He strode up to the cherry red door and rapped lightly.

"Mr. Holt." Eileen McKenna said, her smile warm and friendly as she opened the door. "You're right on time." She dusted her hands on a pink flower-printed apron tied around her ample waist. "I just pulled a batch of lemon cookies out of the oven."

"How did you know lemon cookies were my favorite?" Sam asked. The laugh lines around Eileen's eyes deepened as he shook her hand. Her skin felt smooth and papery, like a grandmother's should. "Please, call me Sam."

"Alright, Sam." She waved him inside. "I'm sorry it took us so long to get back to you. We never expected to be gone so long."

Sam scrubbed the soles of his boots over the welcome mat and ducked under the doorway, eyeing the brochures, souvenirs and chocolates spread out on the coffee table. "Belgium?"

She nodded. "Tom's been wanting to go for years." She looked over her shoulder, her green eyes twinkling. "My husband has a weakness for Belgian beers."

"Let me guess..." Sam held up a basket of truffles. "You have a weakness for their chocolate?"

"Guilty as charged." She grinned, nodding toward the spiral staircase and the faint sound of a radio announcing a local sports game. "But don't tell Tom that half of those aren't actually gifts for anyone."

Sam chuckled as he followed her through a cozy sitting room with a plaid sofa and a worn armchair. A small TV was propped up in the corner. The front windows were open and he could hear the cars passing by on the street.

"How do you take your tea?" Eileen asked.

Sam leaned against the doorway of a kitchen that smelled of melted butter and sugar. "Black. And I appreciate you taking the time to meet with me."

She poured tea into two mugs and added a dollop of cream to hers. She handed him the darker mug and snagged a spatula from the drawer beside the oven. "To be honest, Sam," she said, transferring cookies from the baking sheet to a platter. "I'm glad you called."

"Really?" Sam paused in the act of blowing on the steam floating out of the mug. "Why is that?"

She gestured for him to open the back door and led him out to a rickety metal table painted a cheerful apple green in the back garden. She set the cookies down and settled into the chair opposite him. "I've thought about Brigid a lot over the years. I'm surprised you're the first detective to ask me about her."

Sam nodded for her to go on.

"Brigid was part of the cleaning crew at the college," Eileen began. "She used to come into the library after hours to dust the books. I know it sounds silly—dusting the books. But the library at Trinity College is one of Ireland's finest museums. It's a celebration of our literary culture and heritage. Some of the books go back thousands of years."

"It's an impressive place," Sam admitted.

"Aye," Eileen smiled, straightening her shoulders with pride. "I took care to keep it that way for the twenty years I managed it." Sliding the platter toward him, she waited until Sam took a cookie. "Part of my job was to oversee the cleaning crew. Most of the girls were quiet, hard-working. There wasn't much to manage, really."

Eileen leaned back in her chair, cradling her tea in both hands. "But there was something about Brigid that worried me. I suspected things were not good at home. Every now and then, she'd show up with a fresh bruise on her face. And, despite protests from the other girls, sometimes she would bring her children with her to work."

"Was that allowed?" Sam asked.

"No," Eileen admitted. "But in her case, I let the rules slide a bit. Her two boys were very well behaved. They played quietly in the corner while she cleaned. And I spied bruises on them a time or two. I figured they were safer in the library than they were at home."

Sam thought about the neighborhood where Liam and Dominic had grown up, and imagined their drunk father stumbling home from the bars late at night. No wonder Brigid had brought them into work with her. "How long was she an employee?"

"Less than a year." Eileen broke off half of a cookie and nibbled on the edge. "But it was long enough for me to get to know her. One night, she didn't show up for her shift and didn't bother to call. When she didn't come in the next night, or the night after that, I tried to track her down, but no one seemed to know who she was or where she lived."

"Didn't she have to give an address on her employment form?"

"Yes. But it was a fake one. When I went to check, it was an address of a music shop in Bray. I asked the shop owner and the neighbors who lived around the shop. But they didn't know her. No one had ever seen a woman by the description I gave."

"What else did you do to track her down?"

"I went to the local hospitals." She looked up, her expression sober. "I thought...with the bruises and all, maybe there'd been an *incident*." She swallowed a sip of tea, and looked away. "But no one had checked in under that name."

Sam nodded. He'd done some searching too, hacking into the hospital records of every emergency room in this area. But no one named Brigid O'Sullivan had checked into a Dublin hospital in the winter of 1988.

"After a while, I went to the garda and filed a missing person's report. I was really worried. But they didn't take it seriously. They said her family would have come in, if something was really wrong. I tried to explain that maybe her husband wasn't such a nice man, but things were...different in Ireland back then. Domestic disputes were usually treated as a matter between a husband and wife and the garda didn't want to get in the middle of it."

Sam tapped his fingers over his mug. He was familiar with the situation. It wasn't that different in America still, to this day. It sure hadn't been any different for Tara. He studied Eileen across the table. She had done some digging. He was impressed with how hard she'd tried to find Brigid. It was her missing person's report that first caught his attention when he hacked into the Dublin police files. But a person without proper resources and without the help of the garda could only get so far. "What did the other women in the cleaning crew say?" Sam asked. "Didn't they know where she lived?"

Eileen shook her head. "They were glad she was gone."

"Why?"

Eileen wiped her sugar-dusted fingers on her apron. "Well, besides the fact that they thought she got special treatment, they blamed her for the disappearing books."

"The disappearing...books?"

"Yes." The corner of Eileen's mouth tilted up. "Soon after Brigid started working there, the librarians would come into work in the morning and find that some of the books from the lower shelves were missing." She sent Sam a look over her mug. "You have to understand that every book in the library is shelved with incredible attention to detail according to the topic and time period. This process can take weeks, sometimes months, of extensive research."

Sam nodded. "Of course."

"You can imagine how the librarians felt when their system was... compromised. First, they accused the cleaning crew of stealing, but then they started to find the books shelved in other places. To the librarians, that was almost as bad as stealing and they wanted to fire the entire cleaning staff. But the other girls came to me together and told me it was Brigid. They'd seen her moving books at night without telling anyone. Naturally, being the manager, I confronted her about it."

"And...?"

Eileen paused to take a sip of her tea. "She said she was moving them to their proper place."

Sam's brows shot up.

"I know," Eileen said. "You can imagine how I felt when she said that. It was my job to oversee the proper cataloging and organizing of the books. But Brigid was adamant that the books she moved were shelved in the wrong place and she had corrected the mistake."

"Was she right?"

"Well, you see. That's what's so strange about all this. When I looked into it, I realized she was right. In every case, some small detail had been overlooked and the book belonged exactly where she put it."

"Did she explain why she'd moved each book?"

"No. She never had an explanation. And she couldn't possibly have known without access to the information we had in our archives. She wasn't even a very good reader. But she had some sort of strange sixth sense about it."

Eileen paused as a siren screamed to life a few streets away. She waited for it to die down. "In every case except for one. There was one book—a story about selkies." She glanced up. "You're familiar with them?"

Sam snagged another cookie off the plate as the skin on the back of his neck started to prickle. "Yes."

"Well, there was an old fairy tale—a legend about a white selkie. She insisted it belonged in the section with the mermaids."

Sam paused, the cookie halfway to his mouth. *Mermaids?*

"You see," Eileen went on, "the selkie stories are in one section—under *Irish* mythology. The mermaid stories are in a different section—under *general* mythology. You'd think those sections would be close to each other, but they're not. The Irish have a lot of pride for their *own* culture and legends. And while we respect the legends and myths of the world, we'd rather put our own on special display in our country's premier literary museum."

"Of course," Sam murmured, thinking back to the theory Tara had voiced in the pub yesterday—that maybe Brigid hid the book in a specific spot in the library to give them a clue. "Did she move any of the other selkie stories to the mermaid section?"

"No." Eileen shook her head. "Only the one. Which is why we had such a heated debate about it."

Sam's gaze lifted to the back of the row house edging up to Eileen's back garden, at the long electrical wires hanging out the windows. "But why would she re-shelve only that one? And not the rest of the selkie books?"

"Believe me, I asked the same thing. But she wouldn't tell me. She never had an explanation. But she warned that if I tried to put it back, she'd move it again. After a few days, I gave up. A week later, she was gone and we never heard from her again."

Sam stared at a curved groove in the surface of the rusted table. "Did you put the story back?"

Eileen shook her head. "No."

Sam glanced up. "Why not?"

"I'm not sure," Eileen admitted. "But something about Brigid's sudden disappearance has always haunted me. I've always felt that something bad must have happened to her. And I guess I hoped that maybe one day she would show up again." She looked down, into her tea. "I think I left it there in case she ever came back. So she would know that I...believed her."

"Do you?" Sam said slowly. "Believe her?"

Eileen looked up, her green eyes filled with concern. "I think there's a reason Brigid put that book there. I only wish I knew what it was."

"BRIGID," SISTER EVELYN called softly through the door as she knocked. "We're having a last minute visit from Father McAllister. I wondered if you could put together a flower basket for the dining room?"

Sister Evelyn heard a faint scuffing noise and she put her ear to the door, tapping again. When she didn't get an answer, she sighed and let herself in. A small shaft of light illuminated Brigid's sparse furnishings. Her small single bed was already made—the corners tucked in, not a wrinkle in the material. The pens on her desk were lined up neatly in a row. Her stationery was stacked in a single corner, the edges aligned with the desk.

But the woman on the floor was only half-dressed, her long hair a tangled mess of black waves and knotted river grasses. "Oh, Brigid," Sister Evelyn closed the door and sank to the floor beside her friend. "Not again."

"I thought I heard him," Brigid whispered, her eyes focused on the book beneath her palm. Slowly, she shifted it into a different position. "I thought I heard his voice in the river."

Sister Evelyn brushed Brigid's heavy hair back from her face. The grasses broke off, crackling to the floor. Her friend had gone down to the river last night...again. "But he wasn't there?"

Brigid shook her head, reaching for another book and sliding it behind the last one in the second row. Twelve books on gardening. All hardbacks on loan from the local library. Sister Evelyn had left them in the common room for everyone to look at. She'd been surprised when she walked through the room this morning and noticed they were gone. "What are you doing with the books, Brigid?"

"I need to put them in order."

"How about alphabetically?" Sister Evelyn suggested gently.

Brigid shook her head. "No."

"How about by variety? Or blooming times? Earliest to latest?"

"No."

"Tallest to smallest?"

"No." Brigid shifted another book around. The back cover scraped against the floorboards. A warm wind ruffled the curtains and Brigid paused, lifting her eyes to the rolling green hills outside. "Something's wrong."

"There's nothing wrong." Sister Evelyn picked the river grasses out of her friend's hair. The rest of the nuns might think Brigid was crazy. But they hadn't known her when she was in that hospital. They hadn't seen what those people had done to her. They didn't understand that Brigid's obsession with organization was the only shred of sanity she could claim in a life that had spun wildly out of control.

"The gardens are starting to bloom," Sister Evelyn said cheerfully, shaking more grasses out of her hair while Brigid continued to stare out the window.

Brigid nodded, her gaze following the path of a robin into the forest.

"We might see daffodils for the first time in January."

Brigid shook her head, the grasses rustling around her bare shoulders like tiny bones in the wind. "It's not time."

"It's only a heat wave," Sister Evelyn said gently.

Brigid's pale eyes—the color of storm clouds gathering over the sea—shifted to Sister Evelyn. "It's not time." Her cold fingers wrapped around Sister Evelyn's wrist. "It's not right."

CHAPTER 7

O wen glanced over his shoulder, as he did every night when he wandered down to the beach at sunset. Hardly anyone came here. It was mostly rocks and they could get slippery at high tide. But the coastline was bone dry. Even the lichens crackled under his feet as he picked his way over them.

He paused when he spotted a starfish washed up on the shore. He knelt, scooping it up and carrying it back to the water. Strips of dried seaweed broke off and crumbled under his shoes. His eyes widened when he saw the dozens of pale sea stars stranded on the thin sliver of white sand. He dropped the book he was carrying and scrambled over to them, picking them up and tossing them back into the water.

A lone seal swam into the shallow waters and circled the starfish, swishing her tail fins to help them back into the deeper waters. When Owen and the seal had returned all the starfish back to the sea, Owen glanced up at the horizon. The sun, a copper coin in the distance, was almost touching the hazy edge of the sea.

"I have to get back," he whispered. But the seal swam closer. She lifted her sleek head out of the water and crooned out a sad song. Owen bit his lip. His parents expected him home before dark. He looked at the road leading back to the village. Maybe he could stay a little longer if he ran home.

Picking up the book, he climbed onto the long flat rock that hung over the water and sat with his feet dangling over the edge. He opened to the page where he'd left off last night and started to read.

"'Don't you love me best of all?' the little mermaid's eyes seemed to question him, when he took her in his arms and kissed her lovely forehead.

'Yes, you are most dear to me,' said the Prince, 'for you have the kindest heart. You love me more than anyone else does, and you look so much like a young girl I once saw but never shall find again. I was on a ship that was wrecked, and the waves cast me ashore near a holy temple...'"

He trailed off as Nuala dipped and spun in frantic circles under the surface of the water. She flipped, somersaulting, and then hopped up onto the ledge of the rock, her pale eyes pleading at him to go on. Owen read a few more paragraphs, stumbling over some of the bigger words. He paused when Nuala nudged his fingers with her wet nose.

"What is it?" he whispered. She let out a low whimper and he ran his hand tentatively over her head. He knew she couldn't answer. But she scooted closer, rubbing her nose on the pages of the book. He flipped back a few pages until she stopped nudging the book and he squinted to make out the words through the fading light.

"She saw dry land rise before her in the high blue mountains, topped with snow as glistening white as if a flock of swans were resting there. Down by the shore were splendid green woods, and in the foreground stood a church, or perhaps a convent..."

Nuala splashed back into the water, swimming in frantic half-circles around the rock. Owen paused, his finger on the word as he sounded out the syllables again. "Con-vent?"

She nodded, splashing warm water onto the rock.

"Con-vent," he said again, not entirely sure if he was pronouncing it right. He didn't know what a convent was. But it must be important. He slipped the gold ribbon back between the pages as the sun dipped into the ocean. He stood, waving goodbye to Nuala. "I have to go," he called over his shoulder as he scampered over the rocks to the road. A trail of seawater dripped from the hem of his pants, steam rising up in his wake.

GLENNA LAID A stick of sage across a small driftwood fire. The dried herbs crackled as she stepped out of her cloak. The ocean lapped at her feet, warm as a tide pool on Lunasagh. A swallow darted out of the caves, its black wings beating against the inky blue sky. She lifted her arms, the swell of power building inside her as ripples danced over the surface of the water.

Sky above me, sea below me, fire within me
Give me strength to see more clearly

The sea churned, bubbling around her ankles. Steam floated up from the surface and gathered in Glenna's upturned palms. The air crackled as the mists crystallized, sparkling in her hands.

She bowed her head as her fingers closed over the salt. The tide rose, the water seeping over the scorched sand. It rushed like silk through her toes as she walked to the fire. Slowly, an image began to form in the flames—Sam sitting at a corner table across from a white-haired man in a crowded Dublin pub.

Salt of the earth
Salt of the sea
From seed to birth
I banish thee

She flung the salt into the fire. Sparks exploded from the flames. When the image reformed, the white-haired man was gone and Sam sat alone at the bar, nursing a glass of whiskey.

From the silver chain around her neck, she unscrewed the small glass vial—Tara's tincture—and poured the herbs into her palm. She blew them over the flames and watched as a white light of protection formed around him.

> *By the light of the moon*
> *On this January night*
> *I call on thee*
> *To shield and protect*
> *May no harm be done*
> *No more harm to come*
> *By the power of three*
> *So mote it be*

The ocean receded, and the flames died, leaving only a pile of knotted driftwood inside a circle of stones. Glenna stepped back from the logs and lifted her gaze to the moon.

SAM SNAGGED THE last stool in the crowded bar in Bray—a gritty, working-class neighborhood at the southern tip of Dublin. A hurried bartender wiped the spot in front of him with a wet rag and leaned in, shouting over the jumble of voices. "What's your pleasure?"

"Whiskey."

The bartender pushed back from the bar and filled a glass with a healthy shot, and slid it toward him.

Sam wrapped his fingers around the glass. "Is Padraig Smythe here yet?"

"He left ten minutes ago."

Sam pulled out his phone, checking to see if there was a message. There wasn't. "Do you know if he's coming back?"

"Don't think so," the bartender answered. "He said something came up at home."

Sam knocked back the shot, setting the empty glass back on the counter and pushing it toward the bartender for another. Just when he was starting to catch a rhythm. He shook his head, frustrated. He couldn't seem to catch a break with this case. Every time he picked up a lead, he ran into another wall.

The bartender refilled his glass and Sam gazed out the dingy windows of *Teach Óir*, the dive bar around the corner from the music shop Brigid had listed on her employment form. He'd talked to Padraig Smythe, the owner of the shop, less than an hour ago. Padraig couldn't remember anyone by the name of Brigid O'Sullivan, but he'd agreed to meet Sam here for a pint.

Sam was hoping he might be able to jog the man's memory.

So much for that idea.

"Blackthorn cocktail," a clipped Irish accent called over the swell of voices in the bar.

Sam eyed the girl, probably around eighteen, with short black hair and a lip piercing. She wore black leather cuffs around her wrists, and silver pentagrams winked from her fingers. "Blackthorn cocktail?"

She nodded, picking at her black nail polish.

Sam thought of the roses growing outside his cottage, the thick black vines with long sharp thorns. "What's in that?"

The girl didn't even bother to look at him. "Whiskey, vermouth, bitters and absinthe."

Sam noted the tattoo on her neck, a small crescent moon. "Why is it called a blackthorn cocktail?"

The girl sent him an annoyed glance. Dark eyeliner was smudged around her smoky gray eyes. "Blackthorn's a *plant.*"

"What does it look like?"

The girl glanced back at the bartender, drumming her fingers impatiently over the counter. When the bartender ducked into the back, she picked up Sam's fancy phone and searched the internet. "Here," she showed him a picture of a shrub with thick black stems, long thorns, and tiny white flowers. "It usually blooms around Imbolc."

"Imbolc?" Sam asked when she handed him back his phone.

The bartender walked back out with her drink and she rolled her eyes, laying a few Euros on the counter. "It's a pagan holiday. Look it up."

She turned, disappearing into the crowd. Sam slid his phone into his pocket. He was somewhat familiar with Ireland's pagan celebrations. It was the Midsummer's Eve festival that had led him to Seal Island in search of Tara last summer. But he'd never heard of Imbolc, or blackthorn.

He made a mental note to look into both of them later.

Snagging a day-old newspaper off the end of the counter, he scanned the headlines. The noise in the bar rose to a fever pitch when he spotted the image of an oil painting in the bottom right corner. He checked the page number and flipped to the *Style Section*, taking in the collection of orange rose paintings adorning the walls of a fancy Dublin gallery.

> The Connelly Gallery is pleased to announce the first-ever auction of Glenna McClure's original rose paintings.

Rose paintings? Glenna? Sam stared at the flaming petals and fiery brush strokes. Since when did Glenna paint roses? He glanced at the address, pulling his phone back out and typing it in. The gallery was back in the center of the city, at least an hour's drive from here in rush hour traffic. He stood, pulling out his money to pay.

"Is that what I think it is?" The bartender twisted the newspaper around to face him. His expression went stony as he read the headline. He tore it off the bar, crumpling it in one hand.

Sam paused, his hand on his wallet. "Not a fan of roses?"

The bartender threw the newspaper in the trash. "I'm not a fan of that artist."

Sam slid his wallet back in his pocket. He kept his tone light and neutral. "Any particular reason?"

The bartender nodded, his jaw tight. "She used to live here."

"In Bray?" Sam asked. He knew Glenna was from Dublin, but he didn't expect her to live in a place like this, one of the seediest neighborhoods in the city. He expected her to have grown up in a townhouse along one of the affluent streets north of the river. "When?"

The bartender turned, clearing plates off the bar and dipping them in the sink. "About ten years ago."

Sam lifted a brow. "That's a long time to carry a grudge."

"Not if she killed your brother."

"She...what?"

The bartender dried his hands, flinging the towel over his shoulder. It landed with a sharp thwack. "He wasn't the only one. Three men died in this town because of her."

Sam slid back onto the barstool, signaling the bartender to fill up his glass again. "How old was she when she lived here?"

"Nineteen or twenty." The bartender snagged a pint glass from the rack above the bar, setting it under the taps. "She kept to herself mostly, but my brother couldn't stay away from her." His gaze hardened. "She was beautiful—too beautiful." His hand wrapped around the Smithwicks lever. "No woman should have that much power over a man."

Sam thought of Tara and Brigid—women trapped powerless in relationships with abusive husbands. It went both ways: the balance of power, the struggle for it. When any person got too much, the other was in trouble. "I take it...she didn't return his affections."

The bartender poured himself a shot, leaning his elbows on the bar. "She told my brother she wasn't interested. She told him, and his two friends, to leave her alone. But they were young and madly in love. They started following her around the neighborhood, knocking on her door in the middle of the night, singing her songs from the street when the rest of us were trying to sleep."

"How did she take that?" Sam asked.

"Not well." The bartender pushed back, sliding a pint of Smithwicks down the bar to a customer. "But where other women might have told them off or put a stronger bolt on their door, Glenna locked herself in her apartment and painted those orange roses." He jerked a thumb toward the trash can. "The ones you saw there? Only half a dozen of them in all of Ireland."

Sam reached for his glass and took a long sip.

The bartender's hand shook as he tipped the bottle, topping off his glass. "The same night she painted those roses, real roses grew in the gardens of the men who were after her. It was the middle of winter, but these orange blooms lit up like they were made of sunlight. We had to shut our blinds so we could sleep at night. Some of us went so far as to cross the street so we didn't have to look at them."

Sam thought of the roses growing outside his house, glowing as if their petals were on fire. He thought of Glenna in her robe, desperately trying to destroy them.

"When a week passed and she didn't come out of her home, my brother and the others finally gave up," the bartender continued. "Brokenhearted, they came into the pub and drank themselves senseless."

Sam nodded. That was pretty standard, wherever you lived.

The bartender slid the rag off his shoulder and wiped it slowly over the taps. "At the end of the night, they left and walked home to three different homes along the river. One by one, they fell into the water and drowned."

Sam's hand stilled on the glass. "All three of them?"

"Aye." The bartender nodded. "All three in one night."

Sam fought to wrap his head around it. He'd come here to talk to a man about Brigid. Not find a string of missing persons connected to Glenna. "And...you think this artist killed them?"

"I know she did." The bartender cleared the empty glasses off the counter, stacking them on the shelf under the bar.

"Then why isn't she in jail?"

"We went to the garda and tried to have her arrested, but there wasn't enough evidence against her. There were witnesses who'd seen how drunk my brother and his friends were before they left the pub. It was unlikely, but possible, that they could have stumbled into the river on their own."

"What about bodies?" Sam's gaze fell back to the few sips of whiskey left in his glass. "Surely, they washed up after a while."

The bartender shook his head. "The bodies were never found. But the roses—the day the men died—the roses in their gardens turned black."

THE ROSES FELL, tumbling to the ground. The scent of the petals grew stronger, the sickening sweetness dizzying in the heat. Glenna pushed her heavy hair back from her face, not even noticing the smear of blood on her arms.

She hacked at the stems, her blade severing the vines twisting up the walls of Sam's cottage. She gripped Finn's fillet knife—the sharpest blade she could find on the island—slicing through the thorns.

Sam didn't deserve this. None of them did.

She slashed at the roses, attacking the bush until there was only one long stem left—a thick vine of impenetrable black. She dropped the knife and sank to the ground amidst the knotted thorns.

A single rose bloomed, with one black petal unfurling in the moonlight.

CHAPTER 8

wen chased the football through the rutted streets of the village. It bounced toward Ronan, but Kelsey beat him to it. She squealed as she knocked it away from him and passed it to Ashling.

"Kelsey," Ashling called, as they raced past the pub. "Next time they want to play boys against girls, we should give them a head start."

Kelsey giggled, her blond hair flying out behind her. Owen's sneakers slapped against the pavement, and she glanced over her shoulder, hesitating for a split-second as the ball sailed back toward her.

"Kelsey!" Ashling shouted, but Owen knocked it away and it flew over the edge of the cliff.

"Oh, no," Kelsey groaned. They hurried over to the stone wall and spotted the ball in the water, the waves already pulling it out to sea. "Come on," she said, slipping through a gap in the wall and starting down the path. "My dad will kill me if we lose another ball."

Ashling trotted after her and Owen hung his head.

"Nice one, Fishboy," Ronan muttered, pushing past him and following the girls down the trail. "Maybe you could kick the ball in the right direction if your toes weren't webbed."

"Shut up, Ronan," Kelsey shouted over her shoulder. "I heard that."

Ronan glared at her. "It's not my fault I'm stuck with a teammate who'd rather read fairy tale books for girls than learn to play football."

"Hey," Kelsey snapped, turning. "Knock it off."

Ashling screamed, pointing at the beach. "What is *that*?"

Owen's gaze fell to the shoreline and his eyes went wide. Dozens of fish—tails twitching, silver scales glinting in the sunlight—flopped in the sand, gasping for air. Owen rushed down the path, pushing past the others. His feet slipped in the sand and he kicked off his shoes, racing toward the fish.

"Don't touch them!" Ashling yelled.

Owen scooped as many as he could into his arms and raced to the water. "We have to save them!"

"Ewww," Ashling whined, backing away and scampering back up the path. "I'm getting my mum."

Kelsey ran to help Owen while Ronan waded into the water and grabbed the ball. Hooking it under his arm, he sneered at Owen as he sauntered back to the cliff path. "Have fun, Fishboy."

Owen ignored him, sprinting back to the fish. Kelsey grabbed two and three at a time, tossing them into the water as fast as she could. When they'd cleared the beach, Owen sank to the wet sand at the edge of the surf. He held his breath as the last few fish darted away.

Kelsey sat down beside him. They both reeked of fish and her palms were nicked from the fins. She dipped them in the water, frowning as she washed off the slime. "The ocean's hot."

"Do you think it's too hot for the fish?"

"I don't know. I don't remember it ever being this hot before, even in the summer."

Owen picked up a black rock with little holes in it. Through the eerie yellow haze, he could see the passenger ferry motoring slowly toward the harbor. He wondered if Sam was on it again, bringing back another clue. "Did you know they found our grandmother's pelt?"

Kelsey nodded. "I heard my mum and dad talking about it last night, after they thought I'd gone to bed."

"Me too." Owen lowered the rock, scratching grooves into the wet sand.

Kelsey sat back, drying her hands on her shirt. "Do you think she's still alive?"

"I don't know." The ocean lapped up, leaving a spray of foam at their feet. Sandpipers chased the receding wave, pecking at air bubbles for insects. "Kelsey?"

Kelsey scooped up a handful of sea foam, holding it up to her mouth and blowing it back out into the waves. "Yes?"

Owen looked down at his bare feet, at the thin translucent webbing between his toes. "Do you think fairy tales are only for girls?"

"Of course, not," Kelsey snapped. "Ronan's a jerk." She stood, glaring up at the village where Ronan was kicking the ball against the wall. "And a coward!"

SLICES OF SUNLIGHT pierced the surface of the ocean, illuminating the kingdom of green. Nuala swam south, leaving the glittering spires and gates far behind. Her fins propelled her deeper, into the darkness. Sharp jagged rocks rose up from the sea floor. Fish—the few who dared venture into this part of the sea—floated belly-up, their beady lifeless eyes warning her to turn back.

She knew the risks of entering the sea witch's lair without permission. But she could not let Moira win. Not when she—Nuala—was responsible for putting the selkies in this awful position. The rush of heat seared her seal-skin, but she pushed through the stunted black polyps.

She'd been young and foolish when she'd turned her back on her fate. She'd been born a white selkie—destined to be queen. But instead of honoring tradition, and bringing a land-man into the sea to rule beside her, she'd chosen a selkie lover.

When her lover had died only a few years later, she'd gone to the sea witch for help and she'd made a foolish trade that had cost her everything. She'd thought the sea witch would understand her, would *sympathize* with her. For there was a time, long ago, when Moira had also been willing to turn her back on her kingdom for love.

Nuala skirted the splintered ruins of a ship. Algae dripped from the fractured wood and clung to the bones scattered over the black rocks. Eels slithered through the dark waters, snapping at her with sharp angry teeth. Nuala spun away from them, but the ocean grew thick, making it harder to swim. The heat was oppressive, almost too much to bear. But she kept going, swimming toward the black mountain rising up in the distance.

Nuala and Moira had both lost the ones they loved. But while Nuala's love had been returned, Moira's had not. And the bitterness of that rejection had eaten away at Moira until there was nothing left but darkness inside her.

There were few who knew the truth. But Moira had confided in her in a moment of weakness, when she had been desperate for a friend. And she had confided something else—something she should never have told anyone.

Moira had kept an object that had belonged to her lover—something she'd never been able to part with. She'd hid it in her lair, and it had been safe there. Until now.

No one would dare venture into these waters, except the desperate souls willing to make a trade. Entering the sea witch's lair for any other reason was punishable by death.

But Nuala had not come here to make a trade. And she was not afraid of death. Pockets of boiling lava bubbled up from the rocks and she swam faster, dodging the spitting fire pits. Everything and everyone in her life had been taken from her. Who would miss her when she was gone?

It was up to her to right this terrible wrong. To make sure Moira never claimed the throne. Moira may have stolen her powers and her white pelt, but she had not taken what was inside her. She had survived for ten years outside the protected waters. She had raised

Owen alone, with no help from anyone. And she would not let any more harm come to him—even if she was no longer his mother.

She averted her eyes from the garden of ghostly black roses that undulated in the currents outside the gaping mouth of the sea witch's cave. She swam inside, ignoring the scream of the eels behind her. A black cauldron bubbled and a pool of lava heated it from below. The gleaming ebony walls were covered in iron shelves filled with small glass vials. The vials held anemones, salmon scales, starfish tips, and squid ink—ingredients for her spells.

The cave stretched into the mountain, the dark hallways lit by deep sea glow fish—frozen in glass jars that hung like sconces. She chose the path to the right, her heart beating wildly as every swish of her back fins led her deeper into the caves. There was no way out if Moira returned before she claimed her prize.

A warm light radiated from the end of the hall and she followed it to a chamber of onyx and gold. Jewels from the shipwrecks— diamonds, rubies, sapphires and gold—sparkled from chests and long pearl necklaces dripped from the open drawers of Moira's vanity. A bed carved from volcanic rock and encrusted with thick chunks of gleaming amber took up most of the room. Rich velvet tapestries of white and gold lined the walls. On the floor, a labyrinth of lava twisted around the small glass chest where a crown of blackthorn lay on a pillow of blood-red satin.

The white petals were still in bloom. Even after all this time. Nuala darted through the near-boiling water, whipping her back flippers around in a powerful *whoosh* to shatter the chest. It broke, pieces of glass nicking her skin as she lifted the precious crown carefully into her mouth and carried it from the room.

There were few who knew the secrets blackthorn held in its branches. This crown would give them the truth; the events of the past were written into its thorns. She swam, fast, through the cave, coming back out into the room with the cauldron. She was almost to the mouth of the cave, when she caught her reflection in the broken shards of a ship's mirror.

Pale eyes stared back at her, but her pelt was black now—like the rest of the selkies. She knew Moira had stolen her white pelt, but she had not seen it with her own eyes until now. She edged closer, but a flash of movement behind her had her whirling.

Moira glided elegantly out of the other hallway. "How nice of you to drop by for a visit, my dear."

Nuala cried out in pain, dropping the crown, when a scorching blast of heat seared her skin.

MOIRA CAUGHT THE crown as it fell, biting down lightly on the still-blooming branches. Nuala's limp form lay on the floor of the cave and Moira left her there, carrying the crown back to her bedroom. She laid it lovingly on its bed of red satin, and lifted the precious object to her vanity. She used her flippers to corral the broken glass into a pool of lava, where the shards melted and dipped into the rivers of fire.

She swam back out to the mouth of the cave where her eels waited, their golden eyes glimmering in the darkness. She nodded to Nuala and they slithered toward her, wrapping their long bodies around her like ropes. They bore her from the cave, lifting her onto a dark ledge high on the ridge of the volcano.

She wouldn't kill her. Not yet. She wanted her to suffer—a long, slow, painful death. The scream of the eels in the distance signaled they had left her on the ledge. Where she would stay until the volcano erupted.

Moira turned to the mirror as the broken pieces reformed, rippling in the darkness. The mirror pooled, dripping liquid silver down the ebony walls. An image reflected—her sister entwined in the arms of the man who should have been hers. She hurled a rock at the picture, shrieking with rage.

CHAPTER 9

Tara's face broke into a smile when she spotted Sam walking up the road from the harbor. She lifted her arm in a friendly wave. "I didn't expect to see you back on the island so soon."

Sam climbed the hill, closing the distance between them. "I have some news for Liam."

"About Brigid?"

Sam nodded, pausing beside the sheepdog perched on the stone wall and scratching him behind the ears. "I'm not sure what it means yet, but I want him to look into it."

"I'll let him know you're back."

"Thanks," Sam said. "What are you doing on this side of the island?"

"Brennan said his knees were hurting a bit." She tilted her face up to the sun. "Probably because of this crazy weather."

Sam lowered his hand to his side. "Do you think he's managing alright without me? I don't like leaving him alone on the farm for so long."

"He has help. Dom visits at least once a day and Liam's been lending a hand when he can."

Sam's gaze drifted over the mossy pastures to the gray stone barn. "You didn't happen to notice anything...strange while you were there, did you?"

Tara frowned. "Strange?"

Sam nodded.

"Not that I can recall," Tara said slowly. "Is there anything in particular?"

Sam dipped his hands in his pockets. "Do you have time to walk back with me? I'd like to show you something."

"At Brennan's?"

Sam shook his head. "At the caretaker's cottage."

"Sure," Tara said watching him closely as she fell into step beside him. But Sam kept his expression guarded as they continued up the sloping hill to the farm. Sunlight bathed the rolling emerald fields. A pony stuck its head over a stone wall as they passed, stretching out its neck for a treat.

Sam dug one out of his pocket.

Tara shook her head, laughing. "Have you been spoiling the ponies in Dublin, too?"

"I had them in my pocket when I left."

"Sure, you did."

"Actually," Sam said, glancing sideways at Tara, "I'm the one who got spoiled in Dublin." He pulled out a tin from his satchel, opening it and offering her a lemon cookie. "Compliments of Eileen McKenna."

"The librarian?" Tara asked as she helped herself to a cookie.

Sam nodded. "She said she's been waiting for someone to ask her about Brigid for years."

Tara's hand paused, halfway to her mouth. "She *what*?"

"I know," Sam said, picking a cookie for himself. Between chews, he told her about his conversation with the retired librarian, about how Brigid worked on the cleaning crew at the college and her strange habit of re-shelving books.

"So she didn't borrow the book." Tara snagged another cookie from the tin. "She was part of the cleaning crew."

Sam nodded. "According to Eileen, her habit of moving books caused quite a stir among the librarians. But the only book they couldn't understand was the white selkie legend."

They veered off the road and Tara took in the herd of sheep grazing in a nearby pasture as they walked up the dirt path to Sam's cottage. "And you're hoping Liam can find the connection?"

Sam nodded. "I thought about going to the library myself. But there are thousands of mermaid myths, in hundreds of different cultures. I don't have a clue what I'm looking for." He led her around to the far side of the house. "Liam's got his work cut out for him."

They rounded the corner of Sam's cottage and Tara sucked in a breath at the single black stem climbing up the whitewash. Its sharp thorns dug into the paint and there were marks along the vine, like someone had been hacking at it with a knife. The lone flower was sealed in a tight coral bud, and one of the outer petals was black.

"I was hoping it would be gone by now," Sam said quietly as he knelt down beside it.

Tara took a tentative step toward it. "How long has it been here?"

"Two days," Sam answered. "I might not have even noticed if Glenna hadn't come here at midnight to destroy it."

"Glenna?" Tara's heart began to race. "She knows about it?"

"Yes." Sam reached out, pressing his thumb against one of the thorns. "She wants me to leave the island. To stop the investigation."

"Why?"

"I don't know. That's what I'm trying to figure out."

"Do you think she knows something about Brigid? Something she's not telling us?"

Sam nodded, rising. "How much do you know about Glenna's past?"

"Not that much," Tara admitted. "Only that she moved here a few years ago after a nasty divorce in Dublin."

Sam looked at the black petal on the rose. "I'm afraid there's more to it than that." He took a deep breath. "I went to Bray last night—a small neighborhood on the south side of Dublin. I was following a lead on Brigid that turned up dry, but found out that Glenna used to live there."

"We knew she was from Dublin..."

"Not this section of town." Sam lifted his eyes to hers. "It's not a place you'd want your daughter living alone, at eighteen, looking like Glenna."

"Glenna didn't have much of a mother to look after her," Tara said quietly.

"No," Sam agreed. "But what happened between them? Glenna refuses to even talk about Moira. I'm beginning to wonder if the reason Glenna's so secretive about her past is because it's somehow connected to Brigid's."

When Tara opened her mouth, he nodded for her to follow him around to the front of the house. "We know that both Moira and Brigid are—or *were*—selkies," Sam continued. "And we know Glenna has selkie blood in her from her mother." Sam opened the door, gesturing for her to walk inside. "But don't you think it's odd that Glenna ended up on *this* island after her divorce?"

Tara settled slowly into the worn wooden chair at the rickety kitchen table-for-two. He offered her something to drink, but she shook her head. "I've been thinking about that too, Sam. Wondering how it all connects. But I think we have a better chance of finding Brigid than we do getting secrets out of Glenna."

She laid her hands on the table, spreading her fingers and gazing down at her gold claddagh wedding ring. It was the second ring she'd worn on that finger. But this one would be her last. "I've been struggling with something lately, too," she admitted. "I can't wrap my head around why Brigid would leave her children, how any mother could leave their children in that kind of situation. And I keep coming up with one answer." She lifted her eyes to his. "She didn't."

Sam pulled out the chair across from her, the legs scraping over the dusty floor. "What are you saying?"

"I'm saying"—Tara took a deep breath—"that when I was in that situation and tried to run, I was punished. And it only got worse with every attempt. It could be that she tried to leave with the children first." Tara twisted her wedding ring around her finger. "Maybe she tried to leave *with* them a few times. But every time she tried, she got hauled back and the punishment got worse."

"I checked the hospital records," Sam said. "There's no mention of a Brigid O'Sullivan in any of the Dublin hospitals. Or in any of the surrounding area hospitals for that matter."

"But what about under a name that's not hers?" Tara pressed. "Like a Jane Doe?"

Sam met her eyes across the table.

"It's possible," Tara said softly, "that if she tried to leave enough times, the last time he beat her so badly that she was unrecognizable. She could have been found by someone else, some*where* else, and admitted to the hospital. And if the beating was bad enough, she might have suffered substantial memory loss."

Sam lifted his satchel, laying it on the table and fishing out his small computer. "There could be dozens of Jane Doe's admitted to Dublin hospitals in the winter of '88. The records from the eighties are shoddy at best. They were still paper records then, and most of them haven't even been scanned into the system." But his fingers tapped through several layers of security, pulling up the records of a few hospitals in the area in different windows.

He identified three matches for a woman Brigid's age and shifted the computer so Tara could see the screen. Tara glanced over the first two medical files—a stabbing and a shooting. Possibilities, but not what she was looking for. She paused at the third. A woman in her late twenties was found unconscious and badly beaten on a beach south of Bray.

She looked up at Sam. "Didn't you say you followed a lead to Bray last night?"

Sam nodded and pulled up a larger size of the file. Tara scanned it quickly, but when her gaze locked on a single word in the middle of the page, her breath caught. "Pregnant?"

Sam scrolled through the rest of the file. "It says they transferred her to maternity, but there's nothing else in the file." He clicked again on the scroll bar but the third page of the file was missing. "We don't know where she was discharged."

"Or *if* she was discharged," Tara breathed, staring at the words, *severe hemorrhaging* and *emergency C-section* scrawled in the file. "Sam, if a woman in Brigid's position—with two children already— found out she was pregnant, she would do anything to leave. She may have been so desperate to get away from her husband that she wasn't thinking clearly."

Sam put his hand over Tara's and she realized they were shaking. "I'll go first thing tomorrow. There might be a nurse on staff who remembers her, who can dig up the paper record. It's probably not even her."

Tara's fingers gripped his hand. "The last time a nurse got involved in a situation like this, she was murdered."

Sam squeezed Tara's hand. She was referring to the nurse who'd helped her escape from her own abusive marriage—the nurse who her first husband had killed when he'd found out the truth. "I'll be discreet."

Tara lifted her eyes to his. "I don't know what we're dealing with."

"Dom and Liam's father is dead," Sam reminded her. "He died from a drug overdose years ago. He can't hurt her, or *anyone*, ever again."

"I know," Tara whispered. "But someone doesn't want Brigid found."

SAM TRAILED A finger along the fuchsia vine dripping over the fence post. It wasn't the only flower in bloom on this island. Daffodils were pushing through the hearty soil outside Sarah Dooley's shop and purple irises were budding in Caitlin's back garden. But the roses—the rest of the roses on this island—were still wintered-over. The only rose blooming was the one outside his house.

The one that grew overnight.

He followed the path of a wren to the small stone shed behind Glenna's house. Music played from the stereo propped in the windowsill and Glenna was inside her studio, painting on a large canvas with her back to him. The warm breezes teased the chocolate-brown curls tumbling to her slender waist. The light shining through the door lit the thin material of a pale green dress that skimmed her curves and fell softly to the floor.

She was barefoot, which was rare for her, even in the summer. There was something so disarming about finding her alone like this, when she thought no one was watching. His mouth went dry as his gaze lifted and he took in the outline of her lush figure through the gossamer fabric.

It wasn't hard to imagine how a man could become obsessed with Glenna. He was skirting the edge of it himself. But there was no way in hell that what had happened to those men in Bray was happening to him.

He walked toward her and saw her stiffen when the sole of his boot scuffed against the path of stones leading up to her studio. She turned, paintbrush in her hand, and those sherry-colored eyes locked on his.

Sam fought to keep his balance, as his eyes dropped to where her dress dipped in a low v. She wasn't wearing a bra and an errant paint streak trailed down the pale material, through the track of pearl-colored buttons holding it together. She'd missed a button, and a small piece of green fabric folded over like an invitation. He opened his mouth to say something, but no sound came out.

He lifted his heated gaze to her face. She wasn't wearing any makeup, and a wash of sunlight brushed her flawless skin, high cheekbones and striking almond-shaped eyes. There was something raw and unguarded in her expression and when her full unpainted lips parted slightly, he unhooked his satchel from around his neck and let it drop to the ground.

Screw the roses.

He strode to her, possessing her mouth in a searing kiss. She didn't try to push him away this time. She welcomed it, molding her soft curves to his hard chest and wrapping her arms around his neck. The scent of white sage and sea smoke clung to her hair, and he dipped his fingers into those glorious waves, relishing in the feel of her—any part of her—in his hands.

She kissed him back desperately, as if she were afraid he would disappear if she let go. The air sizzled, crackling between them. But he couldn't get her close enough. He couldn't get enough of her. His lips trailed down her cheek, his teeth scraping the sensitive flesh under her jaw. Her breath caught as he eased one hand free of her hair, his palm gliding down the front of her, closing over her breast.

She arched into him, her lips parting, her tongue tangling with his. A voice in Sam's head warned him to stop. To pull away from her. But his fingers found the opening in the delicate neckline. He could rip the buttons and have her naked, and under him, in seconds.

He cursed, when she bit down, hard, on his lip.

"Christ." Sam jerked back, his hand flying up to his mouth. He tasted blood and his pulse thrummed in his ears as he stared at her. "What the hell was that for?"

Glenna backed away from him, her breath shallow, her face flushed. "You have to stay away from me, Sam."

Sam pulled his hand away, rubbing his bloody fingers together. Glenna reached for the windowsill, steadying herself. Her eyes were still warm with desire, with need for him. A haunting melody played from the speakers and Sam switched it off, flooding the small studio with silence.

He went to her, ignoring the hand she stretched out to warn him away. He cupped her chin in his palm and waited for her eyes to lift back to his. "You could have said 'stop,'" he said quietly. "I would have."

Glenna let out a long breath. "I have trouble...controlling myself around you."

Sam let those words penetrate. It was the first time she'd ever admitted that he had an effect on her. "I need you to tell me the truth, Glenna. Do you have feelings for me?"

Glenna's eyes softened as she reached up, brushing a finger over his bloody lip. "I'm attracted to you, Sam. I won't deny that. But I don't have feelings for you." She lowered her hand and something swam into her eyes—like sadness. "Not in the way you want. Or deserve. I'm not..." She turned away from him, looking back out the window. "I'm not capable of having those kinds of feelings."

He turned her around by the shoulders to face him. "What kind of feelings?"

She lifted his hand, laying his palm over her heart. It was still beating rapidly, and her bare skin was still hot to the touch. But the fingers gripping his hand were cold. "I don't feel that emotion, like others do."

Sam eased his hand free, lifted the strap of her dress that had fallen, slowly inching it back up her shoulder. "Because you can't? Or you won't let yourself?"

When she didn't answer, his gaze dropped to her arms and he saw the scars in the light for the first time. He traced his fingers down her forearms to her hands, where the thorns had drawn long jagged scars into her pale skin. "You were married before, Glenna. Surely you felt something for your husband."

She shook her head. "It was a business arrangement." Her voice grew distant and matter-of-fact. "He was a wealthy Dublin developer. He needed a beautiful woman to take to functions. I wanted to meet all the richest people in the city so they'd buy my art."

"How...romantic."

Glenna pried her hands free from his grip and stepped out of his arms. "Romance was never supposed to factor in."

Sam picked up the edge in her voice and turned, watching her walk back to the easel. Her long skirt dragged over the stone floor. "Supposed to?"

"He was never supposed to fall in love."

"But he did."

"Yes." She looked away. "He did."

"Where is he now?"

Glenna picked up a new brush, but he noticed her hand shook slightly. "I don't keep track of those things."

"Well, I do," Sam said softly, leaning against the windowsill. "Your husband died in a helicopter crash the day your divorce went through. His chopper went down in the English Channel."

Glenna looked up at him, her expression cold. "That's public knowledge. You could read about it in any paper in Ireland that year."

"I know." Sam nodded, crossing his arms over his chest. "What I don't know is why you tried to hide it."

"I didn't hide anything." She dipped her brush in a well of black paint. She had lost a part of herself the day her husband died. She had only divorced him to save him from the curse, when she realized she could not keep him from falling for her. But nothing could save him. "I don't like talking about it."

"Because his body was never found?"

Glenna set down the brush, her eyes hardening. "Why do I get the feeling I'm becoming the subject of one of your investigations."

"Should you be?"

"I think you should leave now, Sam."

"I think I will," Sam said, pushing off the wall and walking toward the door. "But I am curious..." He wandered outside, snagging the strap of his satchel and turning back around to face her. "Is this a single tragic event in your life, or is this a pattern for you?"

"Excuse me?"

"I had an interesting conversation with a bartender in Bray last night."

Glenna's whole body went still. "You're crossing a line, Sam."

"Am I?" Sam walked back toward her. "Good. I plan to cross all of them before this is done." He pulled a small oil painting from his satchel and placed it on the edge of her easel.

Glenna's face went pale when she saw the orange rose. "Where did you get that?"

"There was an auction last night in Dublin. I thought you might be there. That is...until I heard the story behind the paintings." Sam leaned in, his lips a breath from her ear. "Next time you feel like *talking*, I'd like to know what the hell happened to those men."

CHAPTER 10

I t was after midnight when Glenna stole down to the beach. An eerie haze shrouded the moon and her bare feet caught in the snares of kelp twisting over the rocks. A fire burned in the shadow of the cliffs, teasing the hem of her mother's gold dress.

"The roses," Glenna breathed. "They're turning black."

Moira's eyes narrowed at her daughter's knotted hair, paint-streaked dress, and bare feet. "I know."

"I don't understand." Glenna's pale green skirt floated around her ankles as she came to a stop across from her mother. "The curse shouldn't be taking him. I've been so careful—"

"Not careful enough." The flames snapped, snaking dark shadows over Moira's face. "You cannot resist this man, Glenna."

"I can. I need a new spell—"

"No," Moira snapped. "*I'm* taking over now."

"I'm handling it. You have to trust me."

"I'm not good with trust." Moira's lips curved. "Besides, I want Sam. I have a use for him."

Steam whispered over the silent water, drifting like ghosts into the night. "What do you mean? What are you going to do with him?"

"Don't worry about things that don't concern you anymore, darling."

"But this *does* concern me."

"Why?"

"Because he doesn't deserve this."

Moira laughed, a bitter song gliding over the sea. She stepped over the fire, the hem of her dress crackling as it danced in the flames. "You're falling for him, Glenna."

"I'm not—"

"Shhh," Moira murmured, lifting a hand adorned in glittering rubies and stroking it over her daughter's pale cheek. "You've done much for me, Glenna. Much more than you will ever know."

SAM BOLTED UPRIGHT when the door to his cottage flew open. His bare feet met the floor and he fumbled for the lamp, knocking it over as he tried to find the switch.

"Sam!" Glenna grasped the door frame to catch her breath.

Sam righted the lamp, switching it on. "Glenna?"

Her face was pale, and her chest rose and fell as she struggled to breathe. She crossed the room to his dresser, yanking open the top drawer. "You have to leave."

Sam stared at her. "What?"

She shook her head, those luxurious curls snapping around her shoulders. She pulled his clothes out, throwing them on the bed. "There's no time."

Sam stalked up behind her, shoving the drawer closed. "No time for *what*?"

"You need to leave the island." She pushed a small metal object into his hand. "You're not safe here."

Sam looked down at the set of boat keys. "What the...?"

"Donal's," Glenna explained, brushing past him and snagging the strap of the duffel bag stashed under his bed. "Leave his boat at the wharf in Sheridan." She stuffed his clothes into the bag. "Finn can give him a ride there tomorrow."

"Glenna!" He grabbed her by the arms, twisting her around to face him. "Tell me what the hell is going on?"

"You need to leave the island, Sam." Her voice was edged with panic, her eyes wild with fear. "Now!"

"I'm *not* leaving," Sam growled.

"You want to know what happened to those men?" Fear shifted to anger like lightning. "The ones in Bray?" She jerked free of his grasp. "They died!" she shouted. "Because of me. My *husband* died because of me. And there are others—*half a dozen* others—who died because they fell for me."

Sam took a step toward her. "Is this why you've been pushing me away all these months—because you're afraid something's going to happen to me if I fall for you?"

"No," she breathed. But the roses scraped against the window, the long thorns re-growing from where she'd cut them off last night. "Yes."

"Too fucking late, Glenna." He grabbed her, his mouth claiming hers in a searing kiss.

GLENNA FELT HER world tilt. She pressed her palms to Sam's hard chest, sucking in a breath when he lifted her off her feet. Didn't he understand? There was nothing for him here! But when his mouth slanted over hers, forcing her lips to part, she felt the knots of fear in her belly loosen. She pressed her lips back to his hungrily. Not because she was giving in. But because this was the last time she would ever see him.

Sam twisted his hands in the material of her dress, sealing her to him. She could feel his heart hammering—a restless rhythm timed with her own. She ran her hands up his bare chest, over those broad shoulders. His muscles clenched, tightening under her touch.

"Sam," she breathed as his lips trailed down her neck. Sparks danced from her fingertips. Whispers of smoke wafted into the room. A single flame rose up inside her, and the need for him whipped through her like the first rays of a winter sunrise, painting the ocean a glittering gold.

She shuddered as his teeth nipped the strap of her dress, edging it off one shoulder. Her nails dug into the hard muscles of his back as he carried her toward the bed. His foot caught the cord of the lamp. It toppled, the bulb shattering as it crashed to the floor. Fireflies of electricity snapped feverishly at the darkness that fell like a curtain of smoke.

Glenna reached blindly for the headboard, hooking her long legs around Sam's waist as his knees bent and they tumbled together to the tangle of sheets that smelled faintly of mothballs and Sam's sweat. He flipped her until she was on top of him, straddling him. She could feel the pulsing heat of him throbbing under her.

Those tawny eyes lifted, burning into hers as his hands grasped the thin neckline of her dress. The fabric tore, ripping through the silence. Buttons scattered into the folds of the sheets, like the threads of her past unraveling, her darkest secrets spilling into the room.

But he was not afraid of her. He was not afraid of them.

"Glenna," he breathed, his voice hoarse with need. He molded his hands to her breasts and she reveled in the feel of his callused palms gliding over her heated flesh. She dipped her fingers into his thick blond hair—still tousled from sleep, and lowered her mouth back to his.

She had made love with men before, but she had never felt this throbbing ache in her chest—a painful tightening as if her heart would shatter if he pulled away. She deepened the kiss, her fingers twisting into his hair, tugging him closer. His teeth clamped down on her bottom lip greedily—nibbling, savoring, tasting. She wanted more, *needed* more of him.

Glenna's breath caught when he dipped his mouth to the sensitive tip of her breast. Her insides melted, pooling desire between her legs as the heat of his mouth wrapped around her. She pressed herself against him as he peeled the rest of her dress away. It fell to the floor in a whisper of silk.

A low sound of yearning escaped her throat as his heated palms scorched a trail down her back, imprinting on her hips, pulling her closer. She could feel the hardness of him, every inch of him, sliding over her. She reached for the waistband of his black boxers—the only stitch of cloth between them now.

She tugged them down his narrow hips and rose over him. The thorns scraped at the windows, scratching at the paint. The song of the ocean, a whisper of waves in the windless night, floated over the fields. She heard his soft low groan, felt his fingers digging into her hips as she lowered herself over him, as their bodies joined— became one.

The song grew. The sea, quiet for so many days now, began to chant. She felt its power, its voice calling to her. The song built in a cresting surge over the island. And as they began to move, their bodies joined in ecstasy, the waves crashed, beating against the rocks like a drum.

She reveled in the feel of him inside her, in the burning heat that fanned out from her center until her whole body glowed, pulsing toward him like an ember feeding on his every touch. Sam buried himself inside her, setting a breathless, steady rhythm until they were one heartbeat, one flame.

Smoke poured through the window, threatening to swallow them whole. But the roses flashed through the darkness, their brilliant blooms illuminating the sheen of sweat clinging to Sam's chiseled chest. Fire glinted in those whiskey eyes as he claimed her mouth in another scorching kiss.

She struggled to breathe, her hands sliding over his slick skin. She met him beat for beat, her body arching like a bow as the furnace flamed to life inside her. Petals unfurled, the vines clinging to the whitewash, scratching at the glass. She cried out his name as the wave of passion tore through her.

Her head fell onto his shoulder as his body clenched under hers. She shuddered as he pulled the last tremors from inside her. She pressed her hand to the warm glass of the window, streaked with steam. Black petals rained to the ground. He wrapped her in his arms, touching his forehead to hers. "I'm *not* leaving you, Glenna."

CHAPTER 11

When Sam got to the dock the next morning, Glenna was already waiting for him. She stood at the edge of the pier, gazing out at the horizon. Her thick brown tresses were bound, clasped in a copper clip that caught the morning sunlight. A yellow purse was draped over one shoulder and dark jeans tucked into tall leather boots hugged her shapely legs.

The cry of a gull echoed over the harbor as he stepped onto the pier. Glenna turned at the sound of his boots hitting the planks. The sunlight bathed her pale skin in an ethereal glow. Her eyes were guarded, her full mouth—painted scarlet—gave nothing away.

Sam's legs felt heavy as he walked to her. Glenna's black knit top crossed over her breasts and cinched around her slender waist with a knot off to one side. His fingers itched to set her curls free so they tumbled over her bare shoulders. He thought back to the day they'd first met. It was in the bar at *O'Sullivan's* pub during the Midsummer's Eve festival, when he'd come to the island in search of Tara.

He'd asked Glenna if she was a selkie, a woman of the sea who could bewitch a grown man. She'd laughed, but he was only half-joking. Because even then, in the crowded barroom, he'd felt the pull of her, the unmistakable threads of enchantment spinning around him until he was caught in her spell.

He knew the truth now—that the blood of the selkies did run in her veins. And he was bound to her now as a captain was bound to his ship. If one went down, so did the other. He was not afraid of the roses growing outside his cottage. What happened to Glenna's lovers before was not happening to him. They had broken two curses on this island together.

They would find a way to break this one. And he was certain—*certain*—Brigid was the key to unlocking all the clues.

He was close enough now to spy the pale blue crystals that hung from Glenna's ears. The hand that rested lightly on the strap of her purse was adorned in a variety of glittering gemstones. She had her armor back on, Sam mused. She opened her mouth to say something, and he gave into the instinct to lean down and plant his lips on hers.

He felt her stiffen, and grabbed her arms before she stepped back off the edge of the pier. She let out a muffled protest, hooking a hand in the front of his T-shirt to keep from falling. He pulled her to him, deepening the kiss. When he finally let her go, she was out of breath.

"Good morning," he murmured huskily, easing her away from the edge of the pier.

Glenna jerked the strap of her purse back up her shoulder. "Don't do that again," she warned, brushing past him. Her heeled boots clicked over the metal platform leading up to the ferry. Sam turned, watching the sway of her hips. He unhooked his sunglasses from the neck of his shirt and slid them onto his face.

Searching Dublin hospitals for a Jane Doe wasn't exactly how he'd pictured his first date with Glenna. And he had a feeling she wasn't going to make this task any easier. In fact, he was fairly certain the only reason she was tagging along was to try and stop him. He nodded to Finn as he boarded the ferry, and the skipper raised an eyebrow at the spectacle on the pier. Sam smiled. Good thing he knew how to shift her focus.

TARA STOOD AT the window of her cliff cottage, watching the ferry motor toward the mainland. A bouquet of dried lavender hung from a silver ribbon tied to a nail at the top of the window, and she breathed in the sweet floral scent. But it did little to calm her. She could feel the shift in the ocean; the change in the winds.

Dominic had gone down to Sam's to have a look at the roses. The door to the cottage creaked when he opened it. He walked inside, shutting the door behind him.

Tara didn't bother to turn. "Did you see them?"

"Aye." Dominic crossed the room to her. "I saw them."

Outside the window, Tara's seashell chimes clinked in the wind. "How many?"

"At least a dozen."

Tara closed her eyes. "They grew back."

Dominic came up behind her, settling his hands on her shoulders. He pulled her back gently against his hard chest. She could feel his heartbeat through his sweat-soaked shirt. The odor of earth and roses clung to his skin. "You're sure there was only the one rose yesterday?"

Tara nodded.

He wrapped his arms around her waist. "There's nothing underneath the plant."

"How far did you dig?"

"Far enough. And there's no use trying to cut roots. They're as tough as iron."

"Did you see Sam?"

Dominic shook his head. "He and Glenna are on the ferry, headed to Dublin."

Tara looked back at the ferry. Glenna and Sam would be in Dublin by mid-afternoon. The sea surged against the rocks far below, like a slow steady build days before a storm. The waters had finally risen, quenching the parched beaches. But the dried-out kelp and driftwood that had piled on the beaches for days floated off shore—a serpent-like tangle of debris.

"Glenna knows something," Tara said quietly. "I'm sure of it." She turned in Dominic's arms so she was facing him. "Why else would she go with him to Dublin?"

"Sam has a knack for digging out truths. If she's hiding something, he'll find it."

"I'm sick of her leaving us in the dark." Tara stepped out of his arms. She untied the apron around her waist and dropped it over the chair. She turned off the oven, where a pan of sugared rosemary was baking for a new tincture.

Dominic turned, watching her walk to the door. "Where are you going?"

"To Glenna's," Tara said, glancing over her shoulder. "To have a look around."

SAM WHISTLED IN appreciation at the black two-seater Mercedes with buttery leather interior. "*This* is your car?"

Glenna smiled, hitting the unlock button on her remote key pad. The small fishing village of Sheridan was bustling with tourists who'd traveled to the coast at the last minute to take advantage of the sunny weather. Doors to the colorful shops were propped open, beckoning visitors to browse Celtic charms and hand-knit wool sweaters. Lobstermen were pulling up their cages and traps, their frustrated curses echoing over the bay when they found them empty again.

Sam ran his hands over the gleaming finish. "Can I drive?"

Glenna smirked, sliding into the driver's seat. "Not a chance."

Sam folded his tall frame into the passenger seat and she eased the sleek car into the street, steering around a family nibbling on a basket of fish and chips. She pressed on the gas, shifting gears as they climbed the hill leading up to the highway. The mountains of Connemara loomed in the distance.

It felt good to be behind the wheel, to be back in control. Glenna rolled down the window, letting the warm wind play through her hair. She had a lot to think about after last night. Sleeping with Sam might not have been the brightest idea, but it didn't change the fact that she still had to stop him from finding Brigid. The problem was now she had *two* goals—to protect Brigid and Sam. And she wasn't entirely sure how she was going to accomplish both.

She knew she couldn't let Sam out of her sight. Not after what Moira had said on the beach—that she had a *plan* for him. She glanced at Sam out of the corner of her eye when he reached for the radio dial and fiddled with the stations, settling on a mix of folk and country. He stretched his legs and closed his eyes to take a nap. How could he relax at a time like this?

Oh, right, because Sam was certain they could break the curse. Glenna's fingers gripped the wheel. But Sam had only caught a glimpse of what Moira was capable of last November. Now that she had Nuala's powers, there was only one way to stop her.

Glenna scanned the craggy peaks of the Twelve Bens. She needed to draw out the truth. Stealing a glance at Sam to make sure his eyes were closed behind his sunglasses, she reached under her seat and pulled out a long curved blade. With one hand on the wheel, she slid the knife into a hidden cut-out inside her leather boot.

She had sworn to protect Brigid—even if it meant protecting her from the man she was falling for.

CHAPTER 12

Owen's eyes widened as he and Brennan rounded the corner to the harbor. The tide was so high the water had swallowed the pier. Boats floated above the docks, knocking into each other. Brennan leaned on his cane, pulling out his handkerchief to wipe his brow. "Haven't seen a tide this high in years."

Owen offered the elderly man his arm as they walked down the hill to join the rest of the villagers gathered on the hillside. He spotted Ashling, clutching her mother's hand. Kelsey stood in the middle of the crowd with Fiona. Donal Riley shielded his eyes from the sun, gazing out at the driftwood floating at the mouth of the harbor. "We're going to need to move it so Finn can get the ferry back in."

"Aye." Jack Dooley rolled up the legs of his pants. "I'll help you get the nets ready."

Sarah Dooley wrung her hands as the men started walking down the hill to the water's edge. "First, the tides are so low fish are washing up on the beaches, and now this? What's happening to our home?"

When Ashling turned her face into her mother's skirts, Mary Gallagher stroked a comforting hand over her daughter's hair. "Quinn hasn't caught a fish in weeks. He left this morning for Galway to find work."

Brennan took his weight off Owen and hobbled over to Mary. "We've gone through tough times before. We'll get through this one."

Owen lingered in the back of the crowd as Donal and the others sloshed into the water, using the pilings and ropes to balance as they navigated the submerged pier. Owen looked east, to the deserted coastline leading to Brennan's farm. His parents had told him that morning they didn't want him to go anywhere without an adult today, but they wouldn't tell him why.

He'd gone down to the rocks last night at sunset, but Nuala never came. And he needed to know if she was okay. He started to back away from the crowd, but Kelsey turned, catching his eye. Owen put his finger to his lips and shook his head, backing away quietly. As soon as he got to the nearest stone wall, he ducked behind it, breaking into a run.

When he reached the rocks, he kicked off his shoes and waded barefoot into the sea. He fished out the book he'd tucked into a crevasse the night before. He'd left it there as a message for Nuala, so she would know that he'd been there, waiting for her. The book dripped seawater when he lifted it and he brushed a strand of kelp off the cover. The soggy pages clumped together when he opened to *The Little Mermaid*.

He backed out of the water and sat down on the rocks. Maybe if he read a little of the story, Nuala would show up. He turned to the page where they'd left off two days before, glancing up when he smelled smoke. He dropped the book, scrambling back from the water's edge as the ocean wavered, shimmering under Moira's heat.

"It's a lovely day for reading, isn't it?" Moira plucked the book from the rocks and eyed the title of the story. "*The Little Mermaid*? What an interesting choice."

Owen's gaze darted over his shoulder, back to the harbor.

"Expecting someone else?" Moira asked sweetly.

"Wh-where's Nuala?"

"Nuala?" Moira lifted a brow. "You mean, your *mother*?"

Owen's knees started to tremble. "Caitlin's my mother."

"It must be hard, having two mothers." Moira turned, her skirt trailing over the rocks. Sparks snapped up from the lichens as they caught fire in her wake. "I wonder how Caitlin would feel if she knew you came here every night to spend time with Nuala?"

The sea rose, submerging Owen's bare feet. The waves snatched at his discarded shoes, pulling them out to sea. "Where is she?"

"She's gone." Moira said coldly. "You won't be seeing Nuala again."

Owen backed up, slipping on the wet rocks. "What did you do to her?"

She snapped the book shut. "The same thing I'll do to your *mother* if you don't stay away from this story."

Owen scrambled to his feet. "I'll stay away from it. I promise."

"Good." She handed the book back to him. "But first you're going to take it home and tell your parents you're done with fairy tales."

He heard a low keening sound. Moira turned, narrowing her eyes at the young seal watching them from a nearby rock.

"Stop!" Owen cried as she lifted a hand, sending a spark sailing through the air. The spark landed on the seal's fin. A song of pain rose over the waves as the seal slipped under the surface.

"This obsession," Moira hissed as she looked back at Owen, "is over."

SAM BLINKED AWAKE. The midday sun lit up the craggy peaks of a mountain range. He sat up, rubbing a hand over his eyes and looking around at the deserted country road lined with tall grasses and boulders. "Where are we?"

"Connemara National Park."Glenna opened her door, and reached behind the back seat for a small backpack. She slung it over her shoulder and motioned for him to get out of the car.

Sam unfolded himself from the passenger seat and took in the view. They were already pretty high up in elevation. He could see the ocean in the distance behind them. "I thought we were going to Dublin."

"We are." Glenna tossed him a bottle of water. "But we're taking a detour first."

Sam caught the bottle. "To go for a hike?"

"Something like that." She turned, veering off the road and striding into the wild.

He closed the door of the car and heard the alarm system beep as she locked it with her remote. Well, aren't we full of surprises, Sam mused. His boots crunched over the brittle grasses as he followed her. "You realize there's no trail here."

"I don't need a trail."

Sam lengthened his stride until he was hiking beside her. The air tasted fresher, cooler up here. "What are we looking for?"

"A stone circle."

Sam lifted a brow. "What are we going to do when we get to this stone circle?"

"We're not going to *do* anything," Glenna corrected. "I'm looking for a plant that grows there—blackthorn."

Sam scanned the rocky peaks. "This is a hell of a detour for a plant."

"It's a very special plant."

Blackthorn. The girl at the pub in Bray, the one with the tattoo, had ordered a blackthorn cocktail. She'd said blackthorn was a plant that would bloom on Imbolc. He'd forgotten to research the pagan holiday, but he knew better than anyone that answers and clues could come in many forms, including a random conversation at a crowded pub.

Sam looked out at the wide rolling sea, at the cluster of islands in the distance. He thought of the roses, the orange petals fading to black outside his home. "We should probably talk about what happened last night."

Glenna glanced up at him. "There's nothing to talk about."

"Actually, I think we have a lot to talk about."

"I got caught up in the moment, Sam. It's not going to happen again."

"You can't pretend you don't have feelings for me anymore."

"I told you. I'm physically attracted to you. But that's it. And what you feel for me isn't anything other than lust. You can't resist me because of what I am."

"I know you have selkie blood in you. Maybe that's what first drew me to you when I saw you on the island. But it's so much more than that now, Glenna. Besides, Tara has selkie blood in her. You don't question Dominic's feelings for her."

"It's not the same."

"How?"

"I'm different from Tara."

"Okay," Sam said slowly. "Enlighten me."

"Look." She turned to face him. "One of the reasons I moved to Seal Island is because there are so few men there. And the only ones who are even remotely interesting are already taken. It's safe there. I can live. I can breathe without worrying I'm going to hurt anyone."

Sam narrowed his eyes, letting his gaze trail up and down her lush figure. "I have a hard time believing you've completely cut men out of your life."

"I haven't." She looked out at the sea, a light wind blowing a curl across her face. "But I leave my affairs in the city, and I'm very careful about never seeing the same man twice." She lifted her chin, looking back at Sam. "I know that seems cold, but it's the only way."

"So my arriving on Seal Island shook things up for you?"

"Yes." She turned, starting to climb a steep incline.

"Good," Sam called after her. "Because you can't keep living like this."

"This is my life, Sam." She glanced over her shoulder. "I can choose to live it however I want."

"You're afraid," Sam challenged. "You're living in fear. Just like Tara was when she first came to the island. You may not be on the run, but I can see it in your eyes. And I've seen the way you look at Tara and Dominic and at Caitlin and Liam when they're together. You want what they have."

"What I want doesn't matter," Glenna said tightly.

"You want a normal life, but you don't think you can have it. Because of some stupid curse."

"You can psychoanalyze me all you want, Sam. It's not going to change anything."

He caught up with her and put a hand on her arm, turning her to face him. "What if there was a man strong enough to break the spell?"

The grasses shivered, rustling in the wind. Glenna pulled away, shaking her head. "I can't take that risk."

IT WOULD HELP, Tara thought, if she knew what she was looking for. Sitting on the floor in Glenna's bedroom, she blew out a breath. She'd been here for hours: searching drawers and cabinets, checking for loose floorboards, rummaging under sofas and chairs, digging through her friend's closet.

She wasn't a stranger to secrets. She'd learned, during her first marriage, how to hide things so her husband couldn't find them— wads of cash, fake ID's, plane tickets to escape to another country. She'd made mistakes at first, and had been punished for them. But she'd gotten better at it after a while. She'd learned that sometimes the most obvious place was the best place to hide something.

She stood, empty-handed, and walked back to the bookshelves lining the walls behind Glenna's bed. They were filled with ancient myths and legends, books of spells and magic, tales of enchantments and romance. She'd already combed through them once, but something kept nagging her to go back. She ran her hands over the leather-bound volumes, tracing the loopy gold calligraphy along the spines. On the bottom shelf, a collection of black Moleskine sketchbooks took up half the shelf.

She slid one out, then another, dropping them onto the scarlet comforter draped over the queen-sized bed. Maybe there was something in one of Glenna's sketches that would give her a clue. She reached for the last one, frowning at the weight of it. It was the same size and shape as the others, but it felt at least a pound heavier than it looked. She nudged the other sketchbooks aside and edged her hip onto the bed.

A strand of red ribbon peeked out of the top of the pages and she eased it free. It was frayed at the ends, even though the book itself looked fairly new. She ran it through her fingers, noting the threadbare stitches in the material. A movement of curtains caught her eye and she glanced up, but it was only a puff of wind.

She settled back onto the bed, opening the heavy volume. Most of the pages were blank, save a few unfinished sketches of stone circles and moonlit paths. She flipped through the rest of the book, pausing when she spotted the hidden flap tucked into the back cover. She peeled it open and eased out a well-worn, topographic map. She unfolded it carefully and saw that it was a map of a mountain range. There were dozens of spots circled, many of them with a red x slashed through them.

Glenna was searching for something. But what? And where?

Tara froze when the spine retracted, cracking in her hands. The binding quivered. A hot, dry wind gusted in through the open window. Silver necklaces dangling from antique drawer handles clinked and jangled. Tara's heart pounded as the wind caught the pages, blowing them out like a fan. They yellowed before her eyes, crinkling and stiffening with age. They made a dry scraping sound like dead leaves skittering over a city street in the fall.

The leather creaked and stretched in her palms as the pages—blank before—filled with ancient Gaelic letters scrawled in black ink. Her dark hair blew into her eyes as the wind teased the pages open to a rough sketch of a bush with long black thorns and delicate white flowers. Her hand shook as she brushed a finger over the word, *draighean*, under the fading black-and-white sketch.

Every candle in the room lit. Smoke curled up from the wicks. Tara gasped when the window slammed shut and sparks shot out from the cracks in the floorboards. She scrambled to her feet as the curtains ignited, the flames twisting toward her, cutting off her path to the door.

CHAPTER 13

S am knelt, brushing a hand over the scorched earth. "What happened here?"

Glenna balled up the topographic map, crumpling it in her hands. The rugged peaks of the Twelve Bens rose behind them and the Tooreen Bogs stretched out to the sea as she stood inside the crumbling stone circle, known only to a few pagan communities in the area. "My mother."

Sam pushed slowly back to his feet. "The blackthorn?"

Glenna nodded. "I've been searching for this spot for years. I've found nearly every stone circle hidden in these mountains, but this is one of the few I hadn't seen. I thought if there was any blackthorn left, it might be able to help us." A sparrowhawk cried in the distance. "I always knew it was a shot in the dark. But I had to try."

"Are you sure this is the place?"

"This is the place." Glenna pressed her palm to a cool stone. She could sense the energy, the undercurrents of magic hidden deep within the ritual circle. "I've seen it a dozen times in my dreams."

"And this blackthorn..." Sam said slowly as he walked to her. "It holds the truth in its bark?"

Glenna nodded. "If you throw a blackthorn branch into a fire on Imbolc, the true story will be told in the smoke." Her gaze dropped to the blackened soil. "But Moira got rid of it, and made sure none would ever grow again."

Sam stepped inside the circle and Glenna watched him tense. He may not have magic, but his intuition ran deeper than any man she'd ever known. She could tell that he felt things, smelled things that didn't belong here. He reached out, brushing a hand over one of the stones. Whispers and voices danced over the wind.

He jerked his hand back. "What was that?"

A gust rushed over the mountainside, whipping Glenna's ponytail over her shoulder. The tall grasses bent, the wind whistling through their brittle stalks. Sam's eyes locked on hers—clear, sharp and full of questions. "What happened in this place?"

Glenna held out her hand and he walked slowly to her. It was time for Sam to find out exactly who they were dealing with. Her fingers curled around his wide palm and she let the rush of power flow into him. He stood his ground, but she could feel every muscle in his body tighten as the air shifted and the sky changed from blue to vivid red.

Grass sprang up beneath their feet, where scorched earth used to be. A brush fire crackled by one of the stones, and in the middle of the circle a man and a woman lay together, their bodies linked in ecstasy, their bare flesh glistening with sweat. Sam gripped Glenna's hand as the image wavered and shifted. The couple was standing now, and the man reached for his clothes balled up beside the fire. He looked back at the woman with hatred in his eyes. "*I will find her. Wherever she is. I will never stop looking for her. You cannot get away with this.*"

The woman shrieked when he turned and strode away from her. The knife, a flash of silver slicing through the red dawn, caught him in the back of his neck. The man crumpled and the woman's eyes, dark brown only moments ago, glinted green-gold as she pulled the blade free. Her lover's blood covered her hands as he fell, lifeless, to the ground.

Glenna released Sam's hand and stepped away from the stone. The vision that had haunted her since she was a teenager disappeared and the green grass turned black again under their feet. The wind died and the sky transformed back to a brilliant blue.

Sam's eyes lifted to hers. His chest rose and fell, his breathing labored as the last tremors of her power coursed through his veins. "Was that Moira?"

Glenna nodded. "Her appearance changed as her magic grew."

"Who was the man that she killed?"

Glenna looked back at the ground, where the image of the fallen man still burned in the backs of her eyes. "My father."

SMOKE FILLED THE room. The fire crackled and grew. Tara coughed, covering her mouth with her shirt. She staggered to the window, smashing Glenna's lamp into the glass. It shattered, but the hole wasn't big enough for her to climb through. She looked back at the door. It was covered in flames.

The blaze streaked from the curtains to the bookshelves. Tara struggled to breathe as smoke clogged her lungs. Her vision blurred and wavered. The heat of the room became unbearable as she reached blindly over the rug for the spell book.

Her fingers curled over the leather spine, but the ancient pages ignited in her hand. She cried out as the flames grazed her skin. She dropped the book, grabbing a potted plant with both hands and hurling it at the window. More glass broke off and the gap was just wide enough for her to fit through.

Her eyes burned as she crawled through the smoke to the window. The jagged glass sliced into her palms as she fit her shoulders through the narrow opening and pushed her way out. Her jeans tore, ripping down her thighs where the shards bit into the seam. But she climbed out, wrenching away from the glass as her palms met the hot dry soil under Glenna's window.

She stumbled away from the house in a tumble of bloody gashes and burns. The heat of the flames chased her from the cottage until she fell, crawling on her hands and knees toward the open fields. She buried her face in the brown moss, covering her ears as the thatched roof caught fire. A thick stream of black smoke coiled high into the air.

LIAM SAT BACK, rubbing his eyes. He'd been staring at the computer since dawn. But he still didn't have a clue why his mother would re-shelve the white selkie legend with the mermaid books. It didn't make any sense. He glanced up when the door swung open and Caitlin walked into the cottage, her troubled blue eyes locking on his.

Owen trailed in after her and Liam pushed back from the cluttered table when he saw the wet clothes plastered to his son's body. "What happened?"

"I tripped," Owen mumbled. "It was an accident."

Liam stood, worry creasing his brow. "I thought you were at the pub reading with Brennan?"

"He was," Caitlin said, watching their son carefully as he stalked toward his room. "But they went down to the harbor to see the high tide and Owen wandered away."

Liam exchanged a worried look with his fiancée. They'd told Owen not to go anywhere on his own today. It wasn't like him to break the rules. Liam followed his son into the hallway, noting the dripping book in his hands. "Did you drop your book in the water?"

Owen threw it on the ground. "Ronan was right. Fairy tales are for girls."

Liam bent down slowly, picking up the book. It was the one he'd given Owen for Christmas. "I thought this was your favorite book?"

"Not anymore." Owen slammed the door behind him.

Caitlin walked up beside Liam. "He's been like this since I found him wandering along the road leading to Brennan's farm, but he won't tell me what's wrong."

Liam didn't bother to knock. He opened the door and walked in. Owen was across the room, rummaging through his bookshelves, pulling out all his fairy tale books and tossing them on the floor. "What's going on, Owen?"

Owen shook his head, grabbing more books and pitching them over his shoulder. Liam caught one before it fell. It was an illustrated version of *The Little Mermaid*—the same book Owen had been obsessed with since he'd arrived on Seal Island.

Caitlin skirted the growing pile on the floor, lowering herself to the edge of her son's mattress. "Did Ronan say something that upset you today?"

"No," Owen snapped. "I just don't want to read these stupid books anymore."

"Owen," Liam said quietly as his gaze dropped to his son's bare feet. "What happened to your shoes?"

Owen froze, his toes curling under his feet. "I must have...left them at the harbor."

Liam glanced up, his gaze shifting to the window when the scent of something burning drifted over the fields. "Do you smell that?"

"What?" Caitlin asked.

He strode to the window, scanning the sunlit pastures leading to Glenna's cottage. "Smoke."

TARA HEARD VOICES, shouting over the fields. Footsteps pounded toward the flames. She coughed smoke from her lungs, trying to call out to Dominic when the cottage splintered, the thatched roof caving in and the flames swallowing what was left of Glenna's home.

"Tara!" Dominic shouted, his voice echoing over the fields. She heard men cursing, struggling to hold him back from running into the burning cottage. She pulled herself over the grass until she could see him through the wavering flames. He spotted her and broke free, sprinting to her.

"Dominic," she rasped as he scooped her up, pulling her into his arms. She breathed in his warm, salty scent, burying her face in his neck as he carried her safely away from the blazing fire.

She heard more voices, more people shouting over the pastures. He laid her down gently, leaning her back against a stone wall and she blinked when she saw the villagers racing up the path. Fiona covered her mouth at the sight of the fire, then grabbed Kelsey and Owen to keep them safe.

"The house," Tara breathed as orange flames streaked into the air. "It caught fire."

"What happened?" Caitlin sank to the ground beside her.

Tara shook her head, dazed. "I don't know." She coughed, hacking more smoke from her lungs. There was a faint ringing in her ears. "I was looking through Glenna's books." Her fingers scraped over the moss, dry as sandpaper on the ground. The flowers, a cluster of crocuses that had sprouted last night, were wilting in the heat. "It was a book of spells...I think." She looked up at Dominic, into his concerned gray eyes. "It changed shape in my hands."

Dominic smoothed a comforting hand over Tara's hair, clutching her tighter against him.

"There was a word...in the book," Tara whispered. "When I touched the page where it was written, the fire started."

Caitlin balled up Liam's shirt when he handed it to her, pressing it against the deep gash above Tara's knee. "What word?"

"I think"—Tara flinched when Caitlin applied more pressure— "it was written in Gaelic. I'm not sure how to pronounce it."

"Give it a shot," Liam urged.

Tara nodded, squeezing her eyes shut when the skin on her arms started to burn. "Draighean."

Liam looked up at Dominic as the frame of Glenna's house splintered, crashing to the ground. "That's Gaelic for blackthorn."

CHAPTER 14

That man," Sam began as they hiked back to the car. "Your father...was he a selkie, too?"

"No." Glenna shook her head. "But Moira was in love with him, and she risked everything to be with him." A fox streaked through a meadow far below, a blur of red through the green and tan grasses. "Moira wasn't always evil," Glenna explained, picking her way down the rocky hillside. "But she, like every sea witch before her, wanted something badly enough to barter her soul."

Sam shook out his arms. He still felt a faint tingling and he wanted it gone. He had had only a taste of what Glenna lived with every day. And he couldn't imagine how she bore the weight of it. He glanced at her profile. Her skin was still flushed from the rush of power. But she kept her pace brisk and steady, as if she felt nothing.

"There is only ever one sea witch," Glenna continued. "And she must pass on her powers before she dies. If she doesn't, her soul will forever haunt the sea and she will never be at peace."

A flock of starlings alighted from the branches of a yew tree, their black wings beating in a frantic, pulsing rhythm. "The last sea witch," Glenna went on, "the one who came before Moira—she was already dying when she met my mother. She knew Moira was in love with the man you saw in the vision, and she offered to help her run away with him. But she told Moira that if she couldn't convince the man to fall for her, she would have to come and live with her and learn her dark arts."

"A trade for love," Sam murmured. "That sounds familiar."

Glenna nodded. "That's how Moira tricked Nuala the first time. Sea witches find great pleasure in toying with people's love lives. Love makes people desperate and vulnerable."

And that, Sam thought, was why Glenna was so afraid of it. Glenna didn't let people see her vulnerabilities. She didn't show her weaknesses. The best defense she had was closing herself off from love.

"No woman wants to be a sea witch," Glenna explained. "But once the black magic feeds into her soul, she is bound to the dark arts, and there is only one way to break the chain that traps her there." Glenna's eyes looked out at the sea, shining like sapphires in the sunlight. "A sea witch is an outcast, a pariah. The only way Moira can break free of the darkness is if her people welcome her back and choose her as their ruler."

The tingling in Sam's arms gave way to a prickling, like needles over his skin. "That's why Moira wants to rule the selkie kingdom, to be free of the darkness."

Glenna nodded.

"But couldn't Moira take the throne by force if she wanted to? Isn't she powerful enough?"

Glenna shook her head. "A sea witch cannot steal the throne. She has to be *chosen*. Moira cannot escape the curse unless her people ask her to come back."

"What if they did ask her back?" Sam held out his hand when they came to a stream. "Would she turn good again?"

"Possibly." Glenna let him help her over the rocks, drawing her hand free as soon as the rocks gave way to grass again. "But the selkies would never choose her as their queen. Not after what she did to Nuala and Owen. They know the truth, and they could never forgive her for that."

"But she's still going to try," Sam murmured.

Glenna nodded. "She's still going to try."

"The man," Sam said, trying to wrap his head around all of it. "Your father... If she loved him, why did she kill him?"

"Because he rejected her," Glenna said simply.

"He didn't seem to be rejecting her when they were rolling around naked on the ground."

"That's because she tricked him into thinking she was someone else. He didn't know who he was sleeping with."

A flash of sunlight reflected off the hood of Glenna's car and Sam realized they were almost back to the road. "How could he not have known who he was sleeping with?"

"My father was in love with someone else." Rocks skittered out from under Glenna's boots as she picked her way down the final hill to the car. "Someone who looked exactly like Moira."

When Glenna got to the bottom of the hill, she glanced back up at Sam. "My father was expecting to run away with a selkie that night. But he was expecting someone else."

Sam reached the flat stretch of grass. "Who?"

Glenna shrugged out of the backpack. "Moira's twin sister." She pulled out her keys and unlocked the doors with the remote. The lights flashed and the alarm system beeped through the silence. "My aunt Brigid."

THE SUNSET PAINTED the sky a gleaming gold. From her spot on the sofa, curled up in a pair of sweatpants and one of Dom's oversized button-down shirts, Tara watched the sun dip into the sea. Her throat still ached from inhaling so much smoke earlier, and the gashes in her legs stung from where she'd stitched them up. But she'd slathered her arms with a homemade milk and honey salve and the burns were already starting to heal.

She glanced up as Dominic walked out of Kelsey's bedroom, closing the door quietly behind him. "How is she?"

"She's shaken up," Dominic admitted, settling onto the sofa beside her, careful not to shift the cushion and irritate her wounds. "She wants to get rid of all the candles in the house. And no more fires in the fireplace. Ever."

Tara looked down at the bandage on her hand and the red mark snaking up her forearm. "I wish that fire had started from something as simple as a candle or a fire in the hearth."

Dominic cupped her arm in his hand, rubbing a thumb gently over the clear layer of cooling salve. "Caitlin called Glenna and Sam. She told them what happened. Glenna's sure it was Moira."

"Who else could it be?" Tara looked up when she saw Caitlin and Liam walking up the path to the door with Owen. She waved them in through the open window. "I'm worried about Glenna," she said to Dom. "About what Moira wants with her."

Dominic set her arm back down gently. "Glenna can take care of herself."

"But her home," Tara said softly. "It was destroyed."

"I know," Dominic said, and a shadow passed over his eyes. "It almost went down with you in it."

The door opened and Caitlin and Liam walked in, their expressions tense. Dominic stood, ushering them in. He looked down at Owen, ruffling his nephew's hair. "Kelsey's in her room if you want to say hi."

Owen nodded, disappearing into the back.

As soon as the door shut behind him, Tara turned to Caitlin. "What do you know about blackthorn?"

"It's a shrub," Caitlin said, settling into the chair beside Liam. "I think it's relatively common."

"It's one of the first plants to bloom in Ireland—usually on Imbolc," Liam added, already booting up the laptop he'd brought with him. "Which is tomorrow."

"Imbolc," Tara said slowly. "That's a pagan holiday, right?"

Dominic nodded. "It's the half-way point between winter and spring. Pagans celebrate it as Imbolc and Christians as St. Brigid's Day."

"St. Brigid," Tara murmured. "Why does that sound so familiar?"

"There's a church devoted to her in Kildare," Dominic explained. "We stopped there once on a trip back from Dublin. I wanted to show you the spot where the sacred fires used to burn."

"Right," Tara said softly. "The fires that used to burn continuously in her honor. I remember thinking that practice seemed more pagan than Christian.

"It was," Caitlin said. "But many early Christian rituals had roots in pagan traditions. Especially the ones connected to Brigid." Caitlin peered over Liam's shoulder at what he was pulling up on the screen. "There's some debate about this, but many pagans believe Brigid was originally a Celtic goddess. Before the Christians came to Ireland, Kildare was already a holy site devoted to the goddess. When Christianity spread through Ireland, Brigid was 'Christianized,' and she founded a monastery—one that welcomed both men and women—on that same land."

"Isn't it rare for the two religions to come together like that?" Tara asked.

"It is," Caitlin acknowledged. "But Brigid is our strongest link between the old and the new. She is the only Celtic goddess who was embraced by the church. The first of February is a Christian feast day to honor one of Ireland's patron saints and a pagan festival to honor the goddess. Whether you're a pagan, a Christian, or someone who practices a little of both, Brigid is a beloved religious figure."

"And the grounds of Kildare are a powerfully sacred place," Tara finished.

Caitlin nodded as Liam turned the computer around to show her an image of a shrub in full bloom. "This is what blackthorn looks like."

Tara leaned closer. "There was a sketch in the book," she murmured. "It was rough, but it looked like that." She looked up at Caitlin. "Do we have any on the island?"

Caitlin shook her head. "Not that I know of. If we did, it would probably be gone by now. The tourists like to snap off the branches to make wands and walking sticks. They think it has magical powers."

"Does it?"

Caitlin shrugged. "Carrying a blackthorn wand is said to protect you from evil. But who knows if that's true or not."

"It didn't do a very good job of protecting Tara," Dominic said tightly.

"If anything," Tara said slowly, "it's what started the fire." Tara looked down at her burned hands. "I should never have gone there."

"This wasn't your fault." Dominic stood. "I think we should call off the search for Brigid."

"What?" Tara gaped at him. "No. We can't do that now. We have to find her."

"Not if this search is going to put you"—Dom looked at Caitlin and Liam—"put *any* of you, in danger."

"This is our home," Tara said quietly. "We cannot let Moira take it away from us."

"You said the book changed shape in your hands?" Liam asked. "Like it was under some kind of enchantment?"

Tara nodded. "Glenna clearly didn't want anybody to find it."

"But it's gone now?"

"As far as I know," Tara answered. "There was nothing left of the cottage but ash when we left."

ON THE ROCKY shores of a deserted island, a few kilometers south of Seal Island, Moira held the book in her hands. The charred pages crinkled and faded to ash as the wind teased the corners of the ancient spell book. Her tears fell into the sea and steam rose up from the drops as they hit the surface.

Glenna was against her. Her daughter—her own flesh and blood—was against her. She'd been against her all along. Her fingers traced the fading sketch, the long black thorns and delicate flowers. Why? Why couldn't her daughter understand that she was doing this for both of them?

That this was the only way?

She closed her eyes, the memories sweeping over her like a wall of black smoke. She should never have followed that glittering green tail deep into the depths of the sea. She should never have left the selkie boundaries when she was fifteen. But she could not bear to spend her days tending her garden and practicing her songs as her sister did. She'd tested the boundaries for years, pushing the limits to see how far she could go.

The first glimpse of those sparkling fins had been impossible to resist. She'd followed the mermaid to a coral castle with soaring spires and turrets that had stretched high into the undulating currents, as far as the eye could see. She'd slipped past the guards, and through a narrow window looking down into the vast ballroom, she'd seen him—the prince.

He'd been surrounded by a circle of his people; they'd been laughing and cheering as they clapped him on the back. His smile had been radiant, brighter than a Midsummer's moon. His bare chest had gleamed, rippling with muscles, and the strong tail that had propelled him through a crowd that had parted for him to pass had been the color of emeralds dusted in gold.

She'd fallen in love at first sight. She'd known she had to find a way to be with him. She'd believed, in her foolishness, that their love could unite their kingdoms. That their love could break down the borders and restrictions the mermaids had put on them so long ago.

But she had not known then what she knew now. That love made people weak. It made people vulnerable. It made people do things they would never do otherwise.

Moira's nails scraped over the pages as she tore them from the book. She had risked everything to be with him.

And he had chosen someone else.

She hurled the pages into the ocean, and they ignited, bursting into flames. He'd chosen her *sister*. The parchment sizzled, forming sparkling balls of fire floating over the surface. Her pathetic, insipient, malleable twin sister!

The flames twisted, twirling into the night until they transformed into a garden of brilliant orange roses. Moira gazed into the moonlit surface—at the reflection of Brigid shedding her seal-skin on a white beach.

"Are you sure he said this was the place?" Brigid asked, shivering as her bare skin met the cold night.

"I'm sure," Moira urged. "He said he'd be waiting for you just over that hill."

Moira slid from the rocks, into the dark waters, edging back from the beach. She watched her sister wrap her precious seal-skin around her naked body and start up the path.

Toward the man who was watching from the cliffs.

She heard Brigid's panicked scream when he grabbed her, snatching her pelt. She watched her sister struggle, her cries muffled as his big hand covered her mouth.

Moira slid under the surface, into the darkness and freedom of the sea. Her sister's Prince was not waiting for her on the other side of the hill. He was waiting on a beach, several kilometers north along the coast. And he would be getting a different twin.

Moira swept her arm out, the long sleeve of her dress skimming the surface of the sea. She flung the empty leather binding of the book into the circle of roses. The petals shivered, fading to black as the book splashed into the water, sinking like coal.

She had gotten rid of her sister once, and she would get rid of her again. The rocks shook, pebbles skittering into the tide pools as a low rumbling echoed in the distance. The dark sea churned and bubbled as the lava began to flow. The eruption would take care of Nuala, which meant there was only one person now standing between her and the throne. The one person she'd thought was on her side—her daughter.

CHAPTER 15

Glenna twisted her moonstone ring, round and around on her finger. Sam had taken the keys from her over an hour ago when they got the call from Caitlin—the call saying Tara had almost died. She looked up, catching her reflection in the mirror on the back of the visor. Her face was still pale, her eyes wide and haunted. But Tara was alive. She was alive, and that was all that mattered.

Sam cut the engine in the lot of St. James's Hospital in Dublin. "Are you sure it was Moira?"

Glenna nodded. "I'm sure. My mother knows I'm not on her side now. If she got the book—and I'm sure she did—she knows that I've been trying to prove Brigid's innocence for years. But without the blackthorn, I can't prove Moira killed him."

"Then we have to find her," Sam said, opening the door, "and warn her before Moira figures out where she's hiding."

Glenna took a deep breath. "My mother is tracking you, Sam. She's using you to find Brigid."

Sam paused, his hand on the door.

"That's why I've been trying to stop you," she explained. "So you wouldn't lead Moira straight to her."

Sam gazed out the window, at the brightly-lit hospital entrance. A muscle in his jaw began to tick. "That's why I had such a hard time the first couple months," he said, putting the pieces together. "You were using your powers against me."

"To protect Brigid," Glenna explained. "Moira didn't know that I knew the truth. She thought I was on her side. The only reason I knew was because of my visions."

Sam looked back at her. "Do you know where Brigid is?"

Glenna shook her head. "I've been searching for her for years. But she's hidden somewhere where Moira can't see her—somewhere protected." Glenna breathed in the scent of exhaust blowing in Sam's open door. "I thought I had more time. But when Nuala came on land in November, she set things in motion—things that couldn't be undone. Her failure to bring a suitable mate into the sea cost her the throne."

Sam rested his hands back on the wheel. "So you're saying that every trade Moira made with Nuala was to clear her path to the throne?"

Glenna nodded as a nurse wheeled an elderly man out to a van idling by the curb. "Even though I helped bring Liam back, Moira thought I was still on her side—that I would help her reclaim the throne."

"Why would you do that?"

Lights flashed through the parking lot as an ambulance pulled up to the entrance. "Because if my mother cannot release herself from this curse, all her dark powers will pass to me."

"Glenna—"

"It's a sacrifice I'm willing to make." Glenna looked away. She couldn't bear to see the look in his eyes. "Brigid is the eldest daughter of the selkie queen. She is the proper ruler. She is the only one who can restore the balance to the seas, protect the islands, and save us from Moira."

"But—"

"Moira assumed I would do everything in my power to stop you, to save myself. And I let her believe that." She looked up, at the sky, at the pale white moon rising over the city. "But I have always known the truth. As long as Brigid is hidden, she's still a risk to my mother." She looked back at Sam, at the dark shadows playing over the rugged contours of his face. "Moira knows I've been against her all along. She's going to come after us. I'm surprised she hasn't already."

"Glenna." Sam took her hand. "I'm not going to let anything happen to you."

Glenna felt his firm fingers close over hers. Another woman might have welcomed his vow of protection, but Glenna had learned long ago that she was the only one who could save herself. She pulled her hand free. "You should never have gotten involved in this."

"But I did," Sam said, his expression darkening as he stepped out of the car. He kept his eyes on hers as he rounded the hood to the passenger's side. He opened her door and she stepped out into the night.

"We're going to find Brigid," he said, closing the door behind her. "We're going to break this curse. We're going to rebuild your home on the island. And when this is all over, I'm going to take you out on a date to a fancy restaurant in Galway." He took her hand, leading her toward the hospital. "We're going to sit at a table like a normal couple and you're going to order the most expensive dish on the menu and wear something red and slinky that I want to rip off you. And when we get home, you'll let me."

Glenna let out a strangled laugh. She could feel the warmth of him, the strength of him seeping into her palm where he gripped her hand. "I'm glad you have your priorities straight."

"You are my *only* priority, Glenna."

It was dark, but street lamps lit their way to the building. And when she glanced up at him and caught the intensity in his eyes, she felt a strange pulsing, like hesitant wings of hope beating inside her heart. She clamped down on them. *Love is weakness. Love is vulnerability. The only strength you have is yourself.* "What you should be worried about is your own life, and those damn roses."

"I am not afraid of death, Glenna." He paused under a street lamp, pulling her into him. He cupped her face in his hands. "I have never been afraid of death. Because I have never had anything to live for until I met you."

KELSEY LOOKED OUT her window, at the stars twinkling in the night sky. The sun had set over an hour ago, but Uncle Liam and Caitlin were still here. She could hear their hushed voices and her dad clanging around in the kitchen. It sounded like they were staying for dinner.

She glanced at Owen, who was sitting on her floor, throwing black beach stones into a bucket of water at the foot of her bed. He hadn't been himself all night. She'd tried to get him to play a board game, but he just wanted to sulk in the corner.

Plunk. Another stone hit the water. It sank, making a hollow sound as it hit the bottom of the metal bucket. "I won't be able to lift it if you keep adding stones to the bottom," Kelsey muttered.

"You won't be able to lift it anyway," Owen retorted. But he scooted over to the bucket and scooped out two handfuls of stones, dropping them onto her woven rug to dry. He sat back, tossing another one in. *Plunk.*

Kelsey looked back at the window. She'd propped it open with her two tallest books. She wasn't taking any chances. And she was tired of Owen making fun of her fire precautions. Her mother had almost died in that cottage today.

Rolling out of the rocking chair to her feet, she marched across the room and dug the rest of the stones out of the bucket. "Enough," she said, standing between Owen and the bucket. "I might need this later."

"Whatever," he said, turning his back to her and hunching his shoulders.

Kelsey crossed her arms over her chest. "Why won't you tell me where you snuck off to earlier, when we were down at the docks?"

Owen dug at the rug with the stone. "Because it's none of your business."

Kelsey narrowed her eyes. Owen's black hair looked almost blue against the lavender of her walls and his face seemed paler in the lamplight. "Is this about Ronan?"

"No," Owen snapped, his blue eyes sparking as they met hers. "Why does everyone think this has to do with Ronan?"

"Because he's been picking on you for weeks," Kelsey retorted.

"I don't care about Ronan," Owen muttered.

"Then, what *is* the matter?" Kelsey pressed. "Why won't you tell me?"

Owen curled his legs up, wrapping his arms around his knees. "I don't want to talk about it."

"Fine," she snapped, pulling her Hans Christian Andersen fairy tale book from the shelf—the same hardback collection Uncle Liam had given both Owen and her for Christmas—and crawled onto her bed. She sank back into the pillows, scowling. If he didn't want to talk to her, then she'd sit here and read in silence until dinner. That was fine with her.

She read a few pages then glanced up and saw he was watching her. "What?"

"Nothing," he said, looking away.

She rolled her eyes and went back to reading. But she looked up after a few sentences and saw that he was watching her again. "*What?*"

He turned the beach stone around in his fingers slowly. "What are you reading?"

"None of your business."

Owen set the stone down. "Kelsey—"

"What?" Kelsey glared at him. "You won't tell me why you're upset. I'm not telling you what I'm reading."

Owen stood, shuffling over to the bed and peering over her shoulder. The next thing she knew, he was yanking the book from her hands and tearing out the pages.

"Hey!" She scrambled off the bed, grabbing for them. "Stop! What are you doing?"

He turned his back to her, blocking her reach. He shredded the pages into little bits and threw them in the trash. Then he turned, shoving the book back at her.

Kelsey stared at him, wide-eyed, as the door swung open and her dad popped his head in. "Is everything okay in here?"

"Everything's fine," Owen muttered, walking over to the window.

"Kelsey?" Dominic asked, frowning when he saw her expression.

Kelsey looked over at Owen, then back at her dad. "I'm fine," she said quietly, setting the book down on her bed.

"Are you sure?"

"I'm sure," she said.

"Alright," he said slowly. "Dinner's in ten minutes."

As soon as her dad closed the door—leaving it open a crack this time—she turned back to Owen. "*What* is your problem?"

"Why are you reading that story?"

"I'm trying to help Sam find our grandmother," she huffed. "There has to be a reason why Brigid re-shelved the white selkie book with the mermaid books. There might be a clue in there."

"I think you should stay out of it."

Kelsey gaped at him. "Why?"

"Because someone's going to get hurt."

Kelsey pressed her palm to the door, shutting it quietly until she heard the latch click. "Owen, what happened to you today?"

Owen looked out at the ocean, at the reflection of the pale moonlight glistening on the surface. "I saw her."

"Who?"

"Moira."

"*Moira?*" Kelsey's hands began to tremble. "Where?"

"On the rocks, on the way to Brennan's house. Where I usually go at sunset to see my"—he took a deep breath, lowering his voice—"to see Nuala."

Kelsey crossed the room slowly until she was standing beside him. He was two years older than her and at least four inches taller so she had to tilt her head to look up at him. "How long have you been seeing Nuala?"

"Since I started my reading lessons with Brennan. I saw her on my walk home once. She was in the water, but she was looking right at me. I had to go down to her."

"But—"

"My mum and dad don't know." His voice hardened. "And you can't tell them."

"I-I won't," Kelsey stammered.

"I don't want them to think—"

"I know." She took Owen's arm, pulling him back to the bed. He sank to the mattress and she sat beside him. "Tell me."

"I went down to see her last night," Owen whispered. "On my way back from Brennan's. But she wasn't there. That's why I snuck down to the rocks today—to see if maybe she'd come late or somehow left me a message. But Moira was there instead." His fingers curled into Kelsey's pink bedspread. "She said I wasn't ever going to see Nuala again."

"We need to tell my mum and dad."

"No." Owen shook his head. "She said if I ever read that story again—*The Little Mermaid*—she would do to my mum what she did to Nuala. That's why Glenna's house caught fire today. She was trying to warn me."

Kelsey thought of the fire, the billowing smoke and the sight of her mum lying helpless on the ground. "What did she do to Nuala?"

"I don't know," Owen whispered.

"Did she say *why* she doesn't she want you reading the story?"

Owen shook his head.

"There must be a reason." Kelsey rose and went to the trash, digging out the shredded pieces of paper.

Owen shot to his feet. "What are you doing?"

Kelsey looked up. "She didn't say *I* couldn't read it."

"No," Owen said quickly. "I don't want to hurt anyone else."

Kelsey laid the papers out on the floor, piecing them together. "But there *must* be a clue in here if she doesn't want you to read it."

"No!" Owen grabbed the papers and crumpled them into a ball. "We need to stop looking for Brigid."

"What?" Kelsey stared at him. "We can't. She's family."

"But—"

"Maybe Moira was lying about Nuala," Kelsey cut in. "Maybe she was trying to scare you."

Owen shook his head. "She did something to her. Something awful." He let the crumpled papers drop to the floor, hanging his head. "If I hadn't read her that story..."

"What story?"

"*The Little Mermaid,*" Owen whispered. "I used to...read it to her. It was the only one she ever wanted to hear."

"I thought Nuala hated that story? She kept trying to take it away from you before."

"She did. When I thought *she* was the evil sea witch. But now..." He shook his head. "I think Nuala was trying to tell me something." He looked down at the scattered bits of paper. "There were two passages... She used to make a lot of noise and splash around when I read them."

"What are they?"

"There's a word in both of them...a word I don't know." He looked up at her. "Do you know what a convent is?"

"I think it's a place where nuns live."

"Do we have any...nuns on the island?"

"No." Kelsey shook her head. "But the princess in *The Little Mermaid* lived in a convent." Kelsey's eyes went wide. "Our *grandmother* is a princess... Do you think Nuala knows where our grandmother is?"

S orcha," Sam said, pouring relief into his voice as he glanced at the pretty blond receptionist's name tag. "Sergeant Fitzgerald said we should ask for you." He extended a hand over the desk. "I'm John Derringer, and this is my wife Miranda."

Sorcha stood, flustered. "Sergeant...who?"

"Sergeant Fitzgerald," Sam repeated. "With the Donnybrook District... He said he would call ahead." Sam looked bewildered. "You haven't heard from him?"

Sorcha shook her head slowly.

"He's been helping us with...our search." Sam reached for Glenna's hand, lacing their fingers together. "We're trying to find our little girl's grandmother. It's the only thing that might save her life."

The man, Glenna thought, had no shame. She glanced around the records department of St. James's Hospital as Sam spun a story that would pull on every one of Sorcha's heartstrings. A bank of scanners and copiers whirred in the background where employees fed documents into the massive commercial machines. They didn't bother to turn; most of them were tuned into their iPods.

Sorcha's big brown eyes widened in sympathy. "Bone marrow transplant?"

Sam nodded solemnly. "It's our only hope." He pulled Glenna down to the chair beside him, tucking her hand in his lap. "We've been searching for my birth mother for years, but it was only recently that it became...a matter of life or death."

In the hallway, Sam had told Glenna to play along. He'd said he wasn't sure what angle he'd use until he saw who was working at the desk. Now, as Glenna looked around the office, she knew why Sam had chosen it. The receptionist couldn't be more than twenty-three years old, but there was a picture of a baby girl in a pink frame on the corner of her desk and a small gold band adorned her ring finger.

Sorcha shook her head sadly as she clicked through the files on her computer, pulling up records. "I'm so sorry. I can't imagine what you're going through."

No, Glenna thought, glancing up at the florescent lights. *You can't.* But Sam was used to finding people's vulnerabilities and exploiting them to get the information he needed. And though his declaration in the parking lot had left her rattled, who knew what else he might be lying about? For all she knew, he could be using *her* to find Brigid. He might only be doing this to clear his conscience so he could move on from Seal Island. Hadn't he told her that he had no intention of putting down roots?

Sam reached for the picture frame on Sorcha's desk. "How old is she?"

"She's eight months," Sorcha answered, her skin flushing with pride. "Brianna. We named her after my husband's sister."

"Our little girl's name is Alice," Sam said softly, setting the frame back down. "Named after Miranda's mother. They're with her now. They feel terrible that they can't help. But they're not a match. Neither are we."

Sam rubbed a hand over his eyes. "I can't tell you how many nights I've lain awake wishing..." He shook his head. "I keep thinking that if we can find my birth mother—even if she doesn't want anything to do with us—maybe she'd be willing to save her granddaughter."

"Of course," Sorcha murmured. "You said the winter of '88, right?"

Sam nodded.

"There's a file for a Jane Doe who was five months pregnant, but the last page is missing so I don't know where she was discharged." She tapped her fingers on the desk. "But that's the only one who was pregnant." She pushed back from her desk. "Let me see if I can dig up the paper file."

Glenna leveled her gaze at him when Sorcha disappeared into the back. "Alice?"

Sam reached out, tucking a curl behind her ear and the gesture was so unexpectedly tender, she shivered. "I've always loved the name Alice," he murmured, his fingers lingering on her cheek. "And I imagine a child of yours would be nothing short of a trip through wonderland."

Glenna felt her heart skip a beat. She wouldn't be having children with anyone. Not while her mother was still alive. She'd made that decision long ago.

"I found something," Sorcha said. Glenna straightened, pushing Sam's hand away. The receptionist walked back to the desk, setting a file down in front of her. "We haven't sorted all the paperwork for that year, but I found the child's file. On December 27th, a doctor performed an emergency C-section and he was transferred to the NICU. The child was sustained on breathing tubes for about two months before he was discharged to an orphanage."

It was true, Glenna realized as the whirr of the copiers and scanners grew deafening. She had hired a man to hack into the hospital's system and erase the discharge page in Brigid's file years ago. But he hadn't said anything about a child.

"Is there anything in the chart about the mother?" Sam asked. "Did she survive?"

"Yes," Sorcha said slowly.

"What does it say?" Sam pressed.

"There's a note in the file for the social worker," Sorcha said, her expression softening in sympathy. "It says she was deemed unfit to care for the child."

"Unfit?"

"By a psychiatrist," Sorcha explained. "She was admitted to a mental institution."

Glenna stood abruptly, backing away from the desk. How? How had she not known Brigid had a third child?

"Which ward?" Sam asked.

"It wasn't a good place," Sorcha said. "The city shut it down a few years after it opened."

Glenna turned, pushing through the door and walking out into the hallway. She leaned against the wall. She should never have let Sam come here tonight. But she never dreamed he would actually find something. He'd told her about Tara's reaction to the file on his computer yesterday and she'd agreed to look into it with him, only to put Tara's fears to rest.

"Why was the place shut down?" Sam asked, his voice drifting out to the hallway through the open door. "What happened there?"

Sorcha lowered her voice. "Cruel treatment of the poorest people in this city, the ones locked up at the taxpayers' expense."

"What kind of...cruel treatment?"

Glenna closed her eyes, struggling to breathe. She could still hear the scratch of the doctor's pen on his clipboard, the feel of the nurse's papery skin as she wrapped the band around her upper arm, the prick of the needle and rush of serum pouring the wretched drugs into her veins—drugs that made her feel helpless and desperate and afraid.

"From what I've heard," Sorcha answered. "A lot of heavy sedation and shock treatments."

"Does this place still exist?"

"No," Sorcha said. "There was a protest in the mid-nineties that shut it down. It's barred up now, but the empty building is still on the corner of Duke and River Street. They haven't replaced it with anything new."

"Where did the patients go?"

"I imagine to other mental institutions throughout the country."

Glenna heard Sam's plastic chair squeak as he stood.

"I'm sorry," Sorcha said helplessly. "I wish I had better news."

NUALA WOKE TO a low rumbling. She blinked her eyes open and the dark waters churned around the mountain. Trapped beneath several large rocks, she tested her back fins as the volcano shook, the reverberations echoing through the sea.

Liquid fire spewed from the opening, and she fought the urge to panic. She would not let Moira kill her. She would not let Moira win. Black rocks broke off the narrow ledge as she twisted and thrashed. She cried out as her back fin tore.

Blind with pain, she swerved away from the ledge. The eels screamed as they chased her, and she clawed at them with her fore-fins. She swam through the murky waters to Moira's cave, ducking into the eerie blackness. She found the crown, swallowing mouthfuls of dead minnows as she grabbed it with her teeth.

Lava poured into the cave and she flipped, losing the eels in a tangle of their own tails as she shot out of the opening. She dodged the rolling bands of fire, skirting the thick forest of polyps and garden of black roses. The eels shrieked as they unraveled themselves and raced after her, but she didn't look back.

She swam, crossing into the selkie boundaries and passing the kingdom far below. Predator fish picked up her trail of blood, snapping at her with angry teeth. She dove, flipping and switching directions until they were twisted in a circle and couldn't see past the bubbles.

She had lived outside the boundaries long enough to know how to survive.

She swam until the beach and rocks rose up in the distance and she rode the waves to the salty shores of Seal Island. She let out a low whimper as the white sand rubbed into her wounds, but she pulled her broken body onto the beach. She lifted her head, releasing a long howl of distress before she collapsed, the blackthorn crown slipping from her mouth and rolling onto the sand.

SAM CUT THE engine, gazing through the chain-linked fence at the abandoned building. Many of the windows were shattered, and the stark gray exterior made it look more like a prison than a medical facility. Glenna opened the door and stepped out of the car. The wind caught her brown hair, swirling it around her shoulders.

Sam unfolded himself from the driver's seat, locking the vehicle. He followed her to the fence as tacked-up sheets fluttered like ghosts from the windows of the rundown apartment buildings lining the neighboring street.

Glenna slipped through a narrow opening. Weeds snaked through the cracks in the cement, and Sam stepped over a pile of used syringes as he followed her up to the heavy front doors, bound by a thick rusted chain.

"No one should be kept in a place like this," Sam murmured, his boots crunching over shards of glass that had fallen from the broken windows.

"No." Glenna shook her head. "They shouldn't."

Sam gazed at the mold creeping up the door frame. "If Brigid was mentally ill, don't you think Dom and Liam would have picked up on something? I know they were young, but still..."

Glenna pressed a palm to the dirty glass. "There was nothing wrong with Brigid before she came to this place."

Sam turned toward Glenna. A cold knot of fear coiled inside him when he saw the look on her face.

Glenna stared at her muted reflection in the glass, memories floating in her amber eyes. "There was only one person who made it out of here with a shred of her sanity still intact."

Sam stepped back from the window, fighting to keep his voice steady. "Tell me you didn't spend time here."

Glenna lifted her haunted eyes to his. "That's how I met my aunt."

CHAPTER 17

Glenna let Sam into the small one-bedroom flat she kept in the city. He hadn't said a word as they drove away from the barred-up mental institution, and she welcomed the silence. It gave her time to think. "Go ahead," she said quietly, setting her keys on the table. "I'll answer your questions."

He strode to the tall windows overlooking the River Liffey. A steady flow of people were leaving the large stone office buildings and heading home from work. "You would have only been a child in the mid-nineties. Barely a teenager."

Glenna closed the door and strolled through the room, switching on the lamps. "They took teenagers."

"But how did you get there?" Sam gazed down at the arched bridges crisscrossing the murky ribbon of mud and silt. "Who put you there?"

"My first memory of waking up on land was in a hospital—the same one we went to today." Glenna walked to the window where he stood and pulled the brown velvet curtains aside, draping them over an ornate iron hook. "A fisherman found me washed up on a beach and brought me in. I tried to escape. But they kept grabbing me, hauling me back. I told them I needed to go back to the sea. To go home. They thought I was trying to drown myself."

Horns honked and brake lights blinked through the darkness as the crush of commuter traffic streamed by on the road below. Glenna turned away from the window. She rented this place because it was easier than staying in a hotel every time she came into the city for an art show. But it had never felt like home.

Not like her cottage on Seal Island. "I fought them for days, but they strapped me to the bed and shot drugs into me so I could hardly think or speak. The police came and tried to identify me. But no one had filed a missing child report for a girl who looked like me, and I refused to tell them my name."

She picked up her red pillows, fluffing them and setting them back on the plush mocha-colored sofa. "The next thing I knew, I was locked in a windowless room in the building you just saw."

Sam laid his hands lightly on the window ledge, but she could see the bands of tension straining across the back of his shirt. "Do you remember your childhood?"

"I do."

"Did you grow up...underwater?"

Glenna selected two crystal wine glasses from the cherry rack over the sink. "I did. Brigid was the only person in the entire facility who made any sense." She filled the glasses with a rich red Cabernet. "We only saw each other once a week, and even then our time was limited. But they let her come into the common room when she was sedated, and she told stories from the bits of memories she could still piece together—stories about seals and an enchanted kingdom deep under the sea."

Sam turned, his thick blond hair gleaming burnished bronze in the warm lamplight. "What happened to Brigid after the place shut down?"

"I don't know." Glenna set the bottle down. "We were separated."

"What happened to you?"

"I was transferred to another facility." She picked up his glass, walking across the room to hand it to him. "But I'd learned how to act by then. How the doctors *wanted* me to act. I convinced the new

staff I was able to take care of myself and wasn't a threat to society."
He took the glass from her, but didn't drink. "About a year later, they
let me out."

"Could the same thing have happened to Brigid?"

"I doubt it." Glenna shook her head, walking back over to
retrieve her own glass. "The drugs and the treatments erased most of
her memory. She had trouble remembering who she was most of the
time. And the other times, when she wasn't sedated..." Glenna picked
up her glass and sipped, letting the wine calm her.

"What?" Sam pressed.

Glenna carried her glass to the sofa, settling onto the arm. "She
screamed for her children, for her two boys—Dominic and Liam."
Glenna lifted her eyes to Sam's. "She'd wake up screaming in the
middle of the night for someone to save them. But she didn't know
where they were. And when the nurses came to give her another
shot, she wept."

"But she never said anything about a third child?"

Glenna shook her head.

"Is that why you went to Seal Island? To find Dominic and Liam?"

She nodded.

"But you didn't tell them."

"I couldn't," Glenna said. "I looked for Brigid. I searched for her
for years. I knew she wasn't crazy. Or, at least she wasn't before she
went into that place. But she wasn't in any of the other mental institutions. I figured she must have escaped, and I hoped that maybe somehow she found her pelt and was able to return to her home."

"Is that why you didn't want me to search for her? Because you
didn't want them to find out about this?"

Glenna looked down at her wine. Swirling the rich red liquid, she
watched the streaks form in the glass. "They've had so much pain in
their lives already."

"Don't you think they deserve to know the truth?"

"Maybe," Glenna said softly, as the surface of her drink shimmered and an image formed. In a small house behind a white chapel,

a woman stood by the door. She held a bouquet of purple irises and her gray eyes watched the road for the headlights of a black Mercedes.

Glenna's fingers curled around the stem of the glass. How long would Brigid wait for her tonight? How long would she stand by the door?

She closed her eyes. There were too many people watching her now. Too many people following her every move.

Forgive me, my queen.

"OWEN, DON'T YOU like your dinner?" Tara asked across the small kitchen table. "You've hardly eaten a thing."

Owen pushed at the boiled potatoes on his plate. "I'm not hungry."

Kelsey plucked a piece of fish off his plate. "I'll eat it," she said, but she set her fork down when a seal's song drifted up from the beach. "What was that?"

Owen shot out of his seat. He knew that voice. He'd know it anywhere. His utensils clattered to the floor as he pushed back from the table, racing for the door.

"Owen?" Kelsey said, jumping up after him.

He flung open the door, running out into the night. He heard the chairs scraping back, his parents calling for him to stop. But he couldn't stop. He had to find Nuala. She was here on the island. Maybe she was still alive!

He made for the cliff path, his hands grasping the mossy wall to keep his balance as he started down the trail. Rocks slipped out from under his sneakers. Dark waves churned over the surface of the sea. They crested and crashed, sea spray exploding over the rocks.

He scanned the beach. Seashells glowed ghostly white in the moonlight. Sand crabs skittered over the sand, chasing the bubbles as the waves retreated. He stumbled to the sand, tripping over the knotted kelp when he spotted the dark shape curled up by the rocks.

"Is that her?" Kelsey asked, running after him. "Is it Nuala?"

Owen nodded, dropping to his knees and pulling the limp seal into his arms. He could feel her heart beating through her pelt. It was faint, but she was still alive. "We have to save her."

Kelsey knelt beside him, cradling Nuala's head in her lap. Caitlin and Liam caught up with them and Liam called back to Tara. "It's a seal. She's badly injured."

Tara nodded, limping over the sand with Dominic's help. Owen took in the burn marks on Tara's skin—so similar to Nuala's. "It's okay," he whispered, gently stroking Nuala's sleek black neck. "It's okay. Tara's going to fix you."

Waves slid over the sand, blowing froth at them as Tara knelt and ran her hands over Nuala's burned pelt.

"Dom," she called over her shoulder, "bring me my med kit."

He nodded, unzipping the bag he'd grabbed from the cottage at the last minute and set it down beside her.

"I have a salve that might work," she murmured. "It won't heal the burns instantly, but it will at least numb the pain for a while." She pulled out a cloth, and handed it to Kelsey. "Could you dip this in the ocean? I want to wash some of the sand off first."

Kelsey took it and dashed to the water.

Nuala's heartbeat grew stronger as Tara cleaned and dressed her wounds. When she shifted slightly in Owen's arms, he whispered, "It's working. She's waking up!"

Nuala opened her eyes slowly—pale as the light of the moon— and Tara jerked back.

Caitlin let out a strangled cry. "What is *she* doing here?"

Nuala tested her flippers, tapping them against the sand. Owen wrapped his arms around her neck. "I thought you were dead," he whispered. "I thought I would never see you again."

Caitlin staggered back, reaching for Liam's hand.

Tara watched Owen closely. "This isn't the first time you've seen Nuala since we brought Liam back, is it?"

Owen shook his head, still clinging to her. "I thought Moira killed her. She tried to kill both of you today."

Tara's gaze dropped to the burn marks seared into Nuala's pelt. "Moira did this?"

Nuala nodded.

"Why?"

Owen laid his hand on Nuala's whiskered cheek and her gaze slid to the sand by the rocks, then back up. He followed her eyes to where a small object was half-buried and hidden in the shadows. He could just make out the circle of black thorns with small white flowers.

Nuala held his gaze, swimming with a secret message only for him. She didn't want anyone else to know, he realized. She didn't trust anyone but him.

"Does Nuala know what Moira wants?" Tara asked Owen.

"I think so," Owen said. He shifted slightly, kicking sand over the object to cover it from sight, and Nuala relaxed in his arms. "But I don't know what it is."

Tara looked up at Dominic. "Nuala should stay here tonight. One of us will watch over her until the morning and make sure she's okay."

Dominic nodded, but Nuala shook her head, edging away from Owen. Owen reluctantly released his grip on her and she turned in the sand so she was facing the ocean.

"Owen," Tara said. "Help me convince her to stay."

"I can't," he said softly, rising to his feet. He walked beside Nuala as she shuffled to the water's edge. Tara stood, following them. They waded into the warm waves together, until the sea pulsed up to their waists.

Nuala leaned into Owen, rubbing her nose against his shoulder. Owen laid his hand on her sleek head and Nuala let out a soft song before diving and darted away into the depths.

"Where is she going?" Tara asked.

Owen shook his head as the sea swallowed her shape. "I don't know."

SISTER EVELYN WALKED through the house, switching off the lights. When she came to the living room and spotted her friend still standing by the door, her heart sank. Brigid had been standing in the same spot since noon, looking out at the driveway. She held a bouquet of purple irises—flowers she'd grown in the greenhouse.

The gardening books were all perfectly ordered now, displayed in a fan shape on the coffee table. No one dared move them from their proper place. She went to her friend, laying a hand on Brigid's shoulder. "I don't think she's coming."

"She always comes," Brigid whispered, refusing to take her eyes off the driveway. "At noon, on the last day of the month."

"It's almost nine," Sister Evelyn said gently.

Brigid squeezed the flowers. "What if something happened to her?"

"I'm sure she's fine," Sister Evelyn soothed. "She'll probably come tomorrow."

Brigid shook her head. "Something's wrong."

"Come on, Brigid." She pulled her friend gently away from the door. "Let's get you to bed."

CHAPTER 18

S am went for a walk. He wanted to give Glenna some space, and he needed some time to think. He turned onto a crowded cobblestone street in the Temple Bar district of Dublin. Tourists gathered around street musicians that cropped up on every corner. Voices spilled out of the smoky pubs and the scent of hops and malt vinegar clung to the air.

He spotted an outdoor counter selling fish-and-chips and filed into line behind an elderly couple with thick Boston accents. He'd been wandering the city for over an hour and he still couldn't shake the nagging feeling that something in Glenna's story didn't add up. It made sense that she wouldn't tell Dominic and Liam the truth about their mother when she first moved to the island. But after everything they'd been through together, why wouldn't she tell them now?

He put in his order and the battered fish wrapped in brown paper warmed his hands as he wound his way through back alleys and parks. The noise of the city eventually gave way to a quiet tree-lined street lined by tall brownstones with gas lanterns flickering outside the doors. He let himself into her building, climbing the stairs to her flat.

It was odd, Sam thought, as he set the keys on the table inside her door, that she didn't have a single picture or anything that might clue someone in to who actually lived here. It was a nice enough place, and an impressive collection of her artwork—mostly landscapes of the Irish countryside—hung from the walls. But it was more like an extension of one of her galleries than a home.

He set the food down on the counter and settled onto the couch. He could hear water running in the back, so he picked up the untouched glass of wine and booted up his laptop. He typed in the name of the mental institution and clicked through the articles, scanning the accounts of the protest that shut it down. But he leaned forward when he saw the picture of a group of nuns shouting outside the gates of the facility.

Sister Evelyn of St. Brigid of Kildare Parish—one of the nuns spearheading the protest—calls it a "disgrace." She says she won't stop until "the facility is shut down and every patient is transferred to a new home that will care for them properly."

"Glenna," he called when the water switched off.

"You're back," she said through a crack in her bedroom door.

"Yeah," he said distractedly. "Did you know it was nuns who started the protest to shut down the facility?"

He could hear metal hangers clinking together as she rooted through in her closet. "I did."

Sam read the rest of the article and pulled up a new window, typing in the name of the town. "You said you checked every mental institution and Brigid wasn't in any of them?"

A sultry tune played from her speakers when she switched on the music in her bedroom. "Yes."

"Is it possible one of the nuns took her in?"

"I thought the same thing, but I've checked every church in the area. She's not there."

"There's a town," Sam pressed. "Only a half hour's drive from here. It's called Kildare. If any of these nuns are still there, they might be willing to talk to us. They might remember something about Brigid."

"I've been to Kildare a dozen times, Sam. She's not there."

Sam sat back, poking around the town's website. There was a cathedral devoted to one of Ireland's patron saints—Saint Brigid. Now *that* was an interesting coincidence. Sam picked up his wine, took a long sip. He pulled up a new search on the church and skimmed through the articles. St. Brigid's Cathedral was part of the original monastery founded by Saint Brigid in the town of Kildare, on the same site where many believe the Celtic goddess Brigid built a sacred well thousands of years ago.

Sam set the wine down. '*She's hidden,*' Glenna had said. '*Somewhere Moira can't see her.*' His investigative instincts hummed as he toggled back to the church's website and saw they were advertising several special events for a Feast Day in honor of Saint Brigid on February 1st.

February 1st? Wasn't there another Irish holiday on February 1st? He typed in a new search and stared at the screen. Imbolc was a pagan holiday, usually celebrated on Feb 1st or 2nd, that honored the Celtic goddess of fire and fertility—Brigid.

"Glenna," Sam called through the doorway, not taking his eyes off the screen. "I think we should go to Kildare tonight."

"I told you, Sam, I've been there a dozen times. She's not there."

"Maybe you missed something." He checked his watch. "It's not too late. We might be able to catch a few of the nuns at the late service."

He heard the gentle swish of her bedroom door opening. "I didn't miss anything."

SAM GLANCED UP and his hands stilled on the keyboard. Glenna had tied a robe of sheer red silk over her body and he could see every inch, every glorious inch of her, through the material. Her hair was still damp from the shower and it tumbled over her shoulders in rich chocolate curls, teasing the tops of her full breasts.

She walked toward him, her hips swaying in the lamplight. "We'll go tomorrow," she said softly. "If it'll make you feel better. I want to go back to the island and check on Tara anyway, but the ferry doesn't leave until morning. We've both had a really long day."

Sam stayed where he was, but his mouth went dry when she leaned down, sliding his computer off his lap and setting it on the table. His pulse thrummed in his ears as she lowered herself slowly to the couch, with both legs on either side of him. The aroma of sandalwood and vanilla clung to her hair, and his skin burned as she straddled him.

"Sam." She ran her fingers through his hair softly—so softly every nerve ending inside him tingled and sparked. "I want..." she touched her lips to his, a whisper of a kiss. "I want to forget."

A warning went off inside him. This wasn't the first time Glenna had seduced him to get what she wanted. She had lured him back to her cottage the first day they'd met to distract him from finding Tara. His fingers dug into the couch cushions, but the front of her robe was falling open and her breasts were so close to his mouth. She was naked—completely naked—on top of him and he could feel the throbbing heat of her through his jeans.

"Sam." Her fingertips brushed over his cheek, teasing touches that had him yearning for more. "I promise we'll stop by Kildare on the way to the island tomorrow. Tonight, I want to forget."

He knew what it was like to want to forget, to want to cut off the past and run from it. But he was finally starting to get a complete picture of this woman. He needed to back up, to slow down, to find that missing angle and shed light on the whole picture. There was still something missing from her story.

But when she laid her lips on his again, he was lost. Every candle in the room lit, one by one. The lamps flickered off, submerging them in darkness and heat. Her eyes, only inches from his, were honey-colored pools of desire as she reached for the hem of his shirt.

His stomach muscles clenched when her fingers met his bare skin. He ran his hands up her heated thighs until he found the ties binding the robe. He untied the flimsy sash and eased the sheer fabric off her shoulders. It dripped like a scarlet waterfall to the floor.

She was pale alabaster in the candlelight. And even though they were miles from the ocean, he swore he could hear it—the pulsing beat of the sea, the notes of her song twisting into his soul. Seawater dripped from the ends of her hair. Shells threaded through her curls. A string of pearls encircled her throat, and his fingers toyed in the long strands that draped down the front of her, tugging her closer.

Steam rose up between them and her lips, full and soft, brushed against his. "Sam," she whispered, pressing her soft breasts into his chest. "Please. I want to forget."

In one swift motion he stood, hooking her long legs around his waist. The candles hissed as his mouth captured hers. If she wanted to forget, he would make her forget. But he would do it his way, and before dawn she would be begging to tell him the truth.

GLENNA EXPECTED THE soft mattress, expected his hard body to cover hers as they tumbled to the bed. But when her back met the cold hard wall by the door, she felt a wave of panic. No. She needed to do this her way, before she had a chance to change her mind.

She yanked Sam's shirt over his head, exposing his long lean muscles. Her fingers kneaded into his shoulders, trying to push him into the bedroom. But his strong arms pinned her hips to the wall, and his mouth moved warm and insistent over hers. The contrast of his grip on her and the tenderness of his kiss had her mind reeling.

She couldn't do what she needed to do if she let him set the pace, if she let him regain control. But he nibbled and tugged on her bottom lip, changing the pressure from tempting and teasing to desperate and needy. And those traitorous spirals of fire reared until she melted against him.

She ran her hands urgently over his body, imprinting the hard planes of muscles and bare flesh in her palms. His biceps flexed under her touch, his arms molding her body to his as he deepened the kiss. She felt the swell of emotions—those wings frantically beating inside her, desperate to break free of the cage around her heart.

But she fought them back, running her hands down the front of him, branding every inch of him into her memory. After tonight, memories would be all she had left. Her fingers danced down the rippling muscles of his stomach and she unfastened his jeans, pushing them down his slim hips and long lean legs. His eyes, when they opened, burned into hers.

"Sam—"

He silenced her with his mouth, wrapping one hand around that long string of pearls as his other hand came up to cover her aching breast. She fought the urge to wrap her legs around him, to let him take her right here against the wall. She felt herself slipping, tumbling as he skimmed those warm lips down her throat and dipped his mouth to her breast. Desire pooled between her legs.

What would happen if she gave into him, if she allowed herself this one night of passion? Her breathing grew shallow as his mouth moved south. He anchored her to the wall and knelt, the rough stubble along his jaw rubbing the inside of her thigh.

She needed to stop this charade. She needed to stop it now before he got hurt. But then his tongue was on her and she felt herself spiraling—spiraling so far out of control.

Sam.

She had tried to warn him. But he refused to believe her. Couldn't he see that inside, she was nothing but thorns? The sensation built, pulling her under. She sunk her fingers in his hair. She had known from the first moment she saw him that he would be her undoing. That he was nothing like the others who came before him.

The tremors inside her turned to shuddering quakes and her body clenched. His name escaped in a ragged gasp from her lips as he rose, lifting her into his arms and carrying her into the bedroom. Every muscle in her body felt languid and loose. A smoky female voice played from the speakers where she'd switched on a blues station earlier. The candles were lit, the curtains drawn.

He laid her down gently on a bed of burgundy feather pillows and cream sheets. Edging her back, he ran a hand lazily up the curve of her waist, teasing the underside of her breast. "Tonight, Glenna. You are mine."

She lifted a hand, tracing the rugged lines of his face, the hard angles and planes of his jaw and cheek. She brushed her lips back to his, but it was his eyes that had her heart skipping a beat.

There was only one emotion in them. And it was not lust.

LATER, MUCH LATER, when he finally filled her, burying himself inside her as wave after wave of pleasure rolled over them, he whispered the words she had read in his eyes.

And for the first time in her life, she wished she could say them back.

CHAPTER 19

Caitlin eased out of Owen's bedroom, shutting the door quietly behind her. The air in the cottage was warm, but she felt cold—cold all over. Liam was in the living room, stacking their son's fairy tale books into a box. Owen still wouldn't tell his parents why he refused to read the stories anymore, only that he wanted them out of his sight.

Liam glanced up when he heard her come into the room. "Is he asleep?"

Caitlin nodded, wrapping her arms around her stomach. Normally, she would seek comfort in her fiancé's arms. But after Nuala's arrival on the island tonight, she felt like a wall was between them—a wall of bitter memories and foolish regrets. "How could we not have known Owen was seeing Nuala every night?"

"We thought he was at Brennan's," Liam said, setting another book into the box. "And he was. We just didn't know he was leaving early each night to see her on the way home."

"We should have been with him."

Liam looked up at her. "We can't follow him everywhere."

"What if Moira had gotten to him? What if—"

Liam stood, crossing the room to her and rubbing his hands up and down her arms. They could hear the echo of waves through the open windows. "Owen's safe now. He's in his bed. He's okay."

Caitlin stepped back and Liam's arms fell to his sides. "What is Nuala still doing here?" Caitlin asked. "What does she want with us?"

"Maybe she wants to see Owen."

Caitlin looked away, swallowing the lump in her throat.

"He never talks about her," Liam said, lowering his voice. "He's never even mentioned her name. How could we have known that he wanted to maintain contact?"

"We should have asked," Caitlin said helplessly. "We should have offered. So he didn't think he had to sneak around behind our backs."

"Would you have let him see her if he'd asked?"

"I don't know." Caitlin shook his head. "After everything she did to us. To our family..." She fought back a hot rush of anger and walked into the kitchen, filling a kettle with water. "She *stole* our child, Liam. For ten years, Nuala raised Owen as her own, and we didn't even know he was alive."

"And he didn't know *we* were alive." Liam picked up the yellow dish towel hanging over the back of the chair, handing it to her. "Maybe we underestimated the bond that formed between them during those years."

"He asked me to forgive her," Caitlin said, drying her hands. "And I did. To get *you* back. But I don't trust her. I don't want her here." She set the towel down. "And I don't want her anywhere near Owen."

"Owen thinks she might be trying to help us find Brigid."

The gas clicked on the stove as Caitlin lit the burner with a match. "Why would she do that?"

"Maybe to prove to us that she's trying to change?" Liam offered. "That she's on our side?"

Caitlin turned. "I don't want her on our side."

"If Nuala is against Moira, she *is* on our side. She might be able to help us."

Caitlin pushed away from the counter. How could she have been so stupid to think her son would forget about Nuala? Walking over to the box, she picked up the book Liam gave Owen for Christmas, the one that fell in the water. The pages were still damp and stuck together, but she opened them to the story marked by the gold ribbon and wasn't at all surprised to find *The Little Mermaid*. "Have you come up with any ideas about why your mother would shelve the white selkie legend with the mermaid books?"

"I have a theory," Liam admitted slowly. "But it's pretty far-fetched."

"I'm starting to think far-fetched is the norm around here."

Liam walked over to the couch, pulling her down beside him. "Did Owen tell you the story Brennan told him? About the mermaids and the selkies?"

Caitlin nodded.

"I've been searching back, as far back as I can go, trying to figure out when the first white selkie was born. And I think it might have coincided with when the mermaids forced the selkies into these waters."

"But they had queens before then, didn't they?"

"Yes," Liam answered. "But not *white* selkie queens. The siren who almost started the war between the mermaids and selkies was the daughter of a selkie queen. It was that queen's refusal to hand her over to the mermaids that forced the selkies into these waters." Liam's gaze shifted to the book in Caitlin's hands. "I can't help wondering if the white selkie's role was created by the mermaids as a punishment, a sort of twisted test to ensure the selkies maintained the peace between the land and the sea."

Caitlin furrowed her brow. "But a white selkie has to bring a human man into the sea to rule beside her before she can be queen," she argued. "If the reason the mermaids cut off the selkies in the first place was to stop the siren, or any selkie, from luring men into the sea, why would they punish the selkies with something that would essentially make them do the same thing?"

"Think about it." Liam took a deep breath. "It's the *ultimate* punishment. Only one land-man is allowed to be taken every few hundred years, and, yes, he's cut off from his family and friends, but he gets to rule beside the white selkie. He gets to be king. The power is shared. Together they rule these seas and keep the peace between both their people. It's a balance of power."

"But wouldn't that be disruptive?" Caitlin asked. "Wouldn't the mermaids be afraid the ruling family would revolt, if someone didn't want to lose power?"

"Not if the alternative was this." Liam gestured out the window. "There are no fish in these waters, Caitlin. Nothing for the selkies to eat, to live off of. The ocean is growing warmer every day. And the tides..." Liam shook his head. "Donal and Jack spent half the day clearing a path for the ferry to get back in this afternoon. If a storm were to blow in when the tide was as high as it was today, our harbor could be wiped out."

"Our island," Caitlin whispered. "Our home. It's slipping away."

"I think that's what the mermaids want," Liam said quietly. "If the story Brennan told Owen is true, then the selkies are restricted not only by the boundaries under the sea, but by the amount of land they can shape-shift on. Their connection to these islands is the only magic they have left. Without the islands, the selkies would lose their magic. They wouldn't be selkies anymore. They would only be seals."

Caitlin's hands clasped the damp pages of the fairy tale. She had never considered mermaids to be anything other than friendly sea creatures. But now that she looked more closely at the illustrations, she could see the sharp scales on their powerful tales, the elongated fins that could propel them through the sea five times faster than any selkie, and the piercing barbs of the king's trident.

"Nuala couldn't have been the first white selkie to rebel," Liam went on, "to reject the idea of bringing a land-man into the ocean to rule beside her. There had to be others who felt this fate was forced on them."

"Nuala rebelled twice," Caitlin said softly. "First by eloping with her selkie lover, and then by taking Owen—a child instead of a man."

Liam nodded solemnly. "She might have succeeded if Moira hadn't tricked her into stealing *our* child—one with selkie blood in his veins."

Caitlin's gaze dropped to the pearl and sapphire engagement ring on her finger, a gift from Liam's grandmother—the selkie queen who had passed away only six weeks before. "Do you think that's why Nuala was here tonight? To warn us?"

"She's on our side, Cait. I have no doubt of that." He reached for her hand, lacing their fingers together. "As much as we both hate what she did to us, I think we may need her before the end."

Caitlin drew in a shaky breath. "There has to be another way to restore the balance in the selkie kingdom."

Liam lifted his eyes to hers. "The selkies need a queen."

Caitlin gripped his hand as a new fear swept through her. "Nuala?"

Liam shook his head slowly. "I don't think so."

Caitlin searched his face, pale and fraught in the dimly lit room. "Then who?"

"If Nuala hadn't been born," Liam said slowly. "My mother was next in line to be queen."

BRIGID LAY AWAKE, listening to the owl hooting in the woods. The moon was a pale disk of silver shining through her window. The house was quiet, but her fingers worried over the seam of the wool blanket tucked under her chin. She could hear it—the voice whispering to her through the pines—the voice of the sea.

Glenna was the only one who believed her, the only one who said she could hear it, too. But she hadn't come today. And the voice was growing stronger. She could hear it wherever she went on the property now: in the chapel, in the greenhouse, in the dining hall where they ate their meals at night. It followed her like a long winter shadow cast by a frozen sun that would never set.

Glenna had promised her that they would follow it one day, that they would follow the voice together all the way out to the sea. But what if something happened to her? What if she was never coming to see her again?

Brigid slid her bare feet out from under the covers. Moonlight slanted in the small window as she slipped into her habit, fastening the wimple around her throat. She could not ignore it anymore. It was calling to her. If she could follow it, if she could just reach the ocean, everything would be okay.

She slipped silently out of her room and stole down to the river. A warm wind played through the branches of the pines. Clear water rushed over the rocks, twisting and bubbling through the woods. She gathered her stiff black skirt in her hands, lifting the hem as she stepped into the river.

She closed her eyes as the cool water washed over her bare feet. A branch snapped in the forest and an animal skittered through the underbrush. Brigid breathed in the scent of the pines, and with one last look back at the house, she set out alone into the night, letting the voice of the river carry her home.

OWEN WAITED FOR his parents' bedroom door to shut. As soon as their voices faded to whispers, he switched on his flashlight, shining a beam over the crown tucked under the covers. He dusted sand from the crevasses of the braided black vines, tracing the intricate pattern woven into the front. He'd seen it somewhere before—this pattern, like one of the Celtic knots in Brennan's old books.

He didn't know what it meant, or who the crown belonged to, but whoever it was must be special if Nuala risked her life to bring it to him. He switched off the flashlight and pulled back the covers. He wouldn't let her down. He crept out of bed, stuffing pillows down the length of the mattress. The crown couldn't stay here—not if it put his parents in danger.

He padded over to the open window, slipping out and landing softly in the grass. Brennan would know what to do with it. He might even know why Nuala had brought it to him. He hurried across the island, jogging up the hill toward the door of the main house, but a faint orange light coming from Sam's cottage caught his eye. He hesitated as the scent of something sweet mixed with the salty air blowing in from the sea.

He heard tiny branches snapping against the wall, and he crept toward Sam's cottage. His fingers gripped the crown as he rounded the corner. Thick black vines snaked up the walls, latching onto the whitewash, scraping over the glass. Shadows devoured the cracked shudders and the petals on the blooms gleamed iridescent black, like oil spilled into the ocean.

A single rose, at the very top, curled into the thatch. Three of the petals were orange and they radiated light, but the glow faded as another petal turned black. Only two orange petals remained, like the last dying flames of a fire about to go out.

He backed slowly away from the roses. The last time roses had grown on this island, it had meant someone's time was running out. If these roses were growing outside Sam's cottage, did that mean Sam was in trouble? Slowly, he pulled out the crown. They were so similar—this crown and these roses.

His gaze dropped to the soil around the base of the plant. The earth was turned up, as if someone had been digging earlier. His mother had hidden something underneath a rose once, something that meant a lot to her. She must think it was a safe spot to hide things.

He glanced over his shoulder at the barn. He could hear the animals moving around in their stalls. The crown would be safe here. At least until he figured out what the pattern meant. He ran into the barn and grabbed a shovel. Carrying it back out to the roses, he started to dig.

MOIRA FLOATED IN the dark, murky waters outside her cave. The volcano's tremors had subsided, but trails of congealed lava still dripped from the rocky mountainside. Pockets of smoke puffed up from the gray soil, bubbles of sulfur popping and releasing a putrid stench.

With a swish of her tail, she was in her rose garden. She had never liked to garden—not like her sister. She had never seen the point in tending to sea flowers that would wither and fade as the seasons passed. But black roses were different. Black roses had a *use*.

Six black roses with ebony stems and glossy petals undulated in the currents. The soil beneath them glowed like embers. Her flippers wrapped around the black iron rake leaning against the mouth of her lair. She scoured the sharp prongs through the bits of lava rock, preparing a new plot.

Soon there would be seven.

Moira smiled. She had let Glenna think it was the curse taking her lovers all these years. But the truth was, Moira was taking them. Black roses could catch the soul of a dying man in their petals, and the emotions of that soul—the deepest emotion that soul felt when they died—lived on in the rose.

Love was a powerful magic. And without it, Moira would be nothing. She was a fraud, a sea witch with no real powers of her own. A selkie with no ability to attract. These men—her daughter's lovers—they were her magic.

But none of them could give her what Sam would. True love was the most powerful magic of all. And now she was going to have it. She could taste it—the rush of freedom when the selkies crowned her as their queen. The bursting explosion of the volcano in the distance as her lair was destroyed.

She would never come back to this wretched place again. She had thought Glenna understood what was at stake, what Moira was doing for both of them. But her daughter had forsaken her. She had left her with no choice. She would take from Glenna the one thing that meant the most.

The sea pulsed, like a hollow heart beating in her ears. If she could not have love, no one could. A rose snaked out of the soil, its petals a glossy midnight black. A faint swish in the water behind her signaled her eels return. She turned, but they cowered in the shadows at the mouth of her cave, watching her with fearful eyes.

"What is it?" Moira asked dismissively as they entwined their tails, clinging to each other for strength.

"Nuala," one of the eels hissed. "She escaped."

CHAPTER 20

"Owen?" Brennan rubbed his eyes, gazing down at the child sitting on the floor of his living room with a flashlight, surrounded by a pile of books. "What are you doing here?"

Owen shifted his weight. "I needed to look at your books."

"It's the middle of the night," Brennan said gruffly, taking in Owen's torn pajamas and hands caked in dirt. "Couldn't this wait until morning?"

Owen shook his head.

Brennan walked into the room, switching on the light. "Where do your parents think you are?"

Owen reached for another book, the one is his lap slipping onto the floor with the others. "Asleep."

"Don't you think they'll worry if they wake up and find you gone?" Brennan asked, reaching for the phone on the wall.

"No," Owen said, rushing across the room and grabbing the phone from him. "You can't call them."

"Why not?"

"Because I need your help," Owen said quickly, hanging up the phone. "Remember that book you were reading to me a few weeks ago—the one with the Celtic knots in it?"

Brennan nodded slowly.

"Can I see it again?"

Brennan glowered at him, but he ambled over to the wall of books, pulling a heavy volume down from the tallest shelf. He held it away from Owen when the boy reached for it. "Only if you tell me what this is about."

"I need to know what one of the knots means."

Brennan narrowed his eyes, but he handed Owen the book. Owen took it and sank to the couch, flipping through the pages. He paused when he found the one he was looking for. "There it is," he whispered. "Just like I remembered."

Brennan sat down beside him, his knees creaking. He peered at the page. "That's the knot the merprince wears in his crown."

"The...merprince?"

Brennan nodded. When Owen's hands started to shake, Brennan took the book from him. "What's going on, Owen?"

"Nothing," Owen whispered. "I just needed to know what that knot meant."

MOIRA STEPPED OUT of the swirl of smoke. Fingers of fire clung to the sleeves of her dress, sizzling over the seams. She gazed up at the dark homes in the village. She knew the crown was here. She would find it and punish the person who had it.

Nuala couldn't have gotten far. She had no one else in her life but Owen, no one she could trust. She must have given it to him. And Owen would have handed it over to his *real* parents, because he was young and stupid and wouldn't know any better.

She focused on the house with the yellow door, the one next to the pub. She would gladly set it on fire, and burn them all in their sleep. But she couldn't risk the crown being burned and the truth being exposed.

She needed to create a diversion, something else to lure them out of their home so she could search it. She scanned the village, her gaze lingering on every cottage until a swallow flitted out of a cave and swooped over to the harbor.

It landed on the railing of the ferry, and Moira's lips curved.

TARA TOSSED AND turned, drifting in and out of restless sleep. Dreams haunted her. Dreams of her past. Dreams of her future. Dreams of fires chasing her to the highest cliff of the island. She reached for Dominic, burying her face in his warm chest as another dream—a memory this time—pulled her under.

"I wonder why they sell the crosses so far from the church," Kelsey asked, peering over Tara's shoulder to look at the map.

"They sell them at the church, too," Tara explained "But there's a community of nuns who live in the hills. They weave the crosses out of river rushes. I'm curious to see how they do it."

Dominic steered the car onto a long dirt drive, bordered with ewes and knotty pines. Tara rolled down the window, letting in the peaceful sound of birds chirping over the fields.

"What's that?" Kelsey pointed past a modest stone house bordered with cheerful autumn gardens to a small structure with lots of windows and a roof made of glass.

"It's a greenhouse," Tara said. "A place where you can keep plants growing all through the winter."

Dominic parked behind a small gathering of cars. A white chapel sat at the edge of the property, nestled into the hawthorns. Nuns wandered the paths between the unassuming buildings.

"Why are these crosses so special?" Kelsey asked as they climbed out of the car.

Dominic took her hand. "Brigid's crosses are supposed to offer protection to people who hang them above their front door." He ruffled

Kelsey's blond hair. "Who knows if it's true, but we can never have too much protection."

Tara trailed behind them as Kelsey and Dominic wandered over to a small outdoor stand where two nuns were weaving crosses and offering them for sale. The scent of basil and lemon verbena pulled to her and she looked over at the greenhouse. "I'll catch up with you in a minute," she called.

She hadn't known what to expect when they'd decided to stop at a nunnery on their way out of Kildare. But there was something mysterious, almost magical, about this place. The ground hummed beneath her feet, like a force was at work in the soil.

She found a nun alone in the greenhouse, and stepped inside.

"I'm sorry," Tara said quickly when the woman shied away from her. "I don't mean to disturb you."

A curtain of dried lavender and thyme rustled as the woman ducked behind it.

"I like to work with herbs," Tara said, keeping her voice light and friendly. "My mother—she used to take herbs into the farmer's market on the weekend." She touched a colorful spray of foxgloves and marveled at the size of the basil growing beside them. "We had a greenhouse like this when I was growing up. It smells like her."

The woman said nothing, but she watched Tara closely, with eyes as gray as the stones of the cathedral they'd visited earlier that day.

Tara picked up a bouquet of rosemary and sage, tied with a pink ribbon. "Do you sell these?"

"We do," a different voice answered, one that came from behind her.

Tara turned and found herself looking into the brown eyes of another nun—one whose smile was warm and friendly.

"I'm Sister Evelyn," she said. "Would you like me to give you a tour?"

"Sure," Tara said slowly, stealing a glance back at the other nun. The hem of her habit peeked out from beneath the curtain and Tara stared at the intricate pattern of seashells sewn into the seam.

Sister Evelyn stepped into the small greenhouse and started explaining all the herbs and their uses. But as they made their way toward the *back of the greenhouse, the first nun slipped out from behind the curtain. Her hair was tucked into her habit so Tara couldn't tell what color it was, but her skin was pale and the shape of her nose and mouth were oddly familiar. The nun cast her eyes down as she slipped by them.*

Tara frowned, but Sister Evelyn held up a small jar of crushed mint leaves cheerfully. "Have you ever tried adding a pinch of these to a cup of hot chocolate in the winter?"

"I have," Tara said distractedly as the first nun ducked out of the greenhouse. "My mother used to make me that same drink when I couldn't sleep at night."

"Here," Sister Evelyn said when Tara's gaze lingered on the woman walking down the hill. "Have a sniff of this tarragon. It smells a bit like licorice, but better."

Tara took the jar from Sister Evelyn, watching the nun break into a run as she made for the river winding through the pines.

TARA WOKE WITH a start, the image of the woman imprinted in her mind. "Dominic." She sat up, switching on the light. It was still dark and her bedside clock read 5AM. "Dominic, wake up." She shook him, and those gray eyes—the same ones she'd seen in her dream—blinked open. "I think I know where your mother is."

"What?" He sat up, rubbing his eyes. "How?"

"Remember the community of nuns who lived in the hills—the ones who wove the river rush crosses?"

He nodded slowly.

Tara swung her legs over the bed. "I think your mother lives there."

Dominic stared at her. "As a *nun*?"

"I think so." Tara ran to get her computer from the living room. She looked up at the straw-colored cross hanging over their door and clutched her laptop to her chest, rushing back to the bedroom. She crawled back into bed, booting up the computer and waiting for the screen to load. "Remember when I told you about the woman in the greenhouse, how she would hardly look at me?"

Dominic nodded slowly.

"I think that might have been her." She typed in the name of the nunnery and searched for a phone number.

Dominic laid a hand over hers when she reached for the phone. "You can't call there now, Tara. It's the middle of the night."

Tara's fingers stilled on the numbers. "But what if it's her?"

"Call Sam, or Glenna," Dominic said gently. "They're in Dublin already and Kildare's only a half hour's drive from the city. They can go there first thing and take a look around."

"But—"

"Mum?" Kelsey's small voice cut through their conversation.

Tara glanced up at her daughter hovering in the doorway. Her face was pale and her blue eyes were wide and worried. "What's wrong, Kelsey?"

"I..." She looked down. "I need to tell you something."

"What is it?" Tara held out her hand. "What happened?"

Kelsey walked to the bed and Tara helped her crawl up between them. She clutched shreds of paper in her hands and she let them fall.

"What is this?" Dominic said, lifting one of the strips.

"*The Little Mermaid*," Kelsey answered, piecing them together slowly on the comforter

"What happened to it?"

"Owen ripped it up."

Tara set the phone down slowly. "Why?"

"Because Moira told him to."

"When?" Dominic demanded. "When did she tell him this?"

"Yesterday," Kelsey whispered. "He went to see Nuala, but Moira was there instead. Moira told him that if he said anything about it, she'd hurt Caitlin like she hurt Nuala."

Tara looked up at Dominic and saw her own fear mirrored in his eyes.

"I heard what you said," Kelsey admitted softly, "about my grand-mother living in Kildare." She fit the final pieces of paper together. "You're right," she said, pointing to the words. "It's just like in the story. The princess lived in a convent."

CHAPTER
21

C ait!" Liam shook his fiancée. "Caitlin! Wake up!"

"What?" Her eyes flew open, struggling to see in the darkness. "What's wrong?"

Liam switched on the light. He was already out of bed, grabbing his clothes off the floor. "There's a fire in the harbor."

Caitlin kicked at the sheets, scrambling after him. Through the window, flames streaked into the night sky. Their neighbors were waking up, their panicked shouts echoing through the street. "Owen," she breathed.

"I know." Liam tugged a pair of sweatpants over his hips, rushing out into the hallway. He pushed open his son's door, breathing out a sigh of relief when he saw the lump under the covers. "Owen," he said quietly. "You need to wake up. Something's happened."

He walked to the bed, putting his hand on his son's back. But his finger met something soft and squishy—not Owen. He threw back the covers and every muscle in his body clenched in dread. "Owen!"

"He's not in there?" Caitlin breathed, gripping the doorway.

"Come on." Liam grabbed her hand, racing out into the street.

Fiona stumbled out of the cottage on the other side of the pub, tying a robe around her waist. Her gray hair was out of its usual bun and her slippers caught on the pavement as she ran toward them.

"Have you seen Owen?" Caitlin cried.

"No," Fiona said. "He's not in his bed?"

Liam's gaze combed the street. Smoke billowed up from the harbor. Headlights bounced down from the road leading to the cliff cottage. He spotted his brother behind the wheel and ran toward the truck. Dominic slowed and Liam leaned down to peer through the open window. But it was only Dom, Tara and Kelsey in the truck. "Owen's missing."

"What?" Tara helped Kelsey scramble over her lap and climb out the passenger door into the arms of her grandmother. "When?"

"Just now," Liam answered. "We woke up and he was gone."

"Get in," Dom barked at Liam, then looked at Fiona. "Keep Kelsey away from the fire."

Liam ran to the back of the truck, releasing the hatch. He looked at Caitlin. "Stay in the village and search for him here."

Caitlin nodded and Fiona wrapped her arms around Kelsey. But as the trio faded behind them, he could see the fear in his fiancée's eyes. What if Owen had gone down to the harbor to see Nuala? What if he'd gotten on the ferry?

Neighbors ran alongside them, in various states of undress. The wheel caught a pothole and Liam gripped the side of the truck. At the edge of the harbor, Donal was holding onto Finn, struggling to keep the captain back from the pier.

Liam's feet met the pavement before Dominic rolled to a stop. He raced through the gathering of villagers, scanning the harbor. "Owen!" he screamed his name, but his voice was lost in the inferno raging at the end of the pier.

Jack Dooley turned on the harbor hose, spraying it at the ferry, but the fire was already spreading to the other boats. Tara and Dom ran from the truck, yelling at the villagers to get back. The blaze grew, swallowing the pier.

"Liam!" Dominic shouted, wrestling the hose from Jack's hands and throwing it down. "Get away from the pier!"

Liam spotted a child's shoe in the water and he scrambled over the rocks, fishing it out. He remembered Owen came home yesterday without shoes. He said he left them in the harbor. What if he came back for them tonight? What if he was afraid he and Caitlin were angry with him after what happened with Nuala?

Tara grabbed his arm, pulling him away from the water as a blast tore through the night, knocking them both to the ground. Splinters of wood and shards of glass rained down around them.

"Liam, look!" Tara shouted over the aftershocks of the explosion as a beat-up truck rumbled up the road from Brennan's farm. The passenger door opened and Owen jumped from the cab.

"Dad!" Owen cried, running toward Liam.

Liam caught his son when he ran into his arms.

"He's okay," Tara breathed.

Finn staggered down the hill, staring at the destruction, at his livelihood scattered into a thousand flaming pieces in the water. "My boat." He reached out, leaning on Jack Dooley for support. "It's gone."

Dominic strode to Tara, helping her up. "And we're trapped on the island."

CAITLIN'S RELIEF AT finding her son faded as she stood in the doorway of her home, staring at the overturned tables, the contents of her kitchen drawers emptied onto the floor. Books were piled on the floor, entire shelves cleared. The sofa was pushed away from the wall, the floorboards beneath it yanked up.

She walked through her cottage, numb, taking in the damage. Both bedrooms were ransacked, the closets emptied and their clothes and shoes strewn all over the floor. Owen's mattress was shredded and feathers spilled out of the gaps in the seams.

"Moira did this," Liam said grimly.

"But why?" Dominic asked, walking into the cottage. "What was she looking for?"

Caitlin picked her way over her littered bedroom floor to her vanity, checking her small collection of jewelry. She didn't have much, but the gold wedding ring that belonged to her great-grandmother and the pair of sapphire earrings Liam gave her for Christmas were still there. "Whoever it was, she didn't come for jewelry."

"It had to be Moira," Tara said, walking into the kitchen and picking up the shattered glass. "Who else would set the ferry on fire?"

Caitlin walked back out to the living room, taking in the chaos. They'd managed to contain the fire in the harbor after the explosion. The charred remnants of the ferry had sunk into the water and half of their pier was gone, but they'd saved three boats. Many of their neighbors had already made arrangements to leave at dawn.

"Owen," Caitlin said softly as she picked her way across the living room to her son. "You said you didn't know where Nuala went earlier, when we were on the beach. Were you telling the truth?"

Owen nodded, but he wouldn't look at her. He wouldn't meet her eyes.

Caitlin looked up at Tara, her expression grim. "We need to talk to Glenna."

"I know," Tara said, pulling out her cell phone and checking for missed calls. "I've been trying to call her and Sam for hours. Neither of them is answering."

Dominic lifted the kitchen table and slid the rug back underneath it. "Tara had a dream tonight. She thinks she knows where our mother is."

Liam paused in the act of rummaging around in the hall closet, searching for something. "Where?"

"In a nunnery in Kildare," Tara explained. "It's a hunch, but I think I saw her there last fall when we took that side trip to pick up the crosses."

"Kildare," Caitlin murmured, standing and snagging the cross down from where it hung above her door. "It makes sense," she said softly. "It connects the blackthorn, Imbolc, and St. Brigid's Day."

Tara nodded. "I've left messages on both Sam and Glenna's phones, asking them to go to the nunnery as soon as they wake up."

Caitlin looked up. "Today is the first of February."

"Whatever Moira is planning, it's going to happen today," Dominic said as Liam dropped to his knees in the doorway of the closet, tossing clothes out of the way.

"Liam," Tara asked. "What are you looking for?"

All the blood drained from Liam's face as he pulled their metal safe into his arms—the one they kept hidden behind the closet wall. "It's gone."

"What's gone?" Dominic asked. "What's wrong?"

Caitlin gasped when she saw the broken hinges.

Dominic strode to his brother, taking the safe from his arms. "What was inside it?"

Liam lifted his stricken eyes to his son's face. "Owen's pelt."

ALL THE CANDLES had burned down to pools of wax. Glenna watched the last flame flicker and fade as she lay in Sam's arms. She could hear his heart beating, could feel the steady rise and fall of his chest beneath her cheek. Every nerve in her body still tingled from the memory of his touch. But it was getting close to dawn.

Her heart ached as she withdrew from his arms and studied his face for the last time. He looked so calm and peaceful. A small smile played at the corners of his mouth. She touched the lines fanning out from his eyes tenderly, brushing a thumb over the rugged skin of his cheek where a rough layer of golden stubble was beginning to grow.

"Rest," she breathed. "Let your dreams carry you far away from here." She drew two stones from beneath her pillow—amber and jet—and laid them gently in Sam's palm. When he stirred, she swept a hand lightly over his eyes.

Sleep, take thee away
May darkness hold sway
Past first morning light
Shadowed from sight
May no harm be done
No harm come to none
By the will of the sea
So mote it be

A profound sadness consumed her as she eased back, watching his breath deepen and slow. She'd put it off as long as she could. Brigid wasn't safe in Ireland anymore. Two black carry-on suitcases were waiting in the trunk of her car. She'd bought the plane tickets the night before, when Sam was out walking around the city. She'd had a fake passport made for Brigid years ago, in case it ever came to this.

She'd hoped Brigid would be ready by now. But how could Brigid lead the selkies? How could she fight for them, if she didn't know what was at stake? She closed Sam's fingers around the stones. She'd made arrangements with a church in the States. They'd agreed to house Brigid temporarily, until Glenna could find a permanent home for her.

She'd put it off for years, afraid of taking Brigid out of the protected space, even for the short trip to the airport. Any travel outside Kildare would draw Moira's eye to her sister. She'd been doing everything in her power to help Brigid remember who she was, but she had to face the truth now—Brigid might never remember.

She looked back at Sam, tracing the curved outline of his mouth. "If things had been different," she whispered. "I think I could have loved you." She kissed him, letting the memory of him imprint on her lips. She eased back, laying a heavy hand on his chest. "I could have given you my heart."

CHAPTER
22

Glenna's headlights flashed over the small chapel. A single light burned in one of the windows of the communal home; at least one of the nuns was awake. She slowed to a stop at the end of the long driveway, cutting the engine and stepping out of the car. She felt the flow of energy as soon as her boots met the ground.

There were few places in Ireland as protected as these hills on the outskirts of Kildare. They were sacred to both religions—those who honored the goddess Brigid and those who worshiped St. Brigid. It was this powerful convergence of light and love that blocked Moira from seeing her sister.

The reflection of the moon danced over the surface of the river winding through the woods at the bottom of the hill. Snowdrops and crocuses were blooming and the irises were sending up shoots in the hearty garden beds bordering the stone house. She strode to the door and knocked lightly, relieved when Sister Evelyn walked out of the kitchen, drying her hands on a dish towel.

"Glenna," she exclaimed, her brown eyes widening as she opened the door. "What are you doing here at this hour?"

"I came to see Brigid."

"I don't think she's awake yet," Sister Evelyn said, ushering her inside. "Excuse the mess." She waved at the stacks of chairs and folding tables, the plastic tablecloths and dishware the parishioners had dropped off for the celebration following the special St. Brigid's Day mass. "Would you like a cup of tea?"

"No." Glenna shook her head as she stepped into the room. "I'm sorry. I can't stay. I need to see her now."

"Oh." A shadow of worry passed over Sister Evelyn's eyes as she closed the door behind Glenna. "Let me get her up, then."

"Wait," Glenna began when Sister Evelyn started to turn.

"What is it, Glenna?" Sister Evelyn's dark brows furrowed in concern. "Is everything alright?"

Glenna swallowed a sudden lump in her throat. "I wanted to say thank you." The silence of the dark house pressed down on her. "For everything you've done for her."

"Of course." Sister Evelyn looked at her strangely. "Anyone in my position would have done the same thing."

"I'm not so sure about that."

Sister Evelyn smiled and nudged her toward the kitchen. Cast iron pots and kettles hung from simple hooks in the walls. The counters, thick slabs of rough cut wood that doubled as chopping blocks, were covered with loaves of fresh-baked bread and desserts for the feast.

Sister Evelyn pulled out a stool from under the counter. "Why don't you have a seat and I'll go wake her." She laid a hand on Glenna's arm. "She'll be so glad to see you."

Would she? Glenna wondered as Sister Evelyn's footsteps faded into the back. When she told her she was taking her away from her home, from the only friends she'd known for the past fifteen years?

Glenna sat, running a finger over one of the knots in the wood that had been carefully sanded down. When she had visited Brigid as a young woman, without a clue how to survive in this world on her own, the nuns had taught her to read and to cook. They taught her how to make bread, how to harvest herbs, how to store groceries so they kept the longest shelf life.

She knew early on that she could not be one of them, that her own beliefs aligned with the pagan religions of Ireland—ones that worshipped the goddess and the cycles of the earth. But they had never held that against her. They'd welcomed her, as they would their own daughter.

"Glenna?" Sister Evelyn's voice was laced with worry as she rushed back into the kitchen.

Glenna hurried to her feet, the wooden legs of the stool scraping against the cement floor. "What's wrong?"

"She's not here."

"What do you mean, she's not here?" Glenna followed Sister Evelyn into Brigid's empty room. Her bed was made with perfect folds and tightly tucked corners. The floor was spotless, save the pair of black shoes aligned with the edge of the door.

"She was here last night," Sister Evelyn said. "I helped put her to bed."

Glenna strode to the open window. She could hear the river, the song of the water rushing over the rocks. "Where would she go?"

Sister Evelyn's skirt swished as she joined Glenna by the window. She gazed down at the moon sparkling over the bubbling water. "Sometimes she goes down to the river at night."

NEIL LEARY YAWNED, forcing his eyes open as the white lines blurred on the road. He rolled down the window and cranked up the radio to drown out the slabs of slate rattling around in the back. He glanced in the rear-view mirror at the bed of the lorry. He probably should have tied them down better. But he'd been driving all night picking up shipments for his client, and he couldn't wait to get home.

He slowed the truck as the road curved through a stretch of pines and he came to a wooden bridge traversing a river. He blinked when he saw a woman running alongside it, her black hair and dress streaming out behind her. *What the hell?* His rusty brakes squealed as he pulled onto the shoulder and peered down at the rushing water.

He waited for her to appear on the other side of the bridge and when she didn't, he rolled his eyes heavenward. He was probably seeing things. There was nothing but hills and farmland along this road. But he better have a look anyway. He clambered out of the truck. "Hello, there," he called, his deep voice echoing through the silent woods.

There was no answer, but he could hear a faint wheezing. He picked his way down the slope of ferns to the stream bed. Tendrils of fog clung to the pine needles and an icy blue dawn sparkled through the long branches.

Peering under the bridge, he spotted the woman in black cowering behind a metal support beam. "Hello," he said, lifting his hands in a sign of peace. "Are you okay? Do you need help?"

She scrambled to her feet and tried to run away, but she slipped on the wet rocks and fell. Neil hurried to her side and knelt. He could see the whites of her eyes when she tried to pull away from him.

"It's okay," he said again, looking down at her bloody feet, raw from running barefoot along the river for God knows how long. "I'm not going to hurt you. Let me give you a lift home."

She shook her head, and he saw that her whole body was trembling. Her long black hair was knotted with river grasses, and mud streaked across her pale cheeks. She was probably about fifty years old—the same age as him. His gaze dropped to her dress and he stilled. "You're a nun."

She swallowed, her gaze darting over her shoulder to the river. She clutched the top portion of her habit in her hands. River water dripped from the black material.

Neil glanced up at the hills through the trees, as the lightening sky in the east shone over a few houses in the distance. "Where's your home?"

Her voice was raspy, like dried seaweed scraping over sand. "I need to get to the ocean."

He stared at her and that uneasy feeling started to spread. "The...ocean?"

She nodded, and wide penetrating eyes—the color of stormy seas—locked on his. He felt a strange pull, like threads spinning around him and tugging him to her. He coughed when the fog thickened and his lungs constricted. Every sip of air was like swallowing a mouthful of salt water. He staggered back, but he couldn't tear his eyes from her face. "This river," he gasped, "it won't take you to the ocean."

A robin flitted through the forest, landing on the guardrail of the bridge. The woman's gaze lifted and the spell broke. The fog evaporated and Neil pulled dry air into his lungs, pressing his palms to the ground and leaning forward to catch his breath.

"Where will it take me?" the woman asked, watching the robin puff out its orange belly and warble out a solitary song.

"To a system of broken canals," Neil explained. "They used to lead west to the River Shannon, but they got shut down years ago."

"Why?"

"Flooding...through the bogs."

Her gray eyes slid back to his face. "I need to get to the ocean.

"I'm heading to Clifden," Neil said slowly. "It's a town on the west coast, near the Atlantic. I can give you a ride..."

She looked up at his truck, and Neil imagined how it must look through her eyes: the peeling blue paint, the faded *Clifden Construction* logo, the rusted muffler and bumper hanging loose on one side. "It's not much to look at," Neil added quickly, "but it's faster than walking."

"You'll take me to the ocean."

It was a command, not a question. He nodded.

She stood, gathering up her wet skirt. Neil pushed to his feet and offered to help her up the hill, but she edged away from him. At the road, he opened the passenger door. "Sorry," he said, shoving the clutter piled on the seat onto the floor. "It's a bit of a mess."

She put a hand on his arm and he felt the strangest sensation, like water sliding over his skin. He stepped back as she climbed into the cabin. She gathered up the clutter and set it in her lap, sorting through the items and stacking them in tidy little piles.

Neil hesitated for a long moment before shutting the door. He'd gotten a good glimpse of her feet when she climbed into the truck, and he'd seen the thin translucent webbing between her toes. He took a deep breath. "Are you sure you don't want me to give you a ride home?"

She lifted her eyes to his. "I *am* going home."

CHAPTER
23

Light streamed in through the window and Sam opened one eye groggily. He stretched, reaching across the large bed for Glenna. Two small objects rolled out of his hand, clinking together as they fell to the sheets.

He peered down at the two stones—one black, one amber—and he sat up. "Glenna?" he called, his voice echoing through the empty apartment. The refrigerator hummed in the kitchen. A neighbor's door opened and closed as someone left for the day.

Pushing to his feet, he snagged his jeans from the floor and stepped into them. He edged the heavy curtain aside. Traffic flowed along the road by the river and a bright sun shone down on the city, at least four fingers above the tallest building. It had to be close to noon.

Snatching his T-shirt from the floor, he shoved his arms through the sleeves. He'd never slept through a sunrise, even if he hadn't gotten a minute of sleep the night before. He'd always been a light sleeper, haunted by insomnia. The slightest bit of light would jolt him awake.

He glanced at the bed, and saw the stones lying on the sheets. He had a fleeting thought that maybe she'd gone out to get coffee, that maybe they'd both overslept and she was coming right back.

But a quick scan of the counters and table by the door confirmed that she hadn't bothered to leave a note. Her purse and keys were gone. And so was his computer. He spotted the red silk robe on the floor.

"I think we should go to Kildare tonight."
"I've been there a dozen times, Sam. She's not there."
"Maybe you missed something. It's not too late. We might be able to catch a few of the nuns before they leave the church for the late service."
"I didn't miss anything."

Sam dug in his pockets for his cell phone. It was gone. Of course it was. Glenna had seduced him and then she'd put a spell on him—a *sleeping* spell so he wouldn't hear her when she left!

He strode to the door. How much of what she said yesterday had even been true? Was it all lies to get him back to her flat so she could get a head start? He stalked out the door and slammed it behind him. *You can run, Glenna. But you can't hide.*

THE VILLAGERS GATHERED at the pub—those who were left anyway. Dominic didn't blame his neighbors for leaving. They had children to look out for, families to protect. He would have put his own family in the first boat out this morning if they'd let him. But Tara and Kelsey were determined to stay.

Mary Gallagher paused in the doorway, clutching her suitcase and her daughter's hand. Ashling hugged her stuffed bear to her chest, and their family's sheepdog leaned against her legs. Ashling looked across the room at Kelsey. "There's room for one more in the boat."

Kelsey stood and walked over to Ashling. She gave her best friend a hug and then pulled back. "I'll see you soon."

Ashling's eyes filled with tears. "I don't know when we'll be back."

Kelsey patted Clover's furry head and wrapped the leash tighter around Ashling's forearm. "You'll be back in a few days."

"Fiona," Dominic implored, laying his hand on his grandmother's arm. "I beg you to reconsider."

"I'm not leaving this island, Dom." Fiona pulled her arm out from under his. "Stop asking me to leave my home."

Dominic looked across the bar at Brennan.

Brennan turned the crinkly page in the newspaper he was reading, shaking his head. "I won't abandon my animals."

Liam reached across the table for his fiancée's hand. "Caitlin, I'm sure Jack would make room for both of you. Take Owen to the mainland. Stay in our apartment in Galway for a few days until we get this settled."

Caitlin lifted her chin. "We're *not* leaving, Liam. We're a family. We stay together."

Dominic's gaze fell to Owen. His nephew hadn't said a word since last night, and he understood if Owen didn't want to go anywhere near a boat or the open water after what had happened last night. But he still didn't like the idea of his family being trapped here, exposed to whatever Moira was planning.

"Alright, then." Mary took a deep breath, pulling Ashling back out into the street. "Jack's waiting for us at the pier."

Kelsey stood in the doorway, watching them go until their footsteps faded and the faint click of Clover's toenails on the pavement was drowned out by the sound of a boat motor revving up for one last trip to the mainland.

"Don't you see?" Tara asked. "This is what Moira wants. She wants to split us up. She wants us to abandon our homes. She wants us gone." Tara pulled out her phone again, checking her messages. Letting out a frustrated breath, she shoved it back in her pocket.

"Still no word from Glenna and Sam?" Liam asked.

"No." Tara shook her head. "I don't understand why they won't answer."

"**SHE COULDN'T HAVE** gotten that far." Glenna strode out of the woods. "Even if she left right after you fell asleep, she couldn't have gotten that far on foot."

"What if someone picked her up?" Sister Evelyn asked. "Someone who doesn't understand her condition?"

"I'm not even going to think that," Glenna said. "I *refuse* to think that." But they'd been searching the river for hours, and there was still no sign of her. The rest of the nuns were scouring the hills, but no one had seen her. No one had a clue where Brigid had gone.

Glenna had tried, over a dozen times, to pull in a vision, but she couldn't see anything. It didn't make any sense. Her powers should be doubled or tripled on this land. But with every hour that passed, her magic was weakening. She saw a cab turn up the long driveway and hoped it was someone with news. But when she spotted the man in the back seat, she stopped short.

Sam.

The driver braked, and Sam stepped out. She knew it was only a matter of time. He'd made the connection to Kildare last night. She and Brigid were supposed to be on their way to the States by now, but nothing was working out the way she'd planned. She took a deep breath and walked to him, her legs growing heavier with each step.

He slammed the door. "Did you think I wouldn't find you?"

"I was trying to protect you—"

"By putting a *spell* on me?" He stalked to her, taking her elbow and leading her away from the nuns. "You knew where Brigid was all along."

She nodded.

"Why didn't you tell me?"

"I couldn't risk it."

"Because you don't trust me?" Sam's grip tightened around her arm. "Because you don't think I'm on your side?"

"I know you're on my side!"

"Then, why?"

She jerked her arm away. "Brigid is our only hope, but she doesn't understand what's at stake! She doesn't remember who she is!"

"Maybe if you introduced her to her *sons*, she'd remember!"

"No." Glenna shook her head. "I need more time with her. We were supposed to be halfway over the Atlantic by now."

Sam stepped back. "What?"

"I was going to take her to the States, to a church in Ohio. They were going to keep her safe—as far away from Moira as possible—until I could figure out what to do."

Sam stared at her, his expression a mixture of shock and disgust. "What changed your mind?"

"Brigid was gone when I got here," Glenna said quietly. "She left sometime during the night and we can't find her."

Disbelief swam into Sam's eyes as he scanned the sunlit hills, taking in the nuns searching the river. "You *lost* her?"

"We'll find her. I..." She looked down at her hands. "I can't *see* anything. If I could—"

"What?" Sam demanded. "If you could find her, you'd pick her up and run away? Turn your back on your friends?"

"It's not like that!"

"Really?" Sam shouted. "*You* were the one who encouraged Tara to stay and fight for her freedom from her husband. *You* were the one who made Caitlin tell Liam the truth about their child. *You* were the one who believed we could save Liam from Nuala's spell! Why can't you believe in yourself?"

"This isn't about me, Sam! It's about Brigid!"

"Bullshit," Sam spat. "It's *all* about you. When are you going to realize that you can't do everything on your own? That it's okay to ask for help? That your friends *want* to help you?"

"We can't defeat Moira without Brigid! She's too powerful!"

"How do you know unless you try?"

Glenna turned away, shaking her head. "I know what you're thinking—that because of what happened with Tara and Caitlin, love can overcome evil. But you're wrong. In my case, love can only mean death."

"I refuse to believe that, Glenna." He strode to her, turning her around to face him. "And as soon as you do too, we actually have a chance to win this."

She gazed up at him, at the hard set of his jaw and the fierce determination in his eyes. "Why can't you understand that there is nothing for you here but death?"

"Because I love you! And no matter how many spells you put on me, no matter how many times you try to get rid of me, no matter how many roses outside my house turn black, I am *not* leaving you!"

She felt the restless wings beating, the thorns around her heart unraveling and snapping. "Sam—"

"Do you have any idea where Brigid went?"

Glenna looked down at the river. What if he was right? What if there was another way to defeat her mother? What if she had gone about this all wrong, from the very beginning? She could still hear the voices of the nuns searching the river. She followed the path of the water until it faded into the trees. "The ocean."

"East or west?"

"West." Glenna's gaze lingered on the greenhouse, on the piece of her past Brigid had recreated here. It had offered her aunt a small comfort, but it had never truly offered her peace. She had never belonged here. She'd heard the selkies singing to her for years. She'd thought it was her lover's voice in the river, but it was the selkies, calling her home.

Sam took her hand. "Then we'll head west and start there."

"Where? The west coast covers nearly a thousand kilometers."

"We'll start by getting in the car and driving in that direction. If we can't find her by sunset, we'll head back to the island to help our friends."

"Sam..."

"What?" he asked. "Do you have a better idea?"

"No."

"I didn't think so." He lifted her chin, laying his lips on hers.

The air shifted and sparked. The vision came fast and hard—a blue lorry parked beside a bridge and a man helping Brigid into the passenger seat. Glenna pressed her lips to Sam's, bringing the image into focus, sharpening it, and reading the faded words on the logo on the side of the truck—*Clifden Construction.*

She pulled back, breathing hard. "Clifden."

"What?" Sam asked, searching her eyes. "What about it?"

"Clifden," Glenna repeated as hope surged inside her. "Brigid's going to Clifden."

CHAPTER
24

I'm sorry I can't get you closer," Neil said, pulling the lorry into a parking spot across from Clifden's only waterfront restaurant. "But there's a path along the bay." He pointed to the trail leading away from town. "It'll take you to the ocean."

The rusted door creaked as Brigid opened it. The salty breezes lifted the ends of her long black hair as she stepped out of the truck. Neil opened his own door and climbed out. He left the engine idling, afraid it wouldn't start up again if he turned it off. Black smoke streamed from his exhaust pipe.

"Do you want me to walk with you?" Neil asked, rounding the front of the truck.

She shook her head, those captivating gray eyes drifting over his shoulder to the water. "I will go alone from here."

Neil removed his hat as a heart-wrenching sadness gripped him. He didn't want to let her go. Fumbling in his pocket for his business cards, he handed one to her. "If you ever have any building needs... this is my number."

She offered him a small smile and took the card. "Thank you."

A strange ache built in Neil's chest as she walked away. His gaze dropped to her bare feet, his eyes widening when he saw they were healed. A gull cawed, swooping over the bay, and Neil let out a long shaky breath.

If you ever have any building needs...? He turned away from the water. He really needed to get out more. He walked back to the driver's side of the truck, but he spotted her wimple lying across the seat. Reaching through the open window, he fished it out. "Wait," he called, "you forgot your—"

A gray fog swept through the streets. A cold wind rattled the shutters of the homes and knocked over the chairs on the restaurant's patio. Neil grasped the warm hood of his lorry as the notes of a song glided over the water and the woman vanished in the mists.

SISTER EVELYN STARED out the window of the kitchen at the line of cars turning up the driveway. The parishioners were starting to arrive. Behind her, the nuns were pulling dishes out of the refrigerator, making last minute preparations for the feast that would follow the midday mass.

She wanted to believe Glenna. She wanted to have faith in her friend's vision, and trust that she and Sam would find Brigid in Clifden. But what if Glenna was wrong? What if Brigid was still out there, wandering the hills, or lost in the wilderness?

A few of her sisters were still down at the river searching for Brigid, but Father McAllister would arrive any minute. They didn't have much time.

Her gaze lifted to the bell tower in the steeple of the white chapel, remembering something Glenna had told her once, about their two religions—that bells were sacred to pagans as well. In Christianity, they were a call to worship, but to pagans, they were used to drive out evil or seal a spell. Brigid had always loved the bells. Maybe if she rang them, Brigid would hear them and come home.

One of the younger nuns—Sister Catherine—hurried into the kitchen, gathering up the loaves of bread. Sister Evelyn laid a hand on her arm. "Sister, I need you to ring the bells."

"It's not time," Sister Catherine protested, shaking her head. "We're not supposed to ring the bells until the start of mass."

"I need you to ring them *now*."

Sister Catherine set down the loaves and scurried out of the house. Sister Evelyn watched her run across the lawn and dart inside the chapel. As soon as the bells started to ring, she picked up her phone, dialing the office at St. Brigid's Cathedral.

"Sister Margaret," she said when a nun whose voice she recognized answered. "I need you to ring the bells in the cathedral."

"Now?"

"Yes."

"But—"

"I've had a call from the Bishop," Sister Evelyn said. "It's an emergency."

"The Bishop?" There was a long pause on the other end of the line. "What happened? Why haven't I heard anything about this?"

"You will," Sister Evelyn said grimly. But her hands shook as she hung up the phone and started to dial another number. She would get in trouble for this. How much, she didn't know. But right now, all she cared about was finding Brigid.

"Ring the bells in the church," she breathed into the phone when Sister Helen in Tullamore answered. "All of them."

SAM STEPPED ON the gas, passing a car full of tourists. "What color was the truck?"

"Blue," Glenna answered, snagging his laptop case from the back seat. "Will your internet work in the car?"

Sam nodded as she booted it up, searching for information on *Clifden Construction*. She handed him his phone back and he frowned at the screen. "Seven missed calls from Tara. Do you know what this is about?"

She shook her head. "The company's owned by a man named Neil Leary. They're working on a big housing project on the south side of the bay. I think I know where it is, and it shouldn't be that hard to find."

"Good." Sam dialed the pub, and Tara answered on the first ring.

"Tara, it's Sam."

"Sam!" Relief flooded into her voice. "I've been trying to reach you all morning."

"Why?" Sam asked. "What's wrong?"

"Haven't you gotten my messages?"

"I just saw that you called," he said. "I haven't listened to them yet."

Tara took a deep breath. "This is going to sound crazy, but I think I know where Brigid is. I had a dream last night about a community of nuns in Kildare..."

Sam shook his head as she related both the details of her dream and Kelsey's connection to Brigid as the princess living in a convent in *The Little Mermaid*. "You're not crazy," Sam said when she'd finished. "We're leaving Kildare now."

There was a long moment of silence on the other end. "Is Brigid with you?"

"No."

"Where is she?"

Sam gazed through the windshield at the sheep farms and rolling green hills of central Ireland. "We think she's headed to Clifden. Things have gotten," he paused, glancing at Glenna, "complicated. But we're going to find her and catch the last ferry back to Seal Island tonight."

"That's going to be a bit of a problem."

"Why?" Sam asked, putting Tara on speakerphone so Glenna could hear, too.

"We don't have a ferry anymore."

Sam exchanged a look with Glenna. "What happened to it?"

"It caught fire."

Glenna shook her head, dismayed. "My mother did this."

"We think so, too" Tara said. "But that's not the worst of it. She set the fire to get Caitlin and Liam out of their home so she could steal Owen's pelt."

Glenna closed the laptop slowly. "Did she find it?"

"Yes."

Sam gripped the wheel. He accelerated as the lanes widened, passing several cars at once. "How's Owen doing now?"

Through the phone, Sam heard the kitchen door squeak as Tara ducked into the back to hide their conversation from whoever was in the dining room. "He hasn't said a word since last night," Tara murmured.

"I don't blame him," Sam said.

"It gets worse," Tara said softly.

"How could it possibly get worse?" Sam asked.

"He's been sneaking off to see Nuala all winter."

Glenna lifted her eyes to Sam's. "What?"

"We found Nuala injured on the beach last night," Tara explained. "She'd gotten into some kind of fight with Moira. I tried to get her to stay, but she went back into the water. Owen says he doesn't know where she went, but that she's on our side and is trying to help us."

"Can we trust her?" Sam asked.

"I don't know," Tara admitted. "But she still loves Owen and wants to protect him. As long as he's one of us, then I think she's on our side."

Sam downshifted as the tractor trailer in front of him lumbered up the hill. "Has Liam come up with anything connecting the mermaids to the white selkie legend?"

"Yes," Tara said slowly, "but it's only a theory."

"Give us whatever you've got," Sam said.

"Brennan told Owen a story a few days ago," Tara began, "about a powerful siren who almost started a war between the mermaids and selkies."

Glenna tensed, and Sam glanced over at her. He didn't like the look on her face. He didn't like it at all. "Go on," he said slowly.

"The siren was the child of a selkie and a merman," Tara explained. "Because she had both selkie *and* mermaid blood in her, she was very rare and unusually powerful. Men fell helplessly in love with her the moment they saw her."

Sam thought of Glenna, of how he had felt the first time he'd laid eyes on her—the powerful force of attraction that had whipped through him and had left him dizzy with need.

"The siren enjoyed exploiting her powers over men," Tara continued. "She spent her days off the shores of the busy dockyards along the coast, luring men into the sea and watching them drown. After a while, other men realized what was happening and they fought back. They couldn't capture her because she would put a spell on them, so they rounded up dozens of innocent seals and slaughtered them instead. They captured entire families of mermaids in their trolling nets and murdered them."

Sam gazed out at the rolling hills and trees blurring into a patchwork of green. "I read every one of Brennan's books after what happened to you last summer. I don't remember this story."

"Not all myths and legends are written down," Tara said. "When the mermaids finally got word of what was happening, they demanded the siren be handed over to them. The selkies refused, and almost started a war between the two species. As punishment, the mermaids corralled the selkies into the waters around Seal Island and set up boundaries. They took away their freedom to roam the seas, and they said if a child was ever born of a selkie/merman union again, they would destroy it."

Sam looked slowly back at Glenna. He felt a tightening in his chest as he remembered the conversation they'd had while hiking to the stone circle in Connemara.

"...what you feel for me isn't anything other than lust. You can't resist me because of what I am."

"I know you have selkie blood in you. Maybe that's what first drew me to you when I saw you on the island. But it's so much more than that now, Glenna. Besides, Tara has selkie blood in her. You don't question Dominic's feelings for her."

"It's not the same."

"How?"

"I'm different from Tara."

"This siren..." Sam said slowly, looking back at the road. "She was half mermaid and half selkie?"

"Yes," Tara's voice crackled through the phone. "That's why they separated the selkies from the mermaids. They couldn't risk another union between their two kinds because the child would be too powerful."

Sam swallowed. His throat felt dry, like he'd been running for days. "How does this all connect to the white selkie legend?"

"Liam thinks it's possible that the first white selkie could have been born at the same time the mermaids forced the selkies into these waters," Tara explained. "That her very existence is a way for the mermaids to maintain control so that no ruling family stays in power for too long."

Sam glanced back at Glenna. He thought of the man Moira murdered—the man from the vision inside the stone circle, the man who'd been in love with Brigid. Glenna had said her father had been planning to run away with a selkie that night, but he'd been expecting someone else.

Sam had assumed, when Glenna had said her father wasn't a selkie, that he was a human man. But a human man wouldn't have had to run away with a selkie. He could have simply claimed her pelt and she would have belonged to him. A *merman*, on the other hand, would have had to run away from his people to be with a selkie.

"Tara." Sam picked up the phone and took her off the speaker. "I want you to put Kelsey on the phone."

"Why?" Tara asked, surprised.

"I want to ask her a few questions."

A few moments later, Kelsey's small voice came on the line. "Sam?"

"Kelsey, your mother mentioned that you made a connection between Brigid and the princess living in a convent in *The Little Mermaid*."

"That's right."

"Have you made any other connections?"

"Well," Kelsey said slowly, "we know where the princess was hiding. But where is her prince?"

Sam stared out the windshield, at the white lines blurring in the road. "Go on..."

"In the story," Kelsey said, "there was *one* prince and *two* princesses. We know Brigid is the first princess, but who is the other one? And what did she have to trade with the sea witch for a chance to be with her prince?"

CHAPTER
25

Moira paced the rocky shores of Clifden Bay. Her sister should be here by now. She'd felt her twin's presence the moment Brigid had left the sacred grounds of Kildare that morning. She'd seen a vision of her climbing into a blue truck with a *Clifden Construction* logo on the side. It was only a matter of time before Brigid arrived and came down to the ocean.

Her sister would not be able to resist its call.

Moira smiled as she watched the ripples form in the water, the long graceful arc of a merman's tail pushing back and forth under the quiet sea toward the shore. The warrior's bare chest gleamed as he surfaced. Seawater rushed down the rippling muscles of his chest, and his powerful tail flicked effortlessly, suspending him in the deeper waters.

His face was stony, not betraying a hint of emotion as he gazed at Moira with piercing green eyes. "Where is Brigid?"

"We will be at Seal Island by nightfall."

The tip of his sharp silver spear glinted in the sunlight. "Our people are ready."

"The king is prepared to hold up his end of the bargain?"

"He is."

Moira smiled. "The selkies will be pleased."

A shadow crossed the warrior's face. "We have waited a long time to avenge the murder of the king's son."

Moira stepped into the shallow water. A school of minnows darted away, disappearing into the deeper water. "And we have waited a long time to be out from under your rule."

"As soon as we have Brigid in our charge, the boundaries will be dropped and the selkies will be free to roam the ocean."

Moira lifted her eyes to the ocean beyond the wide mouth of the bay. When the selkies found out what she'd done for them, how she'd freed them from the mermaids' rule, they would beg her to lead them. And the moment they crowned her as queen, she would be free of this curse.

"The white selkie?" Moira asked, her voice rising as she related the last deal in their bargain. "Nuala will be the last?"

The merman nodded. "She will be the last."

Moira watched him dive, his long glittering tail propelling him back into the depths of the ocean to deliver her message to the king.

One day, a long time from now, she might find it in her heart to forgive her daughter. Once the mermaids lifted the boundaries, they would not watch the selkies so closely, and she would be able to re-introduce Glenna to the sea. But the mermaids and selkies would never know the truth—the *real* truth—that Glenna was the merprince's daughter and *Moira* was the one who took his life, not Brigid.

Tonight, when the Imbolc fires burned across the islands, the mermaids would come for Brigid. They would take her away and Moira would claim her rightful place on the throne. Nuala would be the last white selkie, and there would never be another white selkie born to usurp the throne. Moira's line would *never* be broken.

Moira gazed out at the sea, at the beautiful sea glistening in the sun. A dark shape swimming beneath the surface caught her eye. She narrowed her eyes as a sleek black head bobbed out of the water. "Well, well, well," she said quietly, "looks like I'm not the only one who came to welcome Brigid back."

Nuala floated in the bay, gazing back at her.

"Perhaps I underestimated you," Moira said, taking another step into the water. "I won't make that mistake again." She lifted her arms toward the sky. Sunlight streamed from her palms and she aimed the blinding beams at Nuala. But the selkie didn't move. She stayed where she was, floating in the water.

A cool wind rolled over the hills, submerging them in a thick blanket of fog.

Bells rang out all over the countryside, and Moira's skin began to burn. Blisters broke out on her arms and neck. She gasped, staggering back to the sand. Nuala watched as Moira disappeared in a puff of smoke.

BRIGID BREATHED IN the mists, letting the cool ocean air fill her lungs. Her toes pressed into the parched earth, the thin webbing between them tightening with every step. Snatches of memories came back to her—memories of the sea, of her childhood, of falling in love.

With every step closer to the ocean, she remembered more. She scanned the surface of the water for a tail, for the flash of green fins. Was her lover still out there? Would he still be waiting for her? Would he still recognize her after all this time?

"Brigid!"

Her long hair swung like ropes around her shoulders as she turned. But it was only the man from the truck, the man who had brought her here.

He held out a folded black cloth. "You forgot this...in my car."

Fog crept up, wrapping around her wrists. The wet air brushed against her cheeks. Church bells rang over the hills, but she shook her head, backing away from him. "I don't need it."

He lowered his hand to his side. "Are you sure you don't want me to walk with you?"

"I'm sure." She turned away from him. She needed to go the rest of the way alone. Lifting the hem of her skirt, she picked up her pace. But she could hear him following her, his footsteps getting closer.

She broke into a run, stumbling over the rocky path as the land dipped and rolled into the sea. She spied a white beach in the distance and she sprinted toward it. She tripped when her feet sunk into the soft sand and Neil caught her elbow, steadying her.

"You said you were meeting someone," Neil said, scanning the deserted beach. "Who were you coming to meet?"

The waves crested, splashing over the beach. Brigid's breath caught as a rush of seawater spilled over her bare feet. She remembered the feeling of weightlessness, of swimming into the arms of her lover. "Someone from my past," she whispered, pulling away from him. "He'll be here."

"I don't see anyone," Neil said.

Brigid's blood roared in her ears as she walked into the waves. The water snatched at the hem of her dress and she waded deeper, until the sea came up to her waist. Her fingertips trailed over the surface, and her heart leapt when a shadow edged toward her through the fog.

But it was only a seal—a lone seal with pale eyes the color of winter frost. She stared at the seal through the mists. Those eyes... they looked so familiar.

Where had she seen them before?

Her wet skirt dragged through the water as she walked closer, but with every step the seal edged away, leading her further down the beach.

"Brigid," Neil called insistently, trailing after her. "I think you should come out of the water."

She ignored him, following the seal until they came to a curved wooden boat pulled up onto the sand.

The seal paused beside it, letting out a quiet croon.

The waves surged and retreated as Brigid walked slowly out of the water. Would this boat take her to him—to her lover?

The seal's eyes pleaded up at her, and Brigid grasped the rope in her hands.

"What are you doing?" Neil asked.

The seal dove into the waves, and Brigid dragged the curragh toward the water. Wherever her lover was, she would find him. They would find a way to be together again.

"Brigid!" Neil grabbed the rope from her. "This is crazy!"

"No," she said, snatching it back and dragging the boat into the surf. "This is where I belong."

"You don't even know if it floats!"

Brigid climbed into the boat, grasping the driftwood paddle lying across the seat. "It floats."

Neil ran after her, splashing through the surf and hooking a hand around the edge of the boat. "Let me take you back to town. Let me get you something to eat, find you a place to rest for the night."

Brigid dipped the paddle into the waves and pushed away from the beach. "I have been resting for far too long."

The seal with the pale eyes surfaced beside the boat. Neil stumbled back as dozens more skimmed through the waves, surrounding her, forming a circle around the curragh, and pushing her out to sea.

Brigid lifted the paddle out of the water. She could hear the swish of fins beneath her, and the ocean lapping at the hull. Behind her, the mists swallowed what was left of the man standing helplessly in the waves.

SAM TAPPED THE brakes of Glenna's Mercedes as the tires skidded on a pile of loose chippings. Tightening his grip on the wheel, he hugged the edge of the narrow road that wound through the hills of Connemara. "Who else knows the truth about you being the daughter of a selkie and a merman?"

"Only my mother," Glenna answered, "I grew up underwater, but I was well hidden. No one knew I existed and no one ever came to the sea witch's lair unless they wanted to make a trade."

She pointed to the right when they came to a stop sign. "Even then, few were lucky enough to make it all the way to the cave. It's not an easy journey."

"How did you end up on land?"

"When I was sixteen, a boy about my age came to trade a priceless family heirloom for a potion to heal his dying sister. My mother was out, and I was not allowed to show myself to anyone. She had warned me that no one would understand what I was, and I could be in great danger if anyone found out the truth. But I was afraid if I waited for her to return this boy would lose his sister, and I knew enough about magic to help him. I fixed the potion and was about to reveal myself and make the trade when she came back."

Glenna kept her eyes peeled for signs leading to a new housing development along the bay as they rounded the final hill into town. "My mother was furious, and she killed the boy on the spot. The next thing I knew, I was in a hospital bed in Dublin and the doctor was telling me a fisherman had found me washed up on the beach." She looked out the window. "You know the rest of the story."

"But Dublin's on the other side of the country," Sam protested. "Wouldn't it have been easier to send you somewhere on the west coast?"

"The more crowded the city, the less likely anyone would try to help. It's easier to lock a crazy person up, to let her slip through the cracks than deal with the issue. My mother knew no one would believe me when I woke up and tried to tell them the truth. She wanted to break me down, to teach me a lesson so that when she finally came back into my life, I would be desperate for her forgiveness and willing to do anything she asked."

"Things didn't exactly work out the way she planned," Sam murmured.

"No," Glenna said. "Not exactly. But if it hadn't been for Brigid—
if I hadn't met her by accident in that institution—my mother might
have gotten what she wanted. Without Brigid's stories, and the bond
that formed between us, the system might have broken me down. I
might have given up and decided I truly was crazy."

Sam put his hand on hers. "I doubt that."

Glenna took a deep breath. "Brigid saved me, Sam. I owe her my
sanity, and my life." She looked out the window, scouring the country roads for a blue lorry. "We have to find her."

"We will," Sam said, pulling into a colorful downtown filled with
pubs and sweater shops. Wisps of fog danced over the mossy green
hills dipping into the bay. "Glenna," Sam asked slowly. "Do you have
a pelt?"

"No."

"Can you go underwater?"

"I can change back, if that's what you're asking."

"Have you ever...changed back?"

"No."

Sam turned onto the road leading down to the bay. "If your kind
is forbidden, what would the selkies and mermaids do to you if they
found out the truth?"

"I don't know what the selkies would do," Glenna admitted.
"But the mermaids..." She trailed off, sitting up as she spotted a blue
lorry with a *Clifden Construction* logo parked in front of a waterfront
restaurant. "There it is!"

Sam braked and they climbed out of the car. "He could be inside,"
Sam said, already striding to the door of the restaurant. But Glenna
paused in the street when she saw all the chairs were overturned and
the potted plants were on their sides, cracked with soil spilling out
of them.

"Wait." She pointed to a man walking toward them from the trail
leading over the hills. He was stumbling as if he was either drunk or in
a daze. She shaded her eyes. It looked like the man she'd seen briefly
in her vision. "I think that could be him."

Glenna raised her voice. "Is this your truck?"

He nodded.

Glenna's gaze dropped to his hands and she saw he was clutching a swatch of black material. "The woman you drove here." Glenna motioned to Brigid's wimple. "Where is she?"

The man paused, all the color draining from his face. He looked back and forth between Glenna and Sam. "I...I tried to stop her."

Glenna glanced down, noting that his jeans were soaking wet and plastered to his legs. She went to him, taking his arm and leading him over to a low-lying stone wall. "Where is she?"

He sat heavily, catching his breath. "She went...to the ocean."

"When?" Glenna asked. "How long ago?"

The man's deep voice shook as he spoke. "About a half an hour, maybe. I don't know. I lost track of time. Are you...friends of hers? Do you know her?"

Glenna nodded. "Tell me what happened."

The man lifted his haunted eyes to hers. "She went out in a boat... with no motor...only a paddle." He pulled a handkerchief from his pocket, wiping his brow. "I-I tried to stop her. But there were seals. So many seals."

Glenna looked up at Sam. They were too late. They weren't going to make it in time.

"She kept saying she was meeting someone," the man said, "but I didn't see anyone else on the beach. Only the seals. And one of them...I've never seen anything like her before."

"What?" Sam asked. "What did she look like?"

"She had these eyes...as pale as glass."

"Nuala," Sam breathed.

Glenna stood. "She knows. She's trying to protect Brigid."

"How can you be sure?" Sam asked, pulling her away from the driver. He lowered his voice. "Nuala could be planning to offer Brigid to Moira in exchange for Owen's pelt."

Glenna shook her head. "Nuala knows what's at stake. She's taking her to the island. She knows we have magic and we can protect her."

"Then we need to go, now!"

"No." Glenna planted her feet, gazing out at the bay.

"What?" Sam stared at her. "What do you mean *no*?"

"I need to help Nuala," Glenna said quietly. "I need to help the selkies protect Brigid."

"Glenna," Sam grabbed her arm. "You said you don't know what the selkies will do to you when they see you, when they find out what you are."

"Don't you see?" Glenna looked up at him. "Without the blackthorn, there's no proof of what Moira did—except for me. *I* am living proof that she slept with my father and murdered him."

Sam shook his head. "No. You can't do this. I won't let you do this."

"I have to show them the truth. This is the only way." She took both of his hands in hers. "Go back to the island. There's still time to catch a ride with Jack if you hurry. Tell the others everything. Tell them I'll be there by nightfall."

"No." He shook his head. "I won't let us be separated."

"We won't be," Glenna said. "I *will* be with you, just not beside you. Now go. There isn't much time."

"Glenna—"

"Do you trust me?"

"Yes."

"Do you love me?"

"Yes."

"Then let me go."

Sam searched her face for some hidden meaning, trying to read in her eyes what she wasn't telling him. "Do you promise to come back to me?"

She nodded. "You asked me out on a date to the best restaurant in Galway. I have to come back."

He pulled her close, holding her tightly against him. She could feel his heart beating through his shirt. "Promise me," he said gruffly.

"I promise," she whispered, tilting her face back up to his.

His mouth captured hers in a possessive kiss, drawing everything out of her. But she forced a smile when he pulled back, gazing down at her. "Glenna, I..."

"I know." She laid a hand on his cheek. "I love you, too."

Sam took her hand as they walked to the cliffs in silence. When they came to the edge, Glenna bent down and peeled off her boots. She turned away from him, so he couldn't see the tears sliding down her cheeks.

She heard his sharp intake of breath as she dove, as her toes pushed off the rock and her body curved toward the water. With a splash, she broke the surface. The salty sea slid over her skin and the sounds of the village faded to a dull echo.

She blinked through the murky water. Sea grasses undulated in the pulsing tide. She pushed deeper, cupping the water with her hands and pulling her body through the bay, awakening the muscles that had been dormant for so long.

A flash of light and a sharp stabbing pain coursed through her as her clothes peeled away, drifting up to the surface. Her bare legs sealed together and her lungs burned as she held her breath, but she pushed deeper, faster, through the dark waters as a powerful mermaid tail made not of scales, but of brown seal-skin, bound her legs.

Schools of fish darted around her as iridescent gold fins fanned out from the tip of her tail. A thin strip of seal-skin banded her breasts. And, for the first time in fifteen years, she opened her lungs to the sea.

CHAPTER
26

D ominic stood at the edge of the splintered pier, watching the last boat motor into the harbor. A winter sunset painted the hazy sky an eerie yellowish-green. He caught the line Sam tossed him. "Watch your step," he warned. "These boards are loose."

Sam nodded, stepping over the charred planks as he climbed out.

"My engine overheated outside Sheridan," Donal said, helping Jack navigate into the crooked slip. "Jack had to tow me in the rest of the way."

Dominic looped the bow line around a piling. "But you came back."

"Aye." Donal gathered up the stern line. "I was born on this island. It's going to take more than a sorceress to scare me off it."

Dominic eyed Jack's small fishing boat. He respected Donal for coming back, but he really wished they had a second boat. "There's not enough room for everyone if something happens tonight."

"No." Jack rubbed a hand over his sunburned face. "But there's enough room for the women and children."

Dominic pushed to his feet. The sea was uncomfortably quiet again, and the tide was rising. The water licked at the bottom of the splintered pier, a hushed lapping sound that set his teeth on edge.

"Fiona's been cooking all day. Go on up to the pub and have something to eat. I'll meet you there in a bit."

Jack and Donal started up the hill to the village, but Sam lingered. They stood for several moments in silence, taking in the destruction of the harbor. "It's worse than I imagined," Sam said finally.

Dominic turned to face him. "Tara told me Glenna knew where Brigid was all along."

Sam nodded.

"Why didn't she tell us?"

"If you had known where your mother was, you would have wanted to visit her," Sam said. "If you and Liam had both started traveling frequently to Kildare, it would have made Moira suspicious. She would have eventually followed you and found out where Brigid was hiding all these years."

Dominic took a step back. "What does Moira want with my mother?"

Sam looked back out at the harbor, at the strands of dried kelp in the water. "I have something to tell you—all of you. But it's not going to be easy."

Dominic frowned. "I don't like the sound of that."

Sam dipped his hands in his pockets. "Is everyone gathered at the pub?"

"Yes."

"Including Owen?"

"Owen?" Dominic raised a brow. "He's not speaking. He won't talk to anyone. Not even Kelsey."

"He needs to hear this," Sam said. "And I think he might start talking when he does."

SAM AND DOMINIC walked into the pub. Utensils clinked and scraped across plates as the islanders—the few who were left—

ate in silence. The boards over the windows blocked out the last of the fading daylight.

"Sam!" Kelsey scrambled off the leather chair in the corner. "Did you figure out who the other princess is yet?"

"I have a hunch."

Kelsey's eyes went wide. "Who?"

"Actually, I want to tell you a story." Sam glanced around the room at the remaining islanders. "All of you."

"A story?" Kelsey wandered back to the chair, her eyes lighting up. "What kind of story?"

"A fairy tale."

Owen looked up, his expression darkening. He was sitting on a wool blanket beside Kelsey, tying strips of rope into knots. He pushed to his feet and headed across the room to the stairs.

Sam blocked his path. "You need to hear this, Owen."

Owen looked down, closing his fingers over the piece of rope in his hand.

Sam frowned at the intricate knots tied into the scattered bits of rope littering the floor. "Where did you learn how to do that?"

Owen lifted a shoulder.

"He's been tying them all afternoon," Caitlin explained, sliding a hardback book across the table to Sam. "Brennan gave him this last night. It's a book of Celtic knots."

Sam took the book, flipping through the pages. "It's written in Gaelic."

"The knot Owen's tying belongs to the merprince," Brennan explained from the armchair in the corner. "It's the symbol he wears in his crown."

Sam bent down, snagging a piece of frayed twine off the floor.

"I think our prince is a merman," Kelsey said, tucking her legs under her, "but there aren't any merprinces in the stories we could find."

"There is in the one I'm going to tell you." Sam set the heavy book back on the table.

Owen went back to his spot on the blanket, but he turned his back so he was only partially facing Sam.

Sam settled into a chair across from the children. He'd agreed to let Glenna go this afternoon, but he knew she was hiding something. He knew how much Brigid meant to Glenna now, and how far Glenna was willing to go to save her. He had a pretty good idea of what she was planning to do.

But there was no way in hell he was going to let it happen.

Every clue he had ever needed had been on this island, and it had always come down to a fairy tale. This time, he knew the fairy tale, but he needed the clue. He looked down at Owen, who continued to twist the ropes into knots, refusing to meet his eyes. Sam knew exactly who was going to give it to him.

"I'm not much of a storyteller," Sam admitted, glancing over at Brennan. "I might need your help."

Brennan packed a fresh pinch of tobacco into his pipe. "If I know the story, I'll try to help."

Sam looked down at Kelsey, taking a deep breath. "Once upon a time," he began, his lips twitching when she gave him a thumbs up, "two identical twin daughters were born to the selkie king and queen."

"Twins?" Tara asked, surprised. She walked out from behind the bar and sat at the table with Caitlin. "But that would mean Brigid has a sister?"

"That's right," Sam replied. And they weren't going to be happy when they found out who she was, but if Owen was hiding something, this might be the only way to get him to talk. "The older twin, and heir to the throne, was quiet and kind. She was content spending her days working in her garden."

"That's Brigid," Kelsey piped in.

Sam nodded as footsteps clattered down the steps. Liam pulled out a chair at the table beside his brother. "The younger twin was more adventurous," Sam continued. "She preferred to spend her days exploring the kingdom, and she didn't understand why she was only allowed to roam so far. When she asked her parents why she couldn't explore the entire sea, they told her that the mermaids ruled the sea and the selkies were given this small part of the sea in exchange for peace between the two species."

"Sam," Brennan cut in. "I didn't realize this was the story you were going to tell. I'm not sure this is a good idea."

"Why?"

Brennan lowered his voice. "I know this story, and it doesn't end well."

"No," Sam admitted. "It doesn't. But you've only heard one side of this story. I'm going to tell you the other side—the one with the *right* ending."

Brennan glanced across the room at Liam and Dominic. A shadow of guilt passed over his eyes. "I don't see what good can come of this."

"Why don't you help me out with some of the details," Sam suggested lightly, "and I'll fill in the rest."

Brennan studied his pipe for a long time before nodding his consent.

Sam stretched out his legs, his boots leaving a trail of dust on the wood floor. "One day, when the princess was sixteen years old, she was exploring the outer edges of the selkie sanctuary and she spied a mermaid. It was the first mermaid she had ever seen and she decided to follow her, deep into the ocean."

Kelsey pulled her stuffed starfish into her lap. "Wasn't that dangerous?"

"It was."

"But she followed her anyway?"

"All the way back to her kingdom." Sam paused, glancing up at Brennan. *Come on. Help me out.*

Brennan shifted in his chair, the leather creaking under his weight. "It was the most beautiful palace she'd ever seen," he said slowly. "The mermaids were gathered in a great hall, dancing and laughing and eating rich spreads of seafood."

"That doesn't sound so bad," Kelsey said.

"No," Brennan agreed. "It wasn't. And the princess longed to join the mermaids, but it was getting late and she knew she should turn back before anyone discovered she was gone. But just as she was about to leave, the princess spotted a young merprince about her age. He had thick blond hair, a gleaming white smile, and a glittering tail that sparkled when he laughed. She fell in love with him at first sight."

"It's like in *The Little Mermaid*," Caitlin murmured, "The princess fell in love with a man she couldn't have."

Sam ran his hands over the knotted wood of the chair, picking up where Brennan left off. "After watching the prince for a long time, the princess swam back to the selkie kingdom and slipped home without anyone noticing she'd been gone. But as the days passed, she kept thinking about the prince, and she dreamed of marrying him and joining their two kingdoms together."

"Ambitious," Tara murmured.

Sam nodded. "Over the next few months, the princess snuck away as often as she could to visit her prince, even though she could only watch him from afar. But one day, as she was swimming back to her own kingdom, she crossed paths with the sea witch—a woman known and feared throughout the ocean for her power, beauty, and dark magic."

Kelsey hugged her starfish to her chest.

"The princess tried to slip away," Sam continued, "but the sea witch stopped her and told her she recognized her. She said she'd been watching her and understood that she was in love with someone she couldn't have. She told the princess that she could help her get what she wanted—the prince—if she would do something for her in return."

"What did she want her to do?" Kelsey asked nervously.

Sam picked up a piece of Owen's knotted rope, toying with it. "The sea witch told the princess that all she needed was a pearl from the selkie queen's crown."

"A pearl from her crown?" Liam asked.

Sam nodded. "The princess was surprised, because that wasn't so difficult. Especially since the queen was her mother and they lived in the same palace. She agreed, and a few days later, she brought the sea witch the pearl and the sea witch was pleased."

Liam reached for the candle in the center of his table, picking at the pieces of wax stuck to the glass. "That was too easy."

"It was," Brennan agreed, lighting his pipe and puffing on it a few times before picking up the story. "Once the sea witch had the pearl, she told the princess that she would help her meet her prince. The princess was overjoyed, but when the sea witch saw how excited the princess was, the sea witch decided to add one more condition. She told the princess that if the prince did not return her love, then the princess would have to come and live with her."

Kelsey's eyes widened. "She wanted the princess to leave her family?"

Brennan nodded. "The princess didn't want to live with the sea witch, but the sea witch told the princess that she was getting tired and needed to teach someone her ways. Who else would help the desperate souls in need when there was no longer a witch in the sea?"

Kelsey shrank back into her chair. "She didn't make the trade, did she?"

Brennan cradled his wooden pipe in his palm, the sweet scent of tobacco filling the room. "The princess was confident she would be able to win the prince's love since she was the most beautiful selkie in the sea, save her twin sister, Brigid. She agreed to the trade and swam away."

Kelsey shuddered. "I think that was a bad idea."

Sam studied the elaborate knots tied into the piece of rope in his hands. "Months passed with no word from the sea witch. When the princess turned seventeen, she began to worry that maybe she shouldn't have made the trade, that maybe nothing was going to happen. But then, one day, everything changed. A new white selkie was born into the selkie kingdom."

Owen glanced up, watching Sam closely.

"As you know," Sam said, "a white selkie is a very unique and special selkie. She is only born every few hundred years and she is always born into a different family than the current ruling family. But she is destined to be queen. As soon as she is old enough to bring her land-man into the sea, the current ruling family must relinquish the throne to her."

"Is this...Nuala?" Caitlin asked.

Sam nodded. "The sea witch had seen a vision of Nuala's coming, and knew it was only a matter of time, so she forced the birth by casting a spell with the enchanted pearl from the selkie queen's crown."

Owen scooted closer to Sam.

"Nuala's birth was a really big deal," Sam continued, "and the selkies invited the mermaids to their kingdom for a celebratory ball in honor of their newest queen. It was the only time their people were allowed to mingle."

"That's how the princess got her chance to meet the prince," Tara said.

Brennan blew out a long stream of smoke, and the air around him grew hazy. "On the night of the ball, the princess knew she had to make the prince fall in love with her or she would have to go live with the sea witch. But the king and queen introduced their eldest daughter to the prince first. The moment the prince laid eyes on Brigid, he fell for her."

Kelsey's eyes widened. "He fell for her *sister*?"

Brennan nodded. "Brigid had no idea that her twin sister had feelings for the prince, and as the prince doted on Brigid throughout the night, she began to fall for him, too. The younger princess watched it happen, desperately trying to think of a way to stop it. But it was too late, and before the end of the night, the prince and Brigid had made plans to meet in secret the following week."

Kelsey squeezed the starfish. "I have a feeling this is going to end badly."

"So do I," Tara said, standing and walking over to join Kelsey. She eased her hip onto the arm of the chair, putting her arm around her daughter.

"The princess was heartbroken," Brennan went on, "but she couldn't tell anyone the truth because of the trade she had made with the sea witch."

"But that night," Sam said, leaning forward, "her sister confided that she and the prince had made plans to see each other again."

"Let me guess," Caitlin said, crossing her arms over her chest, "the princess offered to 'help' them."

"That's right."

"But she wasn't really trying to help them," Caitlin muttered. "She was trying to steal the prince away from her sister."

"That may be," Brennan said slowly. "But things didn't work out so well for the princess. A few weeks later, the prince's parents announced his betrothal to another mermaid, and he and Brigid decided to run away together."

"Run away?" Kelsey asked.

Brennan nodded. "They knew if they remained underwater, there was always a chance they could be found. But if they went on land, they could live out the rest of their lives as humans. They would never see their families again, but at least they would be safe and have each other."

"But mermen can't shed their tails like selkies can shed their skin," Dominic protested.

"No," Sam agreed. "They can't. He had to go to the sea witch and make a trade for human legs."

"Did the princess try to stop them?" Tara asked.

"She did," Sam said.

Brennan frowned, because he didn't know this part of the story.

Sam stood, wandering over to the window and looking out over the dark fields. "On the day of the escape, the princess disappeared pretending to communicate Brigid and the prince's escape plans with the prince's messenger. When the princess returned she told Brigid that the prince had changed their meeting spot."

"But it wasn't true?" Kelsey asked.

Sam shook his head. "That night, after everyone went to sleep, the two princesses snuck out together. They swam to a busy port town and the princess told Brigid the prince was waiting beyond the town. The sisters said goodbye, and Brigid swam to the beach, thinking she'd found a secluded spot behind a boulder to shed her skin."

Kelsey hugged her knees to her chest. "I don't think I like where this story is going."

Sam glanced down at Owen and he saw that the child was watching him intently. "The younger princess had come to this spot many times and there was always a man at the beach this time of night, stringing his nets. He was kind to the birds, feeding them scraps of fish, and he was friendly to everyone. She assumed he would capture her sister's pelt and maybe one day they could love each other. Unfortunately, a *different* man captured Brigid's pelt, and he was nothing like the nice fisherman the princess had seen before."

Dominic glanced up, his expression clouding. "My father."

Sam nodded. "When she realized her mistake, the princess swam as fast as she could to the original meeting spot. The prince was already there, and she shed her pelt quickly, running from the water to tell him everything. But since the two sisters were identical twins, and the prince had never seen Brigid in human form, the prince assumed she was Brigid. He kissed her, and she forgot all about saving her sister and anything other than her love for the prince and how this was all she had ever wanted."

"But he wasn't in love with her!" Kelsey exclaimed. "He was in love with her sister!"

Sam glanced at Brennan. The elderly man was watching him with a pained expression on his face. "Now the prince could tell something was wrong as soon as he kissed her, but the princess said she was just nervous about what they were doing. He comforted her, and they snuck away from the shoreline in human form, deep into the mountains of Connemara."

Kelsey shifted closer to Tara. "I can't believe she left her sister like that!"

Sam took a deep breath. This was going to be the hard part. "When night fell, they built a fire and the prince fell asleep, but the princess laid awake, haunted by terrible grief at what she'd done."

"At least she felt bad about it," Kelsey muttered.

"She did," Sam said quietly, "and the next morning the princess decided to tell the prince the truth, or at least a version of it. She told him her sister had changed her mind at the last minute and she had come in her place. She told him she loved him, had always loved him since she'd first laid eyes on him, and wanted to be with him."

"She told him who she was?" Caitlin asked, surprised.

Sam looked down at the frayed rope in his hands. "She wanted him to know the truth. But the prince didn't react the way she'd hoped. He didn't believe Brigid had changed her mind. He demanded to know where she was and what happened to her. He told the princess he could never love her, and he would never stop searching for her sister."

Owen stared up at him, wide-eyed.

Sam laid the piece of rope on the windowsill. "When the prince turned to leave, the princess realized she'd failed. She'd cost her parents the throne, betrayed her sister, and made a foolish trade with the sea witch—all for nothing. She was unable to live with the idea that the prince might one day find Brigid, that he might recover her pelt and reclaim her freedom from the man who stole it, and that the prince and her sister might live happily ever after."

"Wh-what did she do?" Kelsey asked, leaning into Tara.

Tara put a comforting arm around her daughter's shoulders, exchanging a troubled look with Dominic. "Sam, I'm not sure we—"

"She turned dark," Sam said softly.

"What do you mean...dark?" Kelsey asked.

"She killed him."

Owen recoiled and Kelsey shot up, off the chair. "*What?*"

"She killed him," Sam said, pushing away from the window. "And when she walked back to the sea, the sea witch was waiting for

her at the shoreline, ready to take her home and teach her everything she knew."

"Wait..." Kelsey clung to Tara. "If the princess turned into the sea
witch, then that means..." Her face went pale and the last word came
out as barely more than a whisper. "Moira."

Sam turned, taking in the stunned faces looking back at him.
"You deserved to know the truth."

Kelsey's lower lip started to tremble. "But that means...Moira's
my *great-aunt*?"

Owen scrambled to his feet, shoving the knotted pieces of rope
into Sam's hands. He opened his mouth, trying to speak, but no
sound came out.

Sam knelt in front of him. "What is it, Owen? What are you
trying to tell us?"

Liam crossed the room, gathering up the pieces of rope Owen
scattered over the floor. "If Moira killed the prince, why haven't the
mermaids come after her? Is it because she's too powerful?"

Sam shook his head. "No one knows the truth. Moira let them
believe Brigid and the prince ran away together, and when the
mermaids got word of his death, they automatically blamed Brigid."

Dominic stood, pushing back from the table. "Moira *framed*
Brigid for the murder?"

Brennan looked up at Dominic and Liam. His hands shook as
he set his pipe on the table. "I want you both to know, I had no
idea you were Brigid's children until Liam made the discovery last
fall. If I had known the real truth, I would never have kept it from
you. From everything I'd read and heard up until now, I thought
your mother killed the prince." He shook his head, ashamed. "I'm
so sorry. I was only trying to protect you both from finding out your
mother was a murderer."

"So was Glenna." Sam laid his hand on Brennan's shoulder. "But
Glenna's been trying to prove Brigid's innocence for years. She's been
hiding her from Moira, and protecting her from the mermaids, who

still want vengeance." He looked up at Liam and Dominic. "That's why she never told either of you the truth."

"But how could Glenna possibly clear Brigid's name after all this time?" Tara asked. "When no one saw what happened but Moira and the prince?"

"Glenna's been searching the mountains of Connemara, trying to find the spot where Moira killed him. She's been doing it slowly, careful not to draw any attention to herself. She couldn't risk her mother finding out what she was doing. But she knew if she could find a blackthorn plant growing in the spot where Moira killed the prince, she could burn a branch in an Imbolc fire and it would reveal the true story."

Owen grabbed Sam's hands, squeezing them.

"That's why Moira set Glenna's house on fire when I found the spell book," Tara said. "She realized what Glenna was trying to do."

Sam nodded. "We found the spot on our way to Dublin yesterday, but the blackthorn was gone. Moira had already gotten to it. Glenna thought she had more time, but when Nuala came on land last fall, it set everything in motion. Everything Moira did to Brigid, to Nuala, to you"—he looked at Caitlin—"and you"—he looked at Liam—"and you"—his gazed dropped back to Owen. "Everything she did to *all* of you was to clear her path to the throne."

Thunder peeled through the sky and Kelsey buried her face in her mother's shirt.

"Sam," Tara lowered her voice. "What can we do?"

"I think Moira made an agreement with the mermaids—to give her something in exchange for handing over her sister," Sam said. "They still want justice, and if she hands Brigid over to the mermaids, she will be granted something in exchange that will give the selkies no choice but to choose her as their queen."

Dominic walked over to Kelsey, smoothing a hand over his daughter's hair. "Brigid and Glenna are safe now, right? When you called earlier, you said you'd found Brigid, and that she and Glenna would stay in a B&B in Clifden until we could get there in the morning. The mermaids can't do anything to her when she's on land."

"No," Sam said slowly. "But Moira can. And she's been trying to find Brigid for years." Sam took a deep breath. "I lied earlier, in case Moira was listening. I needed to buy Glenna and Brigid some time. They aren't staying in a B&B in Clifden tonight. They're on their way to the island now."

"How?" Caitlin asked, alarmed. "There aren't any more boats—"

Sam lifted his eyes to hers, and she took a step back.

"You left something out of your story." Tara lowered her voice. "Something else happened between Moira and the prince that night."

Sam nodded. "The night they ran away, Moira conceived a child."

"Glenna," Tara whispered.

"Glenna is the daughter of Moira and the prince," Sam said. "A child of a selkie and a merman is the rarest, most powerful creature in the sea. But no one knows the truth. No one knows she exists. Glenna is going to sacrifice herself in Brigid's place, unless we can find a way to save her."

Owen's nails dug into Sam's wrists. He leaned into him, his voice barely a whisper in his ear. "I have the crown."

"What?"

"The crown," Owen whispered. "The prince's blackthorn crown."

Sam eased back, searching Owen's frightened eyes. "Where?"

"I buried it under the roses last night."

CHAPTER
27

Lightning streaked through the sky, illuminating the flashes of green and silver darting beneath the surface. Brigid's eyes widened as mermaids—thousands of them—came from every direction, carrying sharp spears. Her curragh rocked as they circled, the surface churning with their powerful strokes.

She could see the outline of tall cliffs, the shadow of an island rising through the fog. She fumbled for the paddle, dipping it into the water. This must be where her lover lived now! The seals had brought her to him!

The seals edged closer, barking frantically as a single mermaid broke through their protective circle. Brigid drove the paddle into the ocean, dragging it through the surface. If she could reach him, if she could get to him, everything would be okay.

A hand shot out of the water, grasping the edge of the curragh. A mermaid surfaced, and Brigid dropped the paddle. It clattered to the bottom of the boat. Brigid took in the water running down the mermaid's long brown hair, dripping down her pale face, and clinging to her eyelashes.

"Glenna?" Brigid whispered.

The mermaid nodded, her amber eyes gazing into hers. Brigid's heart began to pound. How had she never noticed how similar Glenna's eyes were to her lover's? How many facial features they shared?

She peered over the edge of the boat and froze when she saw that the long brown tail and gleaming fins belonged to Glenna. She was shaped like a mermaid, but her tail was made of sleek brown seal-skin instead of scales.

"How?" Brigid breathed. "How is this possible?"

Glenna reached for Brigid's hand as the mermaids closed in around them, their movements sharp and practiced. They formed a pattern in the water, an impenetrable knot of silver and green.

"I am with you," Glenna said. "I will not let them hurt you."

SAM DROVE THE shovel into the soil beneath the roses. The flowers, all black now, clung in tight buds to the whitewash.

"Be careful," Owen warned. "It's fragile."

A single black rose fell from the bush. It rolled over the ground to his feet. Tara picked it up, and it crumbled to dust in her hands.

Dominic cut the engine of his truck, angling the headlights at the cottage. More roses fell, their petals fading to ash as they tumbled to the ground. Smoke puffed into the air, mingling with the fog.

Tara stepped back, pulling Kelsey and Owen with her. "How deep did you dig?"

"I don't know," Owen said. "I don't remember."

It had to be here, Sam thought. It was their only hope. He dug deeper, scooping out large chunks of earth.

Liam rushed out of the barn, carrying another shovel. He helped Sam dig until a large pile of dirt grew beside them. "I don't think anything's down here," he said finally, staring down into the gaping hole.

"It has to be," Owen said, breaking free of Tara's grip and dropping to his knees beside the bush. He dug with his hands, exposing a web of gleaming black roots. But he jerked back as they began to move, twisting and bending.

"What's happening?" Caitlin asked as a low wicked laugh cut through the fog.

The door to Sam's cottage creaked as it opened, and Moira strolled out. She smiled, holding up the crown. "Looking for something?"

The roots melted, forming a pool of black oil in the earth. The vines cracked and fell, splashing into the oil.

Sam threw down the shovel, striding toward her. But Moira simply waved her hand, setting the ground around him on fire.

"Owen," she said, walking toward the child. "It's so nice to see you again."

Liam scooped Owen up, holding him tightly in his arms. Moira laughed as the roots bubbled, spitting out a putrid stench of rotting roses.

"You were searching for the crown when you tore our house apart last night," Caitlin breathed. "It wasn't just Owen's pelt."

"Owen's pelt?" Moira arched a brow. "My, my." She eyed the child in his father's arms. "Nuala is *full* of surprises, isn't she?"

"Nuala?" Caitlin took a step back. "You mean...you don't have it?"

"I couldn't care less about Owen's pelt." Moira lifted a sash of gold silk, dripping from a garnet clasp at her waist. "All I cared about was finding the crown." She looped the sash carefully around the crown until it hung like a talisman against her hip. She looked back up at Owen, her eyes narrowing. "Did you think I wouldn't find it?"

Sam edged closer to the fire. The flames shot up, snapping toward him. Moira paused, studying him. "You've been useful to me, Sam. I can almost understand what my daughter sees in you."

"You could *never* understand what your daughter sees in me," Sam said, gritting his teeth as the flames grazed his skin. "Because there is *nothing* inside you."

Moira's eyes flashed. Lightning cracked through the sky. The smell of smoke, thick and suffocating, stretched toward them. Tara gasped when a neighboring island caught fire. One by one, the string of islands stretching south ignited.

"You're burning the islands," Tara whispered, leaning into Dominic and clutching Kelsey to her. "Why? Why are you doing this?"

"I want a fresh start," Moira said simply. "And there's nothing more *effective* than fire to erase the past." Her scarlet fingernails stroked the tiny white petals blooming along the vines of the crown. "When I rule the seas, these islands will belong to the selkies—and *only* the selkies."

"The selkies will never choose you as their queen!" Sam shouted. "They know what you did to Nuala! What you did to Liam and Owen!"

"They will forgive me when they find out what I've done for them tonight." Moira lifted her arms. A sulfurous steam rose from the sea, forming a blinding yellow fog that rolled toward them. She laughed as she faded into a curl of black smoke. "You all should have left the island when you had the chance."

BRIGID CLUTCHED GLENNA'S hand as the air grew warmer and the mists thickened, taking on a foul yellowish tinge. They were within shouting distance of the beach when a blond woman stepped out of the fog. Glenna dropped quickly back into the water, keeping her face barely above the surface on the other side of the boat. Glenna was concealing herself from the woman on the beach, Brigid realized. But why?

The woman on the beach walked into the surf, her long gold dress fanning out in the sea. "Welcome back, sister."

"Sister?" Brigid stiffened. "You're not my sister. You look...nothing like her."

"Don't you recognize me?" The woman smiled, her green-gold eyes glinting through the darkness.

"N-no," Brigid stammered.

Steam rose from the water where the woman stood. She cupped it in her hands and it crystallized, forming into glittering jewels. She let them drop, one by one, into the sea. "Much has changed in both our lives since we last met."

"But..." Brigid shook her head. "You have magic. Moira never had any magic."

The blond woman lifted her eyes to Brigid's. "I have *power.*"

Brigid heard the crackle of flames rising in the wind. She tensed as the mermaids edged closer. "Moira? Is it...? Is it really you?"

Moira laughed. "The mermaids are happy you came back. They've been searching for you for a long time."

"Why? I...don't understand."

"They want you to pay for what you did."

Brigid scanned the misty shores for her lover. If she could find him, if she could look him in the eyes, everything would be alright. "What did I do?"

Moira took a step closer. "You don't remember?"

Brigid shook her head.

Moira let the rest of the jewels slip through her fingers. They splashed into the waves. "You murdered the prince."

"What?" Brigid shrank back. "No!"

The mermaids surfaced, thousands of them all at once in the water surrounding the boat. They raised their spears, pointing them at Brigid. A merman with green eyes and the mark of one of the king's warriors spoke, "We are here to avenge the murder of our prince."

"No!" Brigid cried. "I *loved* him! I would never—"

"Hand over the princess, and your boundaries will be lifted," the merman said, addressing the selkies. "You will be free to roam the seas."

Murder? Brigid grasped the edge of the boat. The selkies stirred, the water churning and bubbling as they tightened their protective circle around her. Glenna squeezed her hand and Brigid looked down, into the deep sadness swimming in her friend's eyes. *No. This is a mistake. He can't be dead.*

"Brigid is innocent," Glenna said, her voice rising over the waves.

Brigid gripped Glenna's hand. "What are you doing?"

"Trust me," Glenna whispered, easing away from the boat.

"No!" Brigid clung to her, refusing to let go. "This is all a mistake!"

Glenna pried her hand free. She dipped beneath the surface, disappearing from sight. The selkies reluctantly parted for her. Brigid struggled to make out her shape as she swam to the outer edge of the circle.

The mermaids jerked back in horror as Glenna surfaced. Moira's anguished scream tore through the night.

"I am the merprince's daughter." Glenna's brown tail shimmered, her gold fins glowing iridescent in the dark water. "It's me you want."

OWEN SCRAMBLED OUT of his father's arms. He needed to find Nuala. He needed to tell her he'd lost the crown. A blinding fog swallowed the cottage, sweeping his mother from sight.

Sam staggered out of the ring of fire as the flames died. "Get inside. All of you!"

Owen felt his father's hand on his back, steering him toward the cottage. But he twisted away, breaking into a run.

"Owen!" Sam lunged, but Owen dodged him. He ducked behind a stone wall and sprinted toward the ocean.

"Owen!" He heard his father shouting his name through the fog. But he kept running. He followed the wall, brushing his hands over the jagged stones as the land dipped, edging into the sea.

He felt for the notches—the markings he'd scratched into the wall. He'd let his parents think that Moira had stolen his pelt, but he'd taken it months ago and had buried it here. In case he ever needed it.

He needed it now.

His hands trembled as his fingers found the grooves. He jiggled the loose stones and they fell away. He reached into the opening and pulled out his seal-skin.

"Owen!"

Sam was getting closer. Owen grabbed his pelt, racing toward the stench of rotting seaweed. He yelped when the rocks started to shake, when they crumbled into the sea. The earth broke off where he was standing.

His feet slipped and he tumbled into the water. He surfaced, spitting out the foul taste of sulfur. Fires were burning in the water, small pockets of oil and smoke.

"Owen!"

More voices—his mother, Tara, Dominic, and Kelsey—they were all calling his name. But the selkies needed him. Nuala needed him.

The surface rolled and twisted as sharp, glinting scales swished beneath the surface. He dove, shoving his hands into his pelt. The seal-skin slid over him, suctioning to his body. He darted after the glittering tails, following them toward the selkies' cries.

CHAPTER
28

S am staggered back from the rocks. The coastline shook, crumbling into the sea. He watched Owen dive, and he saw the pelt in his hands.

Sam cursed as fires ignited all along the coast. He made for the beach to the south, struggling to maintain his footing as the shoreline trembled and quaked. He was almost there when heat lightning streaked through the fog, illuminating the mass of mermaids surrounding a small wooden boat offshore.

The mermaids held spears, but they weren't pointing them at the dark-haired woman inside the curragh. They were pointing them at Glenna. Sam stumbled down the final rocky slope to the beach, racing onto the sand.

"What are you doing?" Moira shrieked as the mermaids seized her daughter. "Don't you want to be rid of this curse?"

"I am stronger than the curse!" Glenna's eyes locked with Sam's as he ran across the beach. "I can fight the darkness!"

"No one is stronger than the curse!" Lighting streaked through the sky, snaking toward the island. A cottage in the village caught fire.

"Leave them alone!" Glenna shouted. "This has nothing to do with them!"

Another bolt hit the cliff by Tara and Dominic's cottage. "I will destroy this island," Moira shouted, "and everyone on it!" The earth broke off, soil and rocks crashing into the ocean. "Until everyone you love is gone, and you realize how little they ever meant!"

"You won't destroy us!" Sam shouted, his voice cutting through the storm.

Moira whirled. Lightning struck the sand at his feet, sparks and bits of glass swirling up into the night.

"Even if you burn this island, and wipe out all our homes," Sam shouted, striding toward her, "we will survive! And when this is all over, we will still have each other!"

More cottages in the village caught fire. Smoke billowed into the sky. But Sam kept walking toward her.

The water receded, rushing over the sand until Moira stood in a tidal pool. Her eels swarmed around her legs, and sparks of electricity shot out of the water. "One step closer and you're dead."

The water almost touched Sam's shoes, but he stood his ground. "Isn't that what you want?" Sam asked, speaking loudly enough so Glenna could hear him. "You want to get rid of us, because you can't stand the fact that Glenna has friends, that she has people who love her. When you have no one."

Moira raised her arms, and lightning cracked from her fingertips. Brennan's cottage and the barn caught fire. Fences splintered as animals pushed their way out, their hooves pounding over the fields.

Sam's gaze dropped to the crown, still looped around the sash in Moira's dress. "Go ahead." He pulled a small knife from his back pocket, hiding the blade in his palm. "Kill me. Isn't that what you want? To destroy another one of your daughter's lovers?"

The eels circled Moira's legs as she walked to him. "You think you're so smart, that you've figured everything out." She paused at the edge of the pool, an eerie yellow steam floating up between them. "But it's too late. Your facts are no match for my power."

"What power?" Sam asked. "You have no real magic. Every power you've ever gotten has been stolen. That is not power."

Moira snapped her wrists and shards of glass rose from the sand. Sam threw his arm over his face, blocking the glass as it rushed toward him. It fell, clinking back to the beach. When he lowered his arm, it was covered in blood.

He straightened back to his full height, towering over her. He didn't believe for a second that there was a curse on Glenna. Not anymore. "Why don't you tell them what really happened, Moira?" He took a step toward her. "Why don't you tell them the *truth*?"

"The truth doesn't matter anymore," Moira hissed. The fog grew tentacles, and they wound like ropes around Sam's neck.

He tore them off, throwing them down. The fog twitched, evaporating in the sand at his feet. "Why don't you tell your sister what really happened the night you led her to the docks? When you said you would help her run away with her true love?"

"You know *nothing*!"

Sam's eyes burned into hers. "I know that you tricked Brigid into believing the merprince changed their meeting spot so you could steal him from her." Sam raised his voice. "Then you tricked him into believing you were Brigid, and you murdered him because you needed his love for *her* to fuel *your* powers."

Moira's eyes flashed as a collective gasp rose from the mermaids and selkies.

"I know you tricked Caitlin into believing her infant child died, and then you stole Owen so you could use him as leverage against Nuala ten years later." Sam side-stepped as flames streaked over the surface of the water. "You tricked Nuala into believing you were on her side, and then you stole her powers when she chose the wrong land-man—a land-man *you* led her to!"

Moira staggered back as he strode into the tidal pool. The sparks faded to smoke around his feet. "I know you tricked your daughter into believing there was a curse on her, and then you stole every man she ever loved." Sam grabbed her wrist, hauling her to him. "*You* stole those men from Glenna. *You* took their lives. Because, without them, *you* would be nothing."

He sliced his knife through the sash of her dress. The material ripped, and he seized the crown, holding it up, high into the night. "It's time they knew the truth."

OWEN SCANNED THE dark waters, searching for Nuala. He struggled to see through the stirred-up sand and broken shells, but he stayed close to the bottom, dodging the sparkling scales of silver and green.

Flashes of lightning lit up the water and he spotted a brown tail amidst the mass of mermaids. He edged closer, transfixed by the long golden fins that skimmed back and forth. She looked nothing like any of the other creatures in the water. Her tail was shaped like a mermaid's, but made of seal-skin.

Another streak of lightning flashed over the surface, and he shrank back when caught a glimpse of her face. Mermaids shot past him, jostling him. His heart pounded in his ears, but he inched slowly forward until he was directly beneath her.

A huge merman held Glenna captive. Her arms were twisted behind her back. The tip of his spear was pressed into her side.

Sam had said the mermaids would take her away and lock her up unless they could find a way to save her. But without the blackthorn crown, they had no way to prove Brigid was innocent. They had no way to prove Moira was behind everything, and all Glenna had ever done was try to stop her.

This was all *his* fault. *He* had lost the crown. *He* had failed them.

The merman tightened his grip on Glenna, and her powerful tail beat against the water as a warning.

Owen narrowed his eyes. He wouldn't let them take her. He wouldn't let them lock her up because she was different. Brennan had said her kind was forbidden, but that was only because she was too powerful and the mermaids were afraid she would use her powers for evil instead of good.

They didn't know Glenna. They didn't know she had almost *died* trying to bring his father back, and that, right now, she was sacrificing herself for Brigid, to save all of them from Moira.

He pushed off the bottom in one swift motion, kicking his flippers up to the surface as fast as he could. He sank his teeth into the arm of the guard. The merman jerked back, releasing Glenna as he cried out in pain.

Owen flipped, darting away. But a searing pain ripped through him as the spear pierced his side. His vision blurred, wavering as the sea of glittering silver and green melted together. He heard Nuala scream before the dark water took him under.

GLENNA FELT FLIPPERS brush against her bare stomach. A small shape darted up from the depths, attacking her guard. Her eyes widened when she saw that it was only a young seal. The guard cried out in pain, releasing her.

Glenna twisted free, peeling away from the merman. Fires broke out over the beach and she saw that Sam still held the crown. His eyes locked with hers.

Sam knew better than to throw the crown into one of Moira's fires, Glenna realized. He knew Moira would enchant it and find a way to block the image. He needed her help.

Her friends' panicked shouts echoed over the fields. Thick black smoke billowed up from the village. She felt her powers burning inside her, building to a feverish peak. She bowed her head, whispering a chant.

She flung her arms from the water. Sparks rained from her fingertips as a bolt of white lightning streaked from the sky, setting the crown on fire.

THE BLACK VINES of the crown unfurled, sparking and igniting in Sam's hand. White flowers bloomed along the braided branches, snapping off and fluttering into the night. The petals floated up, chased by a trail of black smoke. The crown grew hot, burning to the touch, but he held on.

Sam stiffened when Moira's fingers curled around his. He felt the heat sear into his skin—the sizzle of his own flesh burning. The crown unwound, snaking down his forearm.

He jerked back as it twisted around their joined arms, binding them together. His skin blistered. The vines bit into his skin. He looked up, through the flames. The smoke billowed, the white petals swirled like snow through the smoke as the image began to form.

Sam fought to free his hand from the vines, from the flames that coiled up between them. But his hand was trapped, stuck to the vine.

"I can withstand the burns," Moira hissed. "But you can't."

CHAPTER
29

S am!" Glenna shouted as the guard tightened his grip, twisting her arms behind her back. "Let go!"

Whispers and murmurs rose over the waves as an image slowly began to form in the smoke. The selkies edged closer to Brigid, but the mermaids shifted, moving toward the beach.

"Let go of the crown!" Glenna cried.

Brigid's heart pounded as she stared up at the image of a man and woman lying in the grass, their bodies joined in passion. She recognized them—both of them—and her hands grasped the side of the boat for support.

The picture blurred, reforming until the couple was standing. "*I will find Brigid,*" the merprince shouted, looking back at Moira with hatred in his eyes. "*Wherever she is. I will never stop looking for her. You cannot get away with this.*"

Brigid watched the prince turn, striding away from Moira. But a flash of silver streaked through the smoke. She gasped as the blade caught the prince in the back of his neck. Her sister's eyes, dark brown only moments ago, glinted green-gold as she pulled the blade free. Moira's distinctive laugh rang out in the night as the prince crumpled to the ground.

A collective gasp rose from the mermaids, but the selkies could only stare as the smoke vanished. The flames died, and Sam fell to the sand. Moira stood on the beach, unharmed. She laughed—that same low, hollow, wicked laugh—as the mermaids switched direction, heading straight for her.

"Sam!" Glenna thrashed against her captor, struggling to get to the man on the beach.

Thousands of mermaids surfaced, surrounding the beach on all sides. They pointed their spears at Moira, but she only smiled. With a wave of her hand, their spears fell, splashing into the sea. They cried out, their hands burned.

Tears streaked down Brigid's cheeks. All these years, she'd thought her lover was calling to her, searching for her. She'd thought it was *his* voice she'd heard in the river. But it was only the songs of the selkies—her people calling her home.

Her boat rocked in the roiling sea. For so long, she'd feared the prince thought she'd betrayed him, because she'd never made it past the docks where Moira had said he'd been waiting. But he hadn't been waiting on the other side of that town. He'd gone to the first meeting spot—the one they'd agreed on.

The hem of her skirt tore as she shredded it, letting all the grief, all the rage, pour out of her. She blinked through a wall of tears at the frantic tapping on the side of her boat. The selkie with the pale eyes—the one who had met her at the beach in Clifden—carried a small seal by the scruff of his neck.

He hung limp in the water, and Brigid reached for him, pulling him into the boat. She set him down gently, running her hands over his body to feel for a wound. But he drew in a sharp breath the moment she touched him. His little body arched, writhing against the bottom of the boat.

She heard the faint crackling of leather peeling away when his skin began to stretch. The mouth of his pelt widened and a patch of black hair appeared, followed by a small child's head. The skin gave way and the boy wriggled his shoulders through the folds.

Brigid's hands shook as she reached down, edging the pelt back, helping the child. The seal-skin suctioned to him, leaving a thin translucent mucus behind as he forced his hands out. He kicked at the pelt, shoving it down his legs.

Brigid eased back, tearing a long strip of material from her skirt. She wrapped it around his naked body. When he whimpered, clutching at the wound in his side, she fashioned a bandage from the material. "Here," she said, holding it out to him. "Press this against your side."

She grabbed the paddle, driving it into the water when she spotted a man and a woman running onto the far-side of the beach, racing to help the fallen man. "I need to get you to the beach."

A pair of blue-gray eyes blinked up at her, and she almost dropped the paddle. She stared back at the child, frozen. Slowly, she reached out, brushing a wet curl back from his forehead. "L-Liam?"

"No," the boy whispered, shaking his head. "I'm Owen. My father's name is Liam."

Liam. How was it possible this child looked exactly like her son? Was this another one of Moira's tricks? Brigid lifted her eyes to the smoke rising up from the village, the flames swallowing the cottages, the pockets of fire burning in the sea.

She looked back at Glenna, still struggling to free herself from the guard, still desperately trying to reach the man on the beach.

She gathered Owen into her arms, setting him gently on the seat beside her. She may have lost her sons, but she knew the truth about Glenna now. And *no one* was going to take her niece away from her.

Slowly, she pushed to her feet in the curragh. Owen looked up at her as the boat rocked, tipping from side to side. Her sister might not have any *real* magic. But she did. And she wasn't afraid to use it.

She lifted her arms, breathing in the rush of power as the surface of the ocean snapped and stretched. Owen grabbed onto both sides of the boat as the sea surged and a wave—at least three stories high— rushed toward them.

GLENNA BRACED HERSELF as the huge wave crested, crashing over her. The guard's fingers slipped and the powerful force of the ocean ripped them apart. She twisted away, diving into the churning sea.

She spotted Sam floating in the erratic currents. She pushed through the waves, catching him in her arms and hauling his heavy body up to the surface. "Tara!"

"Glenna?" Tara and Dominic ran toward her voice, combing the crowded seas for her.

"There!" Kelsey pointed as lightning streaked through the sky. "She has Sam!"

Dominic rushed into the surf, pulling Sam from her arms. Glenna brushed her tail back and forth in the ocean, treading water helplessly as Dominic carried Sam back to the beach. *Wake up, Sam! Wake up!*

Dominic laid him down, and Tara knelt, interlacing her fingers and pumping the heels of her palms into his chest. The island shook, quaking as chunks of earth tumbled into the sea.

Steam rose from the sand as the water receded, but new fires sprang up as Moira walked toward Glenna. Moira lifted a hand, creating a protective force around her daughter to keep the mermaids at bay. "Let him go, Glenna. He's *mine* now. It's over."

"No," Glenna breathed. She would not believe that. She refused to believe that. "I won't let you take him." Her eyes burned into her mother's. "Sam was right, wasn't he? It was you. You killed all those men."

"I told you," Moira said. "It was for your own good. I always knew love would weaken you." She flicked a glance toward Sam, who still lay unconscious on the sand. "You are just like these humans, blinded by their foolish love."

"No." Glenna shook her head. "You're wrong."

"Am I?" Moira walked into the sea, her gold dress snapping around her legs. "I will offer you one last chance, Glenna. Come with me. Rule with me as my daughter."

Glenna dug her hands deep into the wet sand. Sam wasn't dead. He couldn't be dead. Her fingers closed around a broken oyster shell. She pulled it up, holding it in her hand underwater, where her mother couldn't see. "And if I say yes?"

Moira's eyes glinted triumphantly. "Let us be rid of this curse, once and for all."

Glenna sliced the jagged edge of the oyster shell across her palm. There was only one way to stop her mother now, only one way to save them all.

Moira held out her hand. Glenna reached for her, but as soon as their fingertips met, her good hand shot out, grasping her mother's wrist.

Moira jerked back. "What are you doing?"

Glenna twisted her mother's palm toward her, slicing the oyster shell through Moira's flesh. Moira cried out in pain, but Glenna hung on, clasping her own bleeding palm to her mother's.

By mother's blood
And spring's first bud
I call on thee
To set this woman free
From fire to ashes
Flames to smoke
Dark magic of the sea
Feed into me
By the power of three
So mote it be

Moira gasped, her whole body trembling as she crumpled to her knees in the surf. "What have you done?"

"What I should have done a long time ago." Glenna squeezed her mother's hand, watching her face twist in agony as her powers drained. "All my life you led me to believe that love would weaken me, that it would make me vulnerable. But you were wrong," Glenna said. "Love does not always make people weak. *Love* can make you strong."

CHAPTER 30

How does it feel to be helpless?" Glenna asked the woman trembling in the surf. "To be *powerless*?"

Moira crawled toward the beach, her pale blond hair fading back to black, her eyes transforming from green-gold to gray. "Glenna," she pleaded. "Forgive me."

"Forgive you?" Glenna enjoyed watching her mother's face change shape as lines creased through her smooth skin, revealing her true age.

"I-I didn't know what I was doing," Moira appealed. "It was the curse."

The water around Glenna grew black, festering with oil. Her mother's eels circled her, their bodies brushing against her waist. They were here for *her* now. "The curse didn't force you to trick Brigid into an abusive relationship with a man who beat her *and* their children."

"It was a mistake! I didn't mean to!"

Glenna lifted her eyes to the burning island, taking in the destruction her mother had caused. "You could have gone after her. You could have helped Brigid escape."

"Glenna, please..." Moira trailed off as Liam and Caitlin ran onto the beach, rushing toward the boat Brigid was paddling ashore.

Owen sat beside her, clutching his side. Caitlin pulled her injured son into her arms as Liam helped Brigid—a woman he didn't even recognize as his own mother—from the boat.

Glenna thought of what Moira had done to these people— Brigid, Caitlin, Liam, Owen, Nuala—all the pain and suffering she had caused in their lives.

She looked back at Sam, still unconscious despite all Tara's efforts to revive him. "That's why you hated me," Glenna said, as everything clicked into place. "Because I had everything you wanted." She thought of the men, all the innocent men who'd suffered because they'd fallen in love with her. "You hated that men wanted me, that they couldn't resist me. Even though *you* made me what I am!"

"No!" Moira shook her head, backing away from her. "I was trying to protect you! To keep you from making the same mistakes I did!"

"The only one you were ever trying to protect was *you*!" Spirals of black hatred sprouted roots inside Glenna, dark roots that latched onto her soul bleeding it dry of everyone and everything she had ever known. Her friends' faces began to blur. Their voices, the island, her home faded away until it was only the two of them, until there was nothing inside her but a pulsing black empty heart, begging for revenge.

And she would have it!

Skimming her hands through the surf, she summoned the long strands of kelp and seaweed—debris that had been building off this island for days. A powerful wave built, crashing over her mother's body, trapping her in a net.

"Glenna!" Moira tore at the slick ropes of sea grass as they twisted around her limbs, wrapping around her neck. "Stop! Please!"

"Why? Why should I stop?"

"Because I love you! I have always loved you!"

"You have *never* loved me," Glenna snapped. "The only person you ever loved was my father, and you *murdered* him because he rejected you. If that is your idea of love, I do not want your love." She tightened the kelp around her mother's throat. "I reject you, just like my father did."

"Glenna!" A man's voice—a voice from the beach—broke through the darkness. She kept her palms raised, using magic to hold the kelp to her mother's throat. But her gaze darted over the beach, searching for the source of the voice.

"Don't do this," the voice rasped. "This isn't you."

The eels hissed. They looped around her waist, edging her away from the voice. But she caught a brief movement through the darkness, the shadow of a man crawling over the sand.

"Stay away!" she warned. But a flicker of doubt crept in as the man pulled himself to his knees.

Moira writhed, wheezing. Glenna squeezed the kelp.

"This isn't you," the man said again. His voice was deep and scratchy, but she felt somehow drawn to it. "I *know* you."

"What do you know about me?" Glenna demanded, as the contours of the man's face grew clearer and brighter. A glimmer of recognition sparked somewhere deep inside her, but the black roots dug deeper, forcing him out. "Tell me! What do you know about me?"

"I know that you are not a murderer."

A swell of rage built inside her. Who was this man to tell her who *she* was? She could be anything she wanted to be now! The sand lifted, swirling into a blinding white storm. She laughed as the islanders—these *humans*—covered their faces and huddled in fear.

How weak they are! How fragile! They are nothing like me!

She laughed as the winds died and sand rained back down to the beach. She watched them shrink away from her, their faces pale and frightened. All of them except for this man—this blond man who continued to crawl on his hands and knees to her.

Sam. She remembered now. Of course. How many times had she told him to stay away from her? That he should never have gotten involved in this? But he wouldn't listen! "You fool! Don't you know what I can do to you? To all of you? If you thought my mother was powerful, you have no idea what I can do!"

"Magic is a *choice*, Glenna!" Sam shouted. "You can use it for good or for evil, but it is *your* choice!"

Glenna's eyes narrowed. "Then I choose evil."

She set the sand inches from his hands on fire. But instead of backing away from her, Sam pushed to his feet. "You *used* to use magic to help people, to heal people and protect them! You *never* used it to hurt anyone!"

"I've changed."

"I don't believe that!" Sam's knees gave out when a wave broke over the sand. Another man rushed to his side, hauling him back to his feet. *Dominic.* She recognized him. She recognized all of them now—*Liam, Caitlin, Tara, Kelsey, Owen, Brigid.*

"Don't do this, Glenna," Brigid pleaded. "If you choose this path, there will be no turning back."

But she needed to do it! She needed to! Someone had to pay for all this suffering! Her gaze shifted back to her mother. It was time to end this.

"Glenna," Sam said quietly. "You promised."

"What?" Glenna snapped. "What did I promise?"

Sam leaned on Dominic as he limped into the surf. "You promised to come back to me."

Come back to me? The eels darted in front of her, putting themselves between her and the two men. But as they came closer, Glenna saw Sam—really saw him—for the first time. He had burn marks on his arms. Ash and sand clung to his wet clothes. Dark smudges of soot covered his face.

"You still owe me a night out," Sam said quietly.

A night...out?

"You promised to let me take you out when this was over." Sam waded out until the water came up to his waist. "You said you'd wear a red dress."

A red dress?

"You promised, Glenna." Sam let go of Dominic, using the water to steady himself. "You said you'd come back to me." He kept walking, closing the distance between them. "I'm not going to let you break that promise."

Glenna felt the pull of the darkness, the pulsing beat of the sea witch's lair calling her home. She looked at her mother lying helpless on the sand, then back at her friends.

"It's too late," she breathed.

"No." Sam shook his head. "It's never too late."

A faint light glimmered inside her, cracking through the darkness seeping into her soul. Sam took a step closer. His arms were badly burned. He could barely stand on his own. But he had survived.

"Glenna." Sam took another step closer. "I love you. I will never stop loving you. But this"—he nodded to her mother—"is *not* you."

The glimmer spread inside her, turning into a glow. Hadn't he said that no matter how many spells she put on him, no matter how many times she tried to get rid of him, and no matter how many roses outside his house turned black, he would never leave her?

Sam held out his hand. "I love you. Come back to me."

Kelsey broke away from Tara and ran to Dominic's side. Dominic lifted her into his arms, and Glenna saw that Kelsey was crying.

"You promised," Kelsey whispered brokenly.

"What?" Glenna took a tentative step toward her. "What did I promise you?"

"You promised to teach me to paint."

Glenna felt the eels edging closer. Their eyes blazed up at her— the same color as the light building inside her, flooding through the darkness.

Caitlin rose to her feet at the edge of the beach. She stood between Brigid and Liam, clutching Owen to her side. "You promised to be in our wedding," she said softly, "to be my maid of honor."

Tara crossed the beach slowly to stand beside Dominic and Kelsey. "We love you, Glenna. Come back to us."

Glenna's hand shook as she reached for Sam. The dark roots cracked, crumbling inside her. Sam caught her, pulling her into his arms.

In the distance, an explosion echoed over the sea. The eels screamed as they ignited, turning to ash in the water. Huge black rocks floated up to the surface as the sea witch's lair was destroyed.

Moira fell back onto the sand, gasping for air.

Glenna clung to Sam as the sea waves washed over her, seizing the darkness, scattering it until it was nothing but smoke rising off the horizon. "I love you, too."

CHAPTER
31

Aftershocks of the volcanic explosion rippled through the sea. Black rose petals washed over the sand and Glenna flicked them away with her fins. She could feel Sam's heartbeat through his wet shirt as they lay in the shallow surf.

Dominic and Tara walked over to Moira, gazing down at the woman wrapped in the knotted kelp. "What should we do with her?"

Selkies climbed onto the rocks, barking at the mermaids, no longer afraid of them. The mermaids picked up their spears as one of the guards swam up to the beach. "We will take Moira back to our king. He will decide what to do with her."

Brigid walked slowly across the sand. A few fires still smoldered on the beach and she could see her sister's haunted face in the dying flames. "What do you think he'll do with her?"

"Lock her up," the guard answered. "Somewhere she can never hurt anyone ever again."

Brigid lifted her eyes to Glenna's. They both knew what it felt like to be locked up, to be trapped in a cage. Glenna felt Sam's arms tighten around her as she deferred to her aunt. "What do you want to do?"

Brigid gazed back down at her sister. "We spared her life, but that is all the forgiveness I have inside me."

Moira opened her mouth to scream, but no sound came out. She flailed, gasping like a fish on the sand.

Brigid turned away. "Let them take her."

Dominic grabbed Moira by the elbow, hauling her up. Liam strode over, taking her other arm. Kelp and seaweed slid off her, dripping to the beach. Her heels dug into the sand and she shook her head wildly as they dragged her into the surf.

The guards seized her, shoving her into the waves. They dove, their glittering tails arching out of the water in unison. Moonlight glinted off their fins as they splashed, disappearing beneath the surface.

The sea churned, roiling as the rest of the mermaids dove, following the guards back to their kingdom. Glenna's hand found Sam's as the swish of a thousand fins faded into the night. She gazed at the last two mermen, the king's guards treading water just beyond the breaking point.

"Your king made an agreement with my mother," Glenna said. "To free the selkies and drop the boundaries in exchange for the woman who murdered his son. Will he honor that agreement?"

The guards nodded. "The king has what he wants."

Brigid raised her voice over the waves. "And what about Glenna?"

The guards looked back at Glenna. "We will allow you to live if you promise never to return to the sea."

"I have no desire to return to the sea."

"Then so be it."

Glenna bowed her head and pinpricks of golden light danced over her tail. The veins in her fins flooded with color and streams of sunlight shot out from her tail, covering the sand in a golden dust.

Tara rushed over to Glenna, laying a blanket over her legs as her body arched, seething with pain. Glenna felt her tail sever and she shuddered, her wet hair falling down around her face. A wave crashed over the sand, the bubbling salt water washing away the last peels of seal-skin.

The mermen dove, vanishing into the dark waters. A cool winter breeze blew over the island, and Glenna edged a single foot out from under the blanket, her toes tingling as they curled into the wet sand.

BRIGID AND SAM helped Glenna to her feet as the clouds swept away, revealing a brilliant full moon. Brigid grasped her niece's hand, gazing at the two men walking back up the beach slowly. They were staring at her, their expressions guarded. She felt a strange tightening in her chest when they paused a few feet away from her, looking at her hesitantly, unsure if they should come any closer.

Brigid stared back at them. Moonlight bathed their faces in a silvery glow. She felt a glimmer of recognition when she looked at the one wearing glasses—he was the same man who had helped her out of the boat. He must be the injured boy's father. "Your son," she said, scanning the beach and finding the red-head rocking the dark-haired boy in her arms. "Is he going to be okay?"

The man nodded. "He'll be fine."

"Owen," Brigid said softly, her gaze lingering on the boy and his mother who were both watching her with strange—almost hopeful—expressions. "He said his name was Owen." She looked back at the tall man standing before her. "And his father's name was Liam."

He nodded again and took a tentative step closer. "My name is Liam O'Sullivan. And this is my brother, Dominic."

"Liam?" Brigid breathed, looking back and forth between them. "Dominic?"

Liam nodded.

She lifted a shaking hand to Liam's face, brushing her fingers uncertainly over his cheek. "I had...two sons once...named Liam and Dominic O'Sullivan."

"Mother," Liam whispered.

A sob caught in her throat as she reached for him, as she grabbed both of them and pulled them into her arms. "I thought I'd lost you!"

Tears streamed down her cheeks as she gazed up at their beautiful, precious faces. She took Dominic's face in her hands, tracing every line, every scar. "My children."

Movements—shadows in the sand—had her glancing down. Hundreds of seals pulled their sleek bodies from the waves and slipped from the rocks, gathering around them. "What are they doing?"

Dominic's gray eyes, so bright moments ago, filled with sadness. "I think," he said quietly, "they want to take you home."

"Home?" Brigid shook her head. "No. I want to stay here. With you."

"We have your pelt," Liam said softly.

"No." Brigid continued to shake her head as the selkies surrounded her on all sides. She had just found her sons! Her babies! She could not leave them now! She looked frantically for her niece. "Glenna, I don't understand."

"You are the queen." Tears shimmered in Glenna's eyes. "The queen of the selkies."

Queen? Brigid's heart raced. She combed the beach for someone, anyone who could help her. She spotted a woman separated from the rest of the islanders, wrapped in a wool blanket beside the curragh. Her hair was white-blond and waterfall straight. She was the only one on the beach not looking back at her. Instead, her eyes were locked on Owen.

Brigid took a step toward her. She was the one who'd led her here—the same selkie who'd met her on the beach in Clifden. Those eyes—those pale eyes—she recognized them now. She *remembered.* "Nuala."

Nuala's grief-stricken gaze flickered briefly to Brigid's.

Brigid picked her way across the sand through the crowd of selkies. They lifted their heads, baying confused notes of displeasure as she paused before Nuala. "You are a white selkie."

"I am," Nuala whispered.

"You were the one who was born when I was sixteen."

Nuala nodded.

"Why are *you* not queen?"

Nuala's pale eyes shifted to Liam. "I failed," she said softly. "I failed in my task of bringing a land-man into the sea."

"How is that possible?" Brigid asked. "A white selkie has never failed."

"Moira," Nuala whispered.

Brigid released a long breath. A few small driftwood fires still burned on the beach. Smoke still billowed from some of the cottages along the coast. Was there no end to her sister's destruction? Brigid held out her hand and Nuala took it hesitantly. "I met my true love at the celebration of your birth," Brigid said. "You were the only reason I ever got to meet him."

"It was my fault." Nuala looked down. "If I had not been born—"

"No," Brigid said, taking Nuala's chin in her hand and lifting her face back to hers. "I do not regret that night, or a single moment after. But he is gone, and all I have now is my family." She looked over her shoulder at Glenna, Dominic and Liam. "Let me be with them."

Nuala shook her head, confused. "How?"

"I can never give you back what my sister took from you. But I can give you back what was once yours. What still *belongs* to you."

Nuala's eyes widened, darting around the beach as a distressed baying rose from the selkies. "They will never accept this," Nuala whispered. "I have made mistakes. I have done wrong."

"What?" Brigid pressed. "What have you done?"

"I...I stole a child—an infant—from his home and his family." Her gaze shifted to Owen. "I never meant to hurt anyone. I...I thought it would be better to take a child with no memories, than a grown man. I never wanted to...cause anyone pain."

"This child," Brigid said slowly, realization dawning as she followed Nuala's gaze to Owen. "Is he back with his real family now?"

Nuala nodded.

Brigid squeezed her hand. "Then I forgive you."

Nuala tried to tug her hand away. She tried to back away from Brigid, but Brigid held on. "This," Brigid said, raising her voice so everyone on the beach could hear her, "is my first and last command as your leader." She pulled Nuala to her feet. "You are the last white selkie, and I choose you as my queen."

Nuala opened her mouth to speak, but Brigid knelt, bowing her head. Gradually, one by one, the selkies began to move. They shuffled over the beach, gathering around Nuala. Closing their eyes, they rested their chins in the sand at her feet.

NUALA'S HANDS SHOOK as she reached into the curragh and pulled out Owen's pelt. Across the beach, Caitlin's arms tightened around her son when she saw what Nuala held. But Nuala walked slowly toward them, her heart breaking as her fingers curled around the pelt.

"I am sorry," she said to Caitlin. "For everything I did to you." She looked up as Liam walked up behind Caitlin, laying a protective hand on her shoulder. "To both of you." Tears swam into her eyes as she gazed down at Owen. "I should never have taken you away from them."

He blinked up at her with those sweet, trusting eyes and she felt a tear slip. She released her grip on his pelt, letting it drop into the smoldering fire at her feet.

Caitlin sucked in a breath and Liam jerked back.

"Wait!" Owen tried to scramble away, but Caitlin grabbed him, holding him tight. "What are you doing?"

"What I should have done a long time ago," Nuala whispered. The leather cracked as it went up in flames. "You belong with them, Owen. With your real parents."

Owen struggled against his mother's arms, staring at his burning seal-skin. "But what if I want to visit you?"

"I will always be with you. I will never stop loving you or protecting you from my place in the sea." Nuala knelt, and Caitlin let him go.

Owen rushed to her, wrapping his arms around her neck. She closed her eyes, hugging him back.

The song of the sea rose over the waves, a restless, breathless rhythm calling her home. She pulled back, taking his small face in her hands. "I love you, Owen."

"I love you, too," he whispered, his fingers clinging to the blanket wrapped around her shoulders.

She pressed her lips to his forehead. "Goodbye," she whispered brokenly. She stood, turning away from him. She walked back across the sand to the curragh and pulled out her own pelt. It was white again. It had changed back the moment Moira's powers had drained. Everything that was rightfully hers had been returned.

She lifted her eyes to the sea, to the sparkle of moonlight glimmering over the surface. All around her, selkies slipped into the water, sliding from rocks into the waves, shuffling over the sand to follow her back to the kingdom.

She walked into the waves, wading out into the surf until the cool water lapped at her waist. With one last look back at the island, she dove, letting the song of the sea carry her home.

EPILOGUE

Four months later

Glenna and Sam stood at the railing of Seal Island's brand new passenger ferry. The islanders whistled and clapped as Liam dipped Caitlin under the arch of yellow roses, sealing their marriage with a dramatic kiss. Dominic popped open a bottle of champagne as Caitlin came up blushing. Tara laughed, tossing rose petals on the bride and groom as they made their way through the small gathering of friends and neighbors.

Finn clapped Liam on the back and walked to the helm, revving the engine and steering them out of the harbor for a tour around the island. The pale yellow ribbons and fuchsia vines strung along the rail fluttered in the wind. Seagulls rode the fresh spring breezes, their cries echoing over the soaring cliffs.

"You know," Sam leaned down as they each took a glass of champagne. "This is the second wedding we've been to together."

Glenna arched a brow. "I'm not sure we were *together* at Tara and Dom's wedding."

"No?" Sam asked, feigning surprise.

Glenna took a sip of champagne, eyeing him over the lip of her glass. "All I was thinking about then was how to get rid of you."

Sam smiled. "I guess I'm not that easy to shake, after all."

"No." Glenna lowered her glass. "You're not."

"Maybe that's a good thing," he suggested, the wind blowing his blond hair back from his face.

"I think," she said, lacing their fingers together, "it's one of your best traits."

Sam laughed as Liam and Caitlin walked up to them. Caitlin's red curls were swept back from her face with two pearl-encrusted combs. Her blue eyes were shining and her cheeks were flushed with color.

"The dress is perfect," Glenna said, picking rose petals out of Caitlin's hair.

Caitlin smiled, running a hand down the blue empire-waist coat that Sarah had embroidered for her to wear over Fiona's simple lace wedding dress. "And look," she said, lifting the hem of the dress and wiggling her white satin slipper. "I got away without wearing heels."

OWEN SWIPED A piece of wedding cake from Kelsey and wandered over to the railing. He picked at the almond icing with his fingers, gazing at the wakes fanning out behind the boat. When Ronan walked up to stand beside him, he tensed.

"Hey," Ronan said.

"Hey." Owen continued to gaze down into the water. Ronan's family had moved back to the island a few weeks ago. They'd been staying with relatives in Cork since their house had burned down and had to be rebuilt. So far, he'd kept his distance. But Owen knew it was only a matter of time.

"So..." Ronan hooked his arm over the railing. "I heard you went after one of those mermen."

Owen pinched off a corner of the cake, popping it in his mouth. "Yeah."

"Were you scared?"

"Maybe."

"I heard they had spears, and really sharp scales."

"They did."

Ronan looked down, scuffing his shoe over the deck. "I'm a pretty fast swimmer...but maybe you could teach me a few tricks sometime."

Owen's eyebrows shot up. He turned to face Ronan. "Seriously?"

Ronan nodded.

"Okay," Owen said slowly. "But only if you teach me how to play football so we can beat the girls."

Ronan's face lit up. He pushed off the railing, trotting back toward the stern of the boat. "I think Finn's got some buoys we could practice with now."

Owen set down his plate down on the table where Kelsey and Ashling were cutting the cake.

Kelsey smiled sweetly up at him. "You'll still never beat us."

Ashling grinned. "Never."

BRIGID HOOKED HER arm through Sister Evelyn's. "I'm so glad you came."

"I wouldn't miss it for the world." Sister Evelyn smiled, plucking a bite of cake from Brigid's plate. "I think I might need to ask your granddaughter for this recipe."

Brigid beamed at Kelsey. "Can you believe I have grandchildren? Two of them?"

"I can, and I do." Sister Evelyn wiped her fingers on a napkin, lowering her voice. "Have you heard anything back from Aidan yet?"

Brigid shook her head. They'd tracked down her youngest son—the one who'd been given up for adoption without her consent. His name was Aidan O'Malley and he lived in the States. They'd attempted to make contact weeks ago, but they hadn't heard anything back yet. "Sam said it might take some time."

Sister Evelyn patted her hand. "I know it's not easy to be patient."

"No." Brigid gazed out at the sunlight sparking over the surface of the sea. "It's not."

"He'll come around when the time is right."

Brigid looked back to her friend. "But there is something I've been meaning to ask you." She took a deep breath. "Why did you take me in, when you knew I could never be one of you?"

"When I see someone in need, I help them," Sister Evelyn said simply. "You needed shelter, protection, and friends. I knew I could offer you that."

Brigid searched her friend's kind brown eyes. "Did you know... what I was?"

"I had my suspicions," Sister Evelyn admitted. "You were *very* fond of that river."

Brigid laughed, looking across the deck at Liam and Dominic clinking glasses and joking with each other. "What do you think of my sons?"

"I think your sons are two of the handsomest men in Ireland," Sister Evelyn said, her eyes shifting to Glenna and Sam. "And your niece looks very happy."

They watched Sam lean down, pressing his lips to Glenna's. "They belong together," Brigid said, glancing sideways at Sister Evelyn. "And as you know, I have a knack for knowing where things belong."

Sister Evelyn laughed. "Speaking of belonging together..." She nodded toward the man standing with Brennan and Finn at the helm. "I think you have an admirer."

Neil Leary looked away quickly, blushing. Neil's construction crew had been helping the islanders rebuild the village. As it turned out, Brigid had found a use for his business card after all. "He seems like a good man," Brigid said wistfully. "But I've already had my love."

"So has he," Sister Evelyn said quietly. "From what I understand, he lost his wife several years ago."

"I don't think—"

Sister Evelyn squeezed Brigid's hand. "There are many different kinds of love in this world. Sometimes, the ones that burn brightest are the most fleeting. But a love that grows slowly, building on trust and companionship, can be just as powerful if you give it a chance."

SAM DRAPED HIS arm around Glenna as they gazed out at the sea, sparkling in the sunlight. "Have you had any more ideas about how you want to rebuild your house?"

"Actually," Glenna said slowly, "I was thinking I might like to live in the village."

"In the village?"

"I've always lived on the outside. Even here, on the island, I separated myself. I didn't believe that I belonged." She looked up at him. "I do now."

Sam tugged her gently to him, laying his lips on hers. They'd been dancing around the subject for weeks as they'd split their time between Sam's cottage and Glenna's flat in Dublin. But the rest of the homes on the island were almost rebuilt now. It was time to consider what their future together might look like.

She pulled back, tucking her windblown hair behind her ear. "What about you?" she asked, trying to act casual. "Are you still comfortable in the caretaker's cottage?"

"Sure." Sam lifted a shoulder. "It suits me. I have everything I need."

Glenna looked up at him and when he smiled innocently down at her, she narrowed her eyes. "You're going to make this difficult for me, aren't you?"

His eyes twinkled. "Have I ever made anything easy for you?"

"No."

"Well...?" Sam asked as the ocean lapped at the hull of the ferry. "Do you have something you want to ask me?"

"I'm starting to rethink my decision," Glenna muttered.

"That's too bad." Sam's shoulders shook with laughter as she glared up at him. "Because I've been working with Caitlin on plans for our cottage for two months."

"What?" Glenna pulled back. "*Our* cottage? When were you planning to tell me?"

"When you asked me to move in with you."

Glenna shook her head, but she couldn't help smiling. "You drive me crazy. Do you know that?"

"Good." Sam brushed her hair aside and started nibbling his way up her neck. "Because I plan to continue driving you crazy for the rest of your life."

THE END

ACKNOWLEDGEMENTS

Thank you to my mom and dad for supporting my dreams and believing in me. Thank you to Juliette Sobanet for your friendship, for always being there to listen, and for planning spur-of-the-moment trips to France. Is there anything better than brainstorming ideas for a new book at a riverside café in Lyon? A huge thank you to all of my readers; your support means the world to me. Thank you to Hans Christian Andersen for writing *The Little Mermaid*, and sparking my fascination with the magic of the sea. Thank you to Margot Miller, Martha Paley Francescato, and Kristy Atkinson for reading early versions of this story and providing valuable feedback. And thank you to my amazing design team, Blue Harvest Creative, for transforming the cover and layout of this story into a work of art.

ABOUT THE AUTHOR

Sophie Moss lives in the Mid-Atlantic, where she is currently at work on her next novel. When she's not writing, she's fiddling in her garden, hunting for four-leaf clovers, or trying to convince a friend to have a Guinness with her at lunch. Sophie loves to hear from readers. Email her at sophiemosswrites@gmail.com or visit her website sophiemosswrites.com to sign up for her newsletter.

Printed in Great Britain
by Amazon.co.uk, Ltd.,
Marston Gate.